# SLEEPLESS NIGHTS

*Also in this series*

The Journal by James Allen
The Paradise Garden by Aurelia Clifford

# Sleepless Nights

**Tom Crewe and Amber Wells**

HEADLINE
*Liaison*

First published in Great Britain in 1995
by HEADLINE BOOK PUBLISHING

A HEADLINE LIAISON paperback

10 9 8 7 6 5 4 3 2 1

ISBN 0 7472 5055 3

Typeset by
CBS, Felixstowe, Suffolk

Printed and bound in Great Britain by
Cox & Wyman Ltd, Reading, Berks

HEADLINE BOOK PUBLISHING
A division of Hodder Headline PLC
338 Euston Road
London NW1 3BH

# Sleepless Nights

# Chapter 1

For the best part of five minutes, she had been aware of his eyes watching her as she waited at the edge of the field. They seemed to burn into her, just as the hot summer sun had been scorching her skin all day long. She could feel its glow seeping down inside her, suffusing her body with light and warmth.

He stood about a hundred yards away, on the far side of the cornfield, his pale blue shirt bright against the dark trees. She feigned indifference, sitting with her back half-turned to him on the folding stool she always carried with her on shoots. She could take the occasional sidelong glance at him, knowing her Ray-Bans would hide her eyes. From time to time she would glance up at the clouds that drifted overhead on the distant horizon.

A gentle breeze blew in soft, summer gusts from across the river. It lifted the blonde hair from her shoulders, wrapped it across her cheeks, let it settle again in gentle wraiths. The early evening sunlight was rich and yellow, and it glinted dully on the legs of the heavy tripod that she had set up in a corner of the field.

She got up and, perhaps for the third time since she had first noticed his figure, looked through the viewfinder of her camera. The long lens pulled in the spread of red poppies at the far side of the field, the distant church, the

1

gentle hump of the hill beyond. She could make out the time on the clock quite clearly – almost 7.15. The evening shadows were visibly lengthening now. Soon the setting sun would catch the tower, making it glint like warm honey against the fading turquoise sky, and she would have the photograph she had driven a hundred miles to take.

I wonder what he's after, she thought, glancing back over her shoulder. She lost sight of him for a moment but then, suddenly, there he was, walking around the perimeter of the field, away from her. She had been a professional photographer for four years now and her work had often taken her, usually on her own, into isolated and sometimes dangerous places. Large dogs and other animals she could cope with, but men could and did make her nervous. She had an illegal pepper spray in the cool-bag where she kept her film and she wouldn't be afraid to use it should circumstances dictate.

But this guy seemed OK. She didn't know why, but she knew he wasn't up to anything. He didn't need to be – it was usually only the inadequates who gave trouble. This one was tall, dark-haired, with a tan that was noticeable even from a considerable distance. Maybe she wouldn't mind if he did decide to come across, she found herself thinking. It was extraordinary just how much could be deduced from the slope of a shoulder, the movement of a hip, the way a man stood – perhaps it was a woman's intuition. She took a bottle of Evian water from the bag and had a drink.

At the age of twenty-six Emma Hadleigh was just beginning the final push towards the summit of her chosen profession. In a good year she already earned more than the salary of the Labour MP who, for six glorious weeks the previous summer, had been her lover. Money was the yardstick by which a lot of people in the business in which she worked measured each other's achievement and she found it an irritating but curiously addictive habit – what about the actual work they do, she would find herself arguing at restaurant tables. She didn't really know anything – and didn't care to know anything – about the salary of the consultant obstetrician who had taken her to Venice with him in the spring. He was a nice guy when it suited him, he had good taste, he made love beautifully. What did it matter how much he raked in, as long as he was happy to pay the airfare and the hotel bills for them both?

Though she had a nice flat in St John's Wood and some equally nice things to furnish it with, Emma wasn't terribly into money for its own sake. If you were in demand as a photographer – and she was the first to admit that her work was unashamedly commercial – then serious money was what you expected to make. More important to her was the freedom it could provide, and what it gave her in terms of the kind of life she could lead and the satisfaction she could draw from it. Personal and professional status she had by the vanload. What was clearly missing from her existence, at present, was a partner. And not any old partner, either. Plenty of guys asked her out, but what she wanted was someone who could meet her on equal terms. That was the difficult bit, because men seemed so incapable of being honest with her, and still less with themselves. Sometimes she wondered if the only two emotions men were capable of feeling were contempt and envy.

In the four years since she had left art school she had had six or seven serious relationships, a two-year live-in lover (a graphic designer called Vinnie), a fair few one-night stands and a good number of men who, either literally or euphemistically, were 'just good friends'. The last of the serious ones had departed from her life a year ago. They had, she reasoned, simply grown apart. She valued her new-found independence, the ability to be herself whenever she wanted to be, rather than to have to behave according to someone else's expectations. Since then she had begun to think with increasing frequency that, without significant relationships, even the kind of independence and self-confidence that affluence and a successful career had brought her could still not be entirely satisfying.

It wasn't just the sex, although that was important. Emma enjoyed making love, looked forward to it when it was on offer and thought about it a good deal. There was more to it than that but sometimes, she had to admit, that was all there was. She thought of Jeremy, the obstetrician, in their hotel room in Venice. God, he had known how to drive her wild. Sometimes, alone at night, she masturbated while she thought of some of the things they'd done together. He was desperately good-looking, too, in an actorly sort of way, and fiercely intelligent. He was a big achiever, in his chosen field at least. Everything was seen as a challenge, an opportunity, an object of value. But there hadn't been much more to it than that. They got on quite well, they travelled, they had sex. Theirs was a short-term alchemy that seemed to work only at certain times and under certain conditions. There was the time when, in a quiet midnight street not far from the Doge's Palace, he had drawn her into a darkened doorway and there, with her skirt around her hips and her breasts spilling free, he had given her an orgasm so

4

intense she had shouted out loud, really shouted. But the following day, while he attended the endless round of seminars and receptions demanded by the conference at which he was one of the principal speakers, she had to acknowledge to herself that she didn't find him especially interesting as a person. Fine in bed, rather boring at other times. A highly qualified toyboy, in fact. She wanted more than that – a lot more. And that was the trouble.

His footfall made her jump, even though she had been expecting him to make a move. He seemed to step quite silently along the path that bordered the waving corn.

'Hello,' he said as she turned round.

She smiled quickly, secure behind her sunglasses, but didn't speak.

'Gorgeous light, isn't it?' he added. They were both aware of how unnecessary the remark was.

Rather as Jeremy had been, he was good-looking in an English sort of way. His voice sounded educated, articulate, a vehicle for expression. He made a few casual remarks. She replied in kind. She was happy for him to stay there but she hoped he wouldn't talk at the critical moment when the sun fell just right on the landscape that spread out invitingly in front of them. She murmured some irrelevance, with as much polite friendliness as she could manage. Her preoccupation was with taking the picture, and instinctively she checked the reading on her light meter.

When she turned round to face him again, he was gone.

Oh well, she thought, and concentrated on the camera. Despite herself, she felt her thoughts drifting back to Venice.

They'd been in a gondola. OK, it was corny and

straight out of the ice-cream ads but it had seemed like fun and it was better than making small talk in Euro-English at an early-evening drinks party with all the other delegates. It had been a warm day, much like today, in the middle of the same kind of long, endlessly sultry spell of summer weather. As the sun began to go down, the temperature had dropped noticeably. She had been glad of the thick woollen rug that Jeremy spread over their laps. As they drifted along the waterways of that most magical of cities, she had been aware of his hand on her leg, stealing up her thigh, his fingers delicately insinuating themselves against the outer lips of her pussy. She had been wearing an expensive pair of couture knickers in pale mauve lace that Jeremy had insisted on buying for her from some phenomenally upmarket Venetian lingerie shop. Emma had squirmed and wriggled to make things easier for him, and then his fingers were inside her and, scarcely knowing nor caring whether the boatman knew what they were doing, he brought her off there and then in the middle of the Lagoon, smack opposite the Piazzetta.

It had, as she recalled so often in her night-time fantasies, been a magical experience – but it ended with the last twitching spasm. As she became aware of the lap of the water again, there was no afterglow, nothing to take with her, no mark that had been made in her heart. She still, from time to time, yearned for Jeremy's hard muscular body but the relationship, she knew, was over. Like a butterfly, she had to grow to live and he was just another skin that she had had to shed. With some difficulty she brought her mind back to this Cotswold cornfield and saw, to her alarm, that the moment she had waited most of the afternoon for had almost passed.

\* \* \*

She was walking down the path back to her car, the sun still warm on her shoulders. She'd shot off the best part of four rolls of film on the church tower – extravagant, perhaps, but cheaper than messing it up and having to come back for a reshoot. Her schedule, these days, didn't allow for cock-ups and her clients had come to expect her to get it right first time, every time.

As she was loading the gear into the back of the Volvo, Emma met the guy in the blue shirt for a second time.

'Hello again,' he said. 'Did you get what you wanted?'

Excited by her success, by the warmth of the evening and – as she was fully aware – by the pleasantness of his greeting, she responded warmly.

'Yes I did, thank you,' she smiled. 'It was just what I was after.'

'I think where you were standing was the best position. I keep meaning to get a picture from across that field myself. My place is over by the church.'

'A photographer, are you?' she asked absently, as she stowed the heavy canvas camera bags under an old travelling rug, safe from prying eyes. Like most people who did this for a living, she left the aluminium cases plastered with stickers to the amateurs. At the very least, they said 'steal me' to any tea-leaf who might be passing.

'A sort-of photographer,' he replied. 'But not really. I did a bit of it at college but now I do other things. These days, it's just glorified happy snaps.'

He handed her the big, heavy tripod, evidently surprised at its weight. 'Do you have to carry this lot around everywhere you go?' he asked her. 'It weighs a ton.'

7

'That's why I have the car. I don't go anywhere these days unless I can work out of a car.'

'So you're a professional, then?'

'Yes, this is what I do for a living.'

'What kind of things? Landscapes, is it, or anything else in particular?'

'Mostly landscapes, yes, I travel around quite a bit.'

'So you're not local, then?'

'No, I have a studio in London. I'm down here for a few days – well, until tomorrow.'

'So you're staying nearby?'

'At the Angel in Brampton.'

'It's a nice place. I go there from time to time. Actually some friends run it. The seafood is very good.'

'Yes, I've tried it. Dublin bay prawns. Brilliant. I enjoyed them.'

She swung the tailgate shut. It closed with a solid thunk. She fished in the pockets of her loose, taupe-coloured shorts for her keys.

'Listen,' he said quite suddenly. 'I wonder if you'd like a drink?'

'Now?' she asked, looking at her watch. It wasn't that much after 7 o'clock, it was a lovely Cotswold evening, she was a hundred miles from home and, yes, he was bloody good-looking.

'Yes, now,' he said. 'There's a place in the village if you don't fancy the Angel.'

'All right,' she said. 'I could use a drink. I've been sitting in the sun for two hours and I'm thirsty.'

David – that was his name, David Casserley, he said, introducing himself in a half-bashful sort of way – got in the car beside her. 'I was out for a walk,' he said. 'But it's not very far to drive. You can park right outside.' He had

8

strong legs, Emma noticed, and once in the passenger seat he seemed bigger than he had in the open air. She always felt the Volvo was too large for her to use on her own but it was the right car for her all the same. She valued the space and reliability and its staid, country-cousin qualities didn't bother her – she used it as a working car. It wouldn't be this clean much longer. Her last car, a Subaru estate, looked like something an upcountry farmer would use.

'Follow the road back towards Brampton,' he explained, and she followed his directions. After a quick drive down a quiet lane, the thick tyres scrunching on the stones and pebbles that had been washed down the hill by last night's thunderstorm, they came to a prosperous-looking village and pulled up outside a small restaurant right beside the church that Emma had photographed earlier. It was set back a little from the road, with an informal garden in which a few tables and chairs were set up – it was, after all, perfect weather in which to eat outdoors. Through the heavily mullioned windows she could see warm lights glowing above soft pink tablecloths. Above the door a sign elegantly proclaimed 'The Ancient House'. It was a warm, interesting-looking place and she could feel a welcoming aura that hung about it like perfume. The cars that were parked outside had the quiet authority of wealth and status.

'We can get a drink here,' he said, as though to dispel the doubts that flitted, shadow-like, through her mind. 'The pubs are a bit spit-and-sawdust and you just wouldn't believe the stuff they have on the jukebox.'

'But I'm not dressed,' she protested, suddenly anxious about her white singlet and cotton shorts.

'Nonsense,' he replied with a ready smile that revealed

slightly crooked front teeth. 'They'll take anyone's money here.'

Inside, the restaurant had an atmosphere she could have cut slices off and served with rack of lamb. The ceiling was low and heavily beamed, with clutches of herbs and dried flowers hanging down almost head-high. It was dark and womb-like, with little areas of brilliant colour that twinkled like jewels – candles on the tables, paintings on the walls, alcoves and recesses where concealed lighting picked out casually placed bygones and other bric–a–brac. The effect was both artless and considered at the same time, a statement of personality. It was more like being in someone's home than a public eating house, and just as inviting. It was the sort of place in which practically anyone would feel at home.

'A drink?' said David, motioning her towards the bar that was separated from the restaurant by open studwork. Even at 7.30, quite a few people could be seen eating in there.

'A cold Guinness please,' she replied. 'As cold as it comes.' Many of the guys who had bought her drinks over the years had perhaps been surprised that a long-legged blonde like her hadn't asked for a kir or spritzer but David, she got the impression, wasn't one to pre-judge these things. He ordered a glass of house wine for himself.

'There's a table outside, in the shade,' said David. 'Shall we go and sit there?'

Once they were seated, she took a long drink. She had forgotten how dry her throat was, after the hours she had spent in the cornfield.

'Was this some kind of advertising shoot you were on today?' he ventured.

'That's right,' she said. 'It's for Sainsbury's. I got the job from an ad agency I work for now and then. It's for the Sunday supplements. Actually it's needed pretty quickly – they used someone else but it didn't work out, so it's all being done in a bit of a rush, as usual. I think they want to run the ad in three or four weeks. They want to say something about country living – fresh bread, local cheeses, strawberries and cream. That was the kind of image I was looking for with the church and cornfield. Sunshine, open air, everything very English.'

'I should imagine it has a very strong appeal to Range-Rover owners in Hampstead and Surbiton,' he said with a wry twinkle in his eye.

'Oh, it's all fantasy land,' she admitted. 'We'll forget about the pesticides and stuff. That river of yours is absolutely choked with algae, isn't it? But this is make-believe, and everyone admits that. But if that's what people actually want to believe in, then it's fine by me. All's fair in love and advertising.'

'Do you work on your own or with an agency?'

'I'm freelance, but I do a lot of work for a couple of agencies in town.' She mentioned a few names; he seemed impressed. 'I do my own stuff as well, but it's hard to get the time.'

'What kind of stuff?'

'Photographs of people, mostly. Just ordinary people on the whole, but I like eccentrics as well, people who make their mark. I'd like to do a book of portraits one day, just called *The English* or something. The trouble is that, to do it justice, I'd need about six months and I just can't afford to take that much time off.'

She wasn't normally one to talk much about herself but she noticed how David seemed to be able to draw it

11

out of her. He knew how to talk to women – which meant not saying much about himself. With some guys, you just had to say you were a photographer and they were telling you all about the camera they wanted to buy, all this technical shit that bored her rigid. They didn't ask what she felt about it, or about anything, but David didn't seem to be like that at all. He seemed happy just to listen to her. Smooth he certainly wasn't – the faded denim shirt and the crumpled linen trousers were not the stuff of EC1 champagne bars – but he seemed to be someone, like herself, with an authentic interest in people. He reminded her in some ways, mostly physical, of Jeremy, but he was infinitely more interesting and easy to talk to. There was a pause in their conversation, but it was an open one – she didn't feel the urge she sometimes had, to leap in and fill the gap, to say something inconsequential just to avoid the silence. It was another sign of the growing confidence she had in herself.

More cars had arrived at the restaurant, and groups of kids were messing about on bikes at the far end of the village street. You didn't see kids that young out on their own in her part of the world, that was for sure.

'So you do all right out of your advertising stuff?' he asked her at length. He'd evidently noticed that her clothes were casual, but good. The sandals certainly weren't High Street. And the Volvo had only 5,000 miles on the clock.

'It's not bad,' she modestly conceded. 'Like everything else, it's gone down a bit since the Thatcher years. That was just ridiculous – there was so much money sloshing around, you could just think of the most outrageous sum in your head, double it and clients would still be happy to shell out. But I was fresh from college then and just starting out, so I didn't see too much of it. Some of the people I work with seem almost guilty now about what went on in those days. But still, things don't seem too bad for the time being. I'll tell you what, let me buy you a drink this time.'

He suggested they go back inside and sit in the bar. The sun was going down and the long village street was filling with shadows. It had been pleasant sitting there out of the sun but now it was becoming noticeably cooler. The restaurant was slowly beginning to fill up. Several of the people at the bar seemed to know David, chatting casually to him as they ordered drinks while waiting for friends. A woman she half-recognised from television exchanged banter with him as she and her partner made their way through to their table. He was obviously a popular guy in the neighbourhood.

While David was engaged with a couple of county types – they're not really his sort, she could say to herself with some authority, even after so brief an acquaintance with him – she took the opportunity to slip off to the loo. She was busting; she'd been out in the hot sun for hours with only a bottle of Evian water for company and there was the Guinness and a glass of wine that she'd just knocked back. That's enough now, she told herself. You're driving. She fixed her face and hair and felt a lot better, the sun's glow on her skin beginning to turn into a warm and sensual tingle. She was starting to feel slightly drowsy, but it was a pleasant, relaxed feeling.

When she got back, David was leaning over the bar pointing to something.

'It's in one of the drawers down there, Hannah,' he told the waitress who was rummaging around behind the bottles of fruit juice. 'Just by the phone book. Over there, see. Where that red pen is.'

'Bottle opener,' he said enigmatically over his shoulder. 'We can never find them now that everything's in ring-pull cans.'

Hannah found what she was looking for and flashed a smile of thanks at David.

'And don't forget to put it back where you found it,' he called after her. 'It's the only one we've got.'

Emma looked at him in a slightly puzzled way. He caught her glance, and smiled. Those slightly crooked teeth again, she noticed.

'I own this place,' he said simply. 'Didn't I say? If I'm not here, the whole place falls apart.'

So that was it, she thought as realisation dawned. That explained the crumpled clothes that seemed oddly out of character with the well-heeled diners, the easy familiarity, the suggestion that they have a drink together here rather than anywhere else.

'It's lovely,' she said simply. 'No, I mean it. I spend a lot of my time in restaurants and such places and this one has a lot of character.'

'I do my best,' he murmured quietly. 'But look, would you like to eat with me? I usually have something about this time. Or perhaps you've got something else arranged?.

'No, nothing. I was just going to have a bar snack at the Angel.' She looked at her watch. It was 8.30. She realised with a start that she felt quite famished. 'So yes, I'd love to. That would be very kind.'

'Oh good,' he said, and his eyes seemed to light up. 'We can eat here, or you can come back to my place and I'll knock something up. Sorry, that sounds like too much of a come-on. Let's eat here, shall we? I usually like to stick around in the bar while everyone gets settled. I'll normally eat standing up in the kitchen round the back, if I can't slip away for an hour or so and put something together at home – I live just down the road. It will be nice for a change to actually sit down here, like the paying punters do. So if you don't mind, let's get the main rush over with and then I'll get Hannah to find us a table. Here's the menu. The fish is good, I'm told. Another glass of wine?'

In fact, it was nearly an hour later before they sat down. The food was, indeed, superb. Emma chose humous with pitta bread as a starter, followed by poached salmon in filo pastry, with new potatoes and a big green salad. David had the same. 'You can get *dreadfully* tired of oysters,' he said with a wicked laugh.

The wine was the same newish Australian Chardonnay that David had been drinking earlier. 'You can usually rely on the house wine, can't you?' Emma said as he poured her a glass. 'It's what I usually order.'

'Bang on,' he replied. 'It's the wine that's second on the list that you've got to look out for. You'll get some peasant out with his bird for the evening in the XR3i and the jacket sleeves rolled up, a haircut like a Third Division footballer – not that we get them in here, well not often anyway – and he's out to impress. Now he's obviously not the kind of image-conscious guy who's going to buy the cheapest wine, is he?'

'I don't suppose he is,' said Emma, laughing. There was a guy at one of the agencies she worked for who fitted the bill perfectly. Next time he took her for lunch, she'd check out David's theory.

'But he hasn't a clue about anything else on the list,'

David went on, 'so he buys the one that's the next cheapest. I tell you, it happens time after time. The sharks in the catering business know just what he's going to do, and they have got him trapped. "Hello, sonny, we've got you well sussed," they say in their best joined-up. So they stick the most awful overpriced rubbish second on the list and they sell it by the case, night after night. Not that we'd do that, here, oh dear me no.'

'Well, I could certainly drink this by the case,' Emma said, pushing out her glass for a refill. 'This is really good.'

'Good house wines are always going to sell,' said David, momentarily becoming more serious. 'If you want to build up regular customers, they need to feel they're getting value for money. So you choose a decent one at a decent price. Not everyone is going to spend twenty quid on a bottle, even if it is their anniversary. But some people will choose a wine to go with the food, and hang the expense. It's good when they know their stuff and they're pleased with our selection and they say so. They know what they're buying and they know that their forty quid or so is actually money well spent.'

His features came alive with a rare passion when he spoke about his work. Emma liked a man who was doing what he really wanted to do and felt content. Not smugness, but contentment – it was a value she believed didn't always count for much in an acquisitive age. Square pegs in round holes always made her feel edgy – accountants who wanted to be photographers, photographers (and that included some of the more successful ones) who ought to be accountants. Underneath the bluster, she could sense just how discontented they really were.

'So how did you come to run a restaurant?' she asked between mouthfuls of hot pitta bread. 'I thought you said you were at art school?'

'I was. I started out doing photography, like you, but then I fancied myself more as a wood engraver. That's what I did for my degree show but afterwards there just wasn't the work. I had some reasonable jobs – I did some stuff for Shell, and Body Shop who were just starting up then, and quite a few things for *Radio Times* – but there was just never quite enough to keep everything together. You know how it is. Either you're working like stink but you don't see any money for it for six months, or else you're lying around watching daytime television.

'So I was in the States for a while and then in Australia, helping to run a couple of vineyards of all things, and when I came back this guy I know was just setting up in the restaurant business and he asked would I be interested in joining him. I knew quite a bit about wine from my time abroad and so I said yes. Jim would do the food and I'd look after the wine – that was how we had it set up. We had a little place in Oxford for a while and then we came here nearly four years ago. Eighteen months back he split up with his wife – actually they're back together now, more or less – but I think that was just an excuse to get out of our partnership. We're still friends, but it was obvious his heart wasn't in it any more, so I bought out his share of the business and since then I've run it on my own. We're both happy with the arrangement.'

'And you're doing all right from the look of things.'

'Yes, quite well I guess. We've been in a few of the foodie magazines and last year the *Food Programme* came along and did a piece on us. That gives you a kind of temporary fame – they used the restaurant for a scene in *Inspector Morse* a couple of years back and we were booked solid for weeks afterwards. But I'm more interested in building up regular customers, people who're going to come back again and again. Being a nine-day wonder doesn't pay the bills when it's all gone quiet after Christmas.'

Emma liked the enthusiasm with which he spoke. He was no bullshitter, that was for sure. There were no big hopes, no five-year plans, just a quiet commitment to what he was doing and doing it to the very best of his ability. The more she saw of him, the more she liked what might be on offer.

'And do you have a—?' Emma ventured. 'I mean, are you—'

'Do I have a partner? No, not at the moment. I was with someone when I lived abroad but really, in this business, you're married to the restaurant. How about yourself?'

'Same sort of thing, really, I lived with this guy for a couple of years but that all ended in a bit of a mess. I think he was expecting me to be someone I wasn't. Right now, I'm just enjoying being the person I think I am.'

'Good enough,' he said, raising his glass to her. 'I think that's how I feel at the moment.'

Hannah brought their salmon. It was delicious, the fish flaking so delicately it could have been eaten with a fork alone, the sauce a subtle and understated whirl of flavours. Even the new potatoes seemed to have been the best that money can buy.

'This is absolutely delicious,' Emma exclaimed. 'Your chef's a genius.'

'He is, but he's a temperamental bugger all the same,'

said David. 'Isn't he?' he said to Hannah, who had brought another bottle of the Chardonnay in response to his discreet gesture.

'Isn't who?' said the waitress.

'Louis – isn't he a dreadful old poser?'

'Awful man,' said Hannah, laughing. 'Everything has to be just so or he hits the roof.'

'We get through kitchen staff like you wouldn't believe,' said David with a sigh. 'They just can't work with him. But Hannah's been here since we started. She's made of sterner stuff.'

'I just ignore him,' retorted the waitress over her shoulder. 'It goes in one ear and out the other.'

'How'd you like a job washing up? David suddenly said to Emma. 'You can start Monday.'

'Me?' she laughed. He didn't seem to be drunk. 'I'm the original slut in the kitchen. I'd drive your man Louis nuts. I'm happy with what I'm doing, thanks all the same.'

'You are, aren't you?' he said quietly.

'How do you mean?'

'You seem to get a lot out of it. It's very satisfying, what you're doing. That's obvious to me.'

'It's not always like that. Sometimes I feel like packing the whole thing up.'

'No job worth doing ever is roses all the way. But if things go wrong, we think about them and try and do them better. In fact, we're always looking for things that go wrong. That's what makes people good at what they do. Things go wrong and they work damn hard to put them right. The things that go right, they can ignore. They just happen, they don't need to bother about them.'

They talked on, long into the evening. She felt increasingly drawn towards him, as if to confirm the attraction to him she had felt the first time she had spotted him across the cornfield that afternoon. When they had first exchanged greetings, she was struck by his openness, the genuine quality that hung about him. She liked that in a man, and she liked him in a physical manner too, the way his hair fell across his temples, the upturn at the corners of his mouth. He looked at her with a steady gaze, betraying a confidence in himself. At one point she was sure he had noticed how her nipples had poked up against the soft cotton of her top and she felt a sharp, momentary stab of desire for him. And yet, despite herself – she was, as she would readily admit if pressed, no shrinking violet – she hadn't consciously set out to let him pick her up.

By the time they finished the fish, she fancied him like mad. Calm, funny, sensitive, intelligent – she wished there were more men like him. He had a nice bum, she noticed – Emma was into bums, and liked a nice, tight, hard one. In her early twenties, she had gone to bed with guys for their bodies as much as anything else. Now, at twenty-six, she was after other things, like personality and charisma, but having a nice butt was no disadvantage for a guy.

Despite the wine dancing gaily through her inhibitions, Emma noticed how much closer they seemed to be getting. They had started off facing each other across the table, but now he was halfway round towards her side. Body language, she reflected, could tell you a lot about what was going on in someone's mind. His legs were stretched straight out in front of him, directly towards her. Without thinking too much about it, she found herself crossing and uncrossing her own legs. She was a little out of control.

They didn't finish the second bottle of wine, only a glass or two from it. 'No, I've had plenty already,' she protested. 'I've got to get up in the morning. Oh God,' she said, remembering the Volvo parked outside. 'How am I going to get back?'

'I can run you back if you'd like,' he said after what she was sure was the very briefest of pauses. Was he expecting her to stay with him? Was he hoping to ask her back to his place, or something? Were things starting to move a little too fast?

'Would you mind?' Emma said with all the authority she could muster, clearing her head. 'But I'm worried about all the camera gear I've got in the car.'

'We'll look after it. It's no trouble,' he said with a genuine willingness to help. 'Take out all the valuable stuff and I'll lock it in the cellar. We spent six grand on alarm systems and they'll beat a better class of burglar than we usually get round here. Anything else you can leave in the car and park it out back.'

After that, they both could relax again. He wasn't going to make a play for her, not yet, anyway, though she was still aware of her own feelings for him. They skipped puddings in favour of cups of coffee – real French coffee cups, Emma noticed – and he told her about his time out in Australia.

'But what about the art school stuff?' she asked. 'What happened to that?'

'Oh, I've put it to some use,' he said in his usual quietly dismissive way. 'I even did some wine labels out in Oz. I did the menu here, too – we change the design every six months or so.'

She'd wondered who'd done the illustration on the front – a strong, confident image of the Ancient House itself. It was difficult for any artist to inject a building with personality but David had done it superbly. The engraving had an impromptu, off-the-cuff quality that Emma knew must have taken hours to achieve, and it made the restaurant seem warm, animated, somehow alive.

'It's brilliant,' she said simply. 'And I love the illustrations inside, all these fruits and shrimps and things. Can I take one?'

'Of course you can – I'll put it on the bill. Just kidding.'

As ever, she thought. It seemed the cue to make a move, and Emma got to her feet. David disappeared through a back entrance while she waited outside. Emma heard a car engine fire, and then a pair of enormous headlights swung into view. It was an old Citroen, like the one Maigret used to drive. She knew instinctively he would have a car like that.

'That was an absolutely lovely evening,' Emma said later as David swung the Citroen into the Angel's car park. The feeling was genuine, but she was aware of a slight thickness in her voice. That Australian wine, she thought. Jeremy had always insisted on French wine, she recalled. Bloody colonials can do a good party wine, he had declaimed, but that's about the level of it. He could be a dreadful snob about some things, and that was one of the aspects of his personality that she had liked least.

'I'm glad you enjoyed it,' he replied, touching her hand. 'I certainly did. And don't worry about your car. It'll be perfectly safe behind the restaurant. Maybe I'll see you when you come to pick it up in the morning?'

Emma was aware again of the implication of that slight catch in his voice.

'Have lunch with me,' he said. 'If you've got time.'

'Of course I'll have time. But it will have to be a late lunch. I have work to do in the morning.'

He said that was fine, he had things to do too. There was a brief pause. Emma was about to reach for the door handle when she sensed a sudden electricity and then he kissed her, very quickly, on the lips.

'See you tomorrow then,' he smiled with his crooked teeth, half-embarrassed, as she got out of the car.

And then she was standing alone in the car park, watching the taillights of his Citroen disappear down the long, straight road. Inside, Emma felt a warm glow despite the chill of the evening air on her bare arms and legs. She could still taste his mouth on hers and her fingers strayed across her cheek, where his lips had grazed them. As she turned towards the entrance to the old coaching inn, her senses seemed strangely alive, defying the long day and the wine.

David's car was almost out of sight when Emma turned round for a final glance. She watched the faint red pinpricks tracing their way through the black Cotswold night. Black and red, she thought, the colours of desire. And then, suddenly, the brake lights pulsed with surprising brightness and Emma could see the car stop and reverse.

He pulled up alongside her, pushing open the passenger door.

As the old car rattled down the country lane she experienced elation, anticipation and desire in wildly fluctuating measures. She realised she had not felt so sexually aroused in weeks, months even. A strange kind of exhilaration seemed to surge through her, and she sensed a delicious trembling that appeared to afflict her very nerve-ends. She put a hand on David's knee and squeezed. He grunted gently. No words were necessary.

'Stop the car,' she said at length. Moths fluttered out of the darkness towards the speeding windscreen.

He looked at her and saw the meaning in her eyes. With a reckless swerve, he brought the old Citroen shuddering to a stop at the entrance to a field.

And then Emma was in his arms and their tongues were together, hands pushing up under clothes. All the language of abandoned passion, of fierce thirsts desperate to be saked.

'This is a bit bloody uncomfortable,' she murmured. 'Let's go into the field.'

She felt the thrill of an unexpected surprise. She could hardly wait to get home with him but, my goodness, this was something else. He leaned across and pushed open the passenger door for her – women had never seemed to be able to get the hang of how the handle worked, he told her later, even if their need had not always been so urgent – and Emma ruffled his hair and kissed him again as he did so.

And then they were pressed together against the side of the car, their bodies urgent and eager in the gathering darkness. He took her hand and led her into the field, rich with ripening promise. Corn, barley, what was it? She didn't know, and cared even less.

There was a flattened patch where a tractor had turned round. Here he kissed her really hard for the first time, breathing in the faint musk of her perfume that had been undetectable amid the oil-and-leather smells of the car. As though of one accord, they sank to their knees and then he was lying beside her on the grass, one hand under her, the other under her cotton vest, feeling for her breasts. The points were hard with desire.

Her fingers were in his hair, on his neck, across his chest under the buttons of his denim shirt. Emma pulled him over until he was half on top of her.

'Undress me,' Emma hissed with unexpected urgency. Her hand lightly brushed against his cock through the crumpled linen of his trousers. He undid the button on her shorts – how soft and cool her belly felt – and the zip and pulled them off. Her tongue was in his ear as he did so. Then her pants, white cotton, as Emma moved her backside to make it easier for him to shuck them off.

He tugged off his shirt, his shoes and socks. He said he always felt absurdly self-conscious in socks and nothing else. If he had any control over it, they were always almost the first things to come off. Then he too was naked beside her, his cock pressing hot and hard against her flank, his arms around her. Her cotton vest was rucked up so that her breasts were crushed against his bare chest, and his tongue was seeking the nipple like a young animal.

All of a sudden Emma stopped, and looked him full in the face.

'Do you have anything?' she asked.

For a moment he seemed to wonder what she meant. He took a guess and got it right.

'No, I don't. I wasn't really expecting this,' he said. His heart was pounding like an engine.

'Well, don't worry,' Emma soothed. 'It'll be OK. It's not that time yet. I just wanted to be extra sure.'

David felt hot and male in her arms as she relaxed

and her tongue sought his. A car went past a hundred yards away. Its headlights speared the field but they scarcely registered the fact. All Emma was aware of – apart from the raw energy of their desire – was what came through her reeling senses, a delicious cocktail compounded of the coolness of the evening, the soft breeze against her naked skin and the earth rubbing against her body every time she moved. Each sensation added only to the totality of the feeling – there were no such concepts as pleasure and pain any more.

He pushed her on to her back, forcing his knee between her legs. They parted willingly for him. And he his was on top of her, his cock unmistakably there against her groin, urgent, insistent, ready. Emma took hold of it and guided it to her pussy.

'Wait,' she said, aware of his urgency. She moved her hips to accommodate him, this strangely exciting new lover she had not even met six hours ago. And yet, in some deep recess of her mind, she felt she had known him all her life.

'Now,' Emma breathed, but it was not a word, more a sigh of glad surrender. And then he was inside her, filling her, his breath warm and urgent against her cheek and shoulders. She gasped with the release that penetration gave her. God, it had been so long. Spreading her legs to take more of him in, she looked up and saw the stars twinkling in the black heavens as he began to push now with greater passion.

Their lips sought each other and Emma ground her hips against his, slowly and rhythmically in the primordial rhythm, all the while her eyes, normally closed while making love, gazing out into the unseeing, sparkling blackness. And then she was thrusting against him with more and more urgency until she felt she was falling over an abyss into deep space, scarcely formed words escaping from her lips and floating away, the smell of the night keen in her nostrils. Her climax was short, inevitable and intense, butterfly flutterings that grew into something inevitable and irresistible, the big pulse, the rhythm of the universe. For an instant, in that field beneath a coal-black glittering sky, time stood still and then David was pumping his seed into her, murmuring something incoherent, his breath ragged as he ground his belly against her. And then they were still.

It had seemed so right, there out among the stars on that hot summer night, and they made love again when they reached David's house. They had scarcely spoken on the short journey back to the village. Words seemed an unnecessary intrusion, small talk an irrelevance when neither had anything to say. Instead Emma wound the window down and felt the cool of the passing breeze against her bare forearms, saw the fat moths that fluttered momentarily in the headlights and then vanished into oblivion. The twin beams scoured the fields like searchlights as they twisted and turned down winding country lanes, picking out rabbits and other bright-eyed denizens of the night. Once, she fancied, she caught a glimpse of a fox on a high banking above the road. She was surprised at how small it was – not much bigger than a terrier.

The interior of the restaurant, as they passed by, was dark now, the table lamps switched off, the floodlights playing on the honey-coloured stone of the church opposite. David's house was a large stone cottage on the edge of the village, very cluttered inside but with that distinctively individual stamp that had caught her eye at the restaurant. A biggish dog – half border collie, half something else – greeted David by jumping up, as he let himself in, its bushy tail wagging furiously. He looked at her with initial suspicion but a few words from his master soon allayed the doubts.

'This is Guy the Gorilla,' he said, laughing. 'He means well.'

In the kitchen lights Emma was aware of how flushed she must have looked, the bits of stalk still sticking to her flesh, her hair ruffled. Was it that slight puffiness about her face where the blood had so lately pumped hot and fierce, or merely the myriad, infinitesimal adjustments to the set of the features that proclaimed the unmistakable signs of a woman just fucked?

'Would you like a bath, perhaps?' he ventured as he played with the dog's ears. 'I'm afraid I don't have a shower here. I've got all the bits – it's just that I've never got round to getting it all plumbed in.'

'Yes,' Emma said. It was as if he had read her mind. 'That would be lovely. I feel so sticky.'

She smiled at him, hot and sultry on this warm summer night, aware that there was little to say. What was important was to experience, not to think and interpret. Even now, with her thirtieth birthday beginning to approach over the once-distant horizon, Emma found it not always the easiest thing to talk to a man with whom she had just made love for the first time. She had learned enough by now to know that there were times – and this was one of them – when you didn't need to say much. It was what you didn't say that mattered most.

'Right then,' he said, wakening her from the reverie into which she had sleepily sunk. 'You make friends with

Guy here and I'll go and get things sorted out for you.'

While he was gone Emma looked around her. The first thing that had struck her inflamed, over-aroused senses was the aroma. The kitchen was small, but evidently well used. It had that indescribable smell of all kitchens where there is a love of cooking – a faint, almost human patina of garlic and olive oil and pan juices and good coffee. It was not dissimilar, in a curious sort of way, to the scent of sex. The worktops were heavily scored with use and everywhere were those same little touches Emma had noticed at The Ancient House – lemons in a hand-thrown bowl, an old wooden candle box filled with salt, eggs in a wire basket hung from the ceiling, something she had rarely seen outside France. Great bunches of herbs were festooned from the ceiling.

Emma pushed open the heavy oak door into what was evidently the living room – scrubbed floorboards, a big inglenook with the ashes of a log fire, lots of books, an Edward Bawden print over the hearth. There were Kelim rugs of varying antiquity on the floor, on the walls, even thrown over the furniture. The curtains were undrawn and on a small Georgian table in front of the window, moonlight spilled on to a huge vase of flowers – campanula, marigolds, honeysuckle. She looked at the CDs on another table – jazz from the 1950s by people she'd never heard of, Verdi's *Requiem*, a not-so-new Annie Lennox album. The dog came in and stood next to her, panting, quickly followed by David himself.

'It's all ready for you,' he said. 'It's at the top of the stairs. There's plenty of hot water. I just need to get some fresh towels.'

Upstairs Emma stretched out in bubbling luxury. The bathroom was large, surprisingly so, and she was fascinated by the collection of mirrors along one wall, mostly old, gilt-framed ones that had reached a fair degree of shabbiness but which, in this context and in such abundance, looked amazing. Before she got in, she had inevitably looked at her reflection – it was possible, by discreet posturing, to see every inch of her body. Not bad, she thought. But must keep it up.

The tub itself was equally commodious – David told her later he had picked it up from a local hospital. 'They're used for washing down the geriatrics,' he explained. 'After a bad night at the restaurant, I sometimes feel like one myself.' She experienced a mixture of numbness and elation as the hot water eased away the day's aches and pains. She somehow felt drowsy and revitalised at the same time. The progress of the last few hours had been quite extraordinary. What else was going to happen, she found herself wondering. God, she had really wanted David out there in the field. When he first went into her, Emma had nearly died. It had hardly been an Olympic performance from either of them – basically a snog and a quick screw when she came to think of it – but my goodness, she recalled with a thrill, she'd gone jetting off a million miles beyond the stars when she came and that wasn't something that very often happened the first time, if at all.

She heard a tap on the door. 'Only me,' said David's voice. 'Mind if I come in?'

'Sure,' Emma said, almost laughing aloud, aware of the extraordinary Englishness of a situation when a man who has just made violent love to her felt he had to ask permission to come into the bathroom.

He came in sideways, pushing the door open with his backside. He had towels over one arm and was clutching in one hand a bottle of champagne and two glasses. He put them down carefully on the edge of the bath and produced a bowl of kalamata olives, the best.

'What's this?' Emma asked. 'You're not trying to seduce me, are you?'

'Thought you'd like a drink,' he said simply as he popped the cork. 'Mind if I get in too?'

The big bath might have been designed with love-making in mind. Emma climbed on top of him, her thighs straddling his, and he eased his cock into her.

'That's nice,' Emma said. 'Let's just stay like this for a while.'

He poured the champagne and they sipped it, quietly kissing each other from time to time. It was good stuff, served at just the right temperature. He touched her nipple with his cold glass and it hardened up almost instantly, pert and luscious like fruit. David began to trace little wet trails around her aureolae with his tongue, gently licking the tip of the nipple before taking it in his mouth. Emma moaned softly, grinding her hips against the cock that was deeply embedded inside her. Then he sucked her other breast, she clasping him around the neck while, with her other hand, she continued to sip her champagne. Her blood was rising again. She caught a glimpse of the two of them in the mirror and Emma felt thrilled, hot, abandoned. Sex and champagne in the bath with a stranger – it was the very image of reckless, lustful wantonness.

His cock continued to press insistently into her as he tongued her nipples. Emma put down her glass and kissed him long and hard, smack on the mouth.

'Let's do it differently now,' Emma breathed. 'I'll show you how I like it.'

She got off him and turned round so that her backside was facing him, her elbows resting on the end of the bath. He caught a glimpse of a snatch of pubic hair and vaginal lips in the cleft between her legs and it seemed to fire him up all the more. In a great tidal wave of scented bubbles he changed position and came up behind her, his cock pressing hard against the cheeks of her backside.

She reached down, guided the dome of his glans to the entrance of her vagina. 'Now push,' she murmured and she felt herself being penetrated with breathtaking urgency. Her muscles gripped him like a vice as he entered her from behind, almost crying out with the pleasure of the sensation. Emma pressed hard against him, grinding her hips against his groin, her breasts swinging free.

Oblivious to the hot water that surged around them, they began to move in the ancient rhythm, their bodies locked together, minds emptying fast of everything but the pleasure of cock sliding in cunt and of warm, tantalising desires. Kneeling down behind her, he placed his hands on her hips to steady himself and arched his torso. Now his pushes were hard and insistent, and Emma felt her stomach flattened against the cool enamel of the bath. Even as he powered into her from behind, Emma felt herself being forced down towards the turbulent water. She turned her head, and watched him in the mirror as he drove himself against her. Her mind was on fire; trapped by his arms and the unyielding smooth surface, she could do little but abandon herself to his invasion of her body. Emma somehow got her hands on the edge of the bath and pushed back against him, burying him ever deeper inside her as he pulled her to him.

A sunburned forearm brushed against her breasts as they swung free, the nipples standing up firm and erect. She wanted him to grab them, squeeze till they hurt, she wanted him to bite her neck, she wanted to suck his cock and do anything, anything he wanted, and to do anything she wanted to him. Her mind reeling, lost to the intensity of sensation within her body, her whole vaginal area seemed to have become one enormous glow. Feeling every movement by her engorged nerve endings, Emma could sense the approach of his climax long before she arched back her head. With what seemed like half a sob and half a cry of elation, he pulsed five or six times inside her and she came too, shuddering into orgasm as her reflection in the mirror shattered into a million glittering fragments.

Later, as they lay together on his bed, he went down on her, long and slow. Awash on a sea of sensation, Emma never felt that it was always necessary for her to come to be content but here, with the warm night breezes stirring the curtains and the moonlight stealing in through the open window, it seemed the perfect end to the day. He licked her long and expertly, never too insistently, but slow and gentle as Emma had always wanted it to be done to her. Hard fucking was one thing but she knew that so often, as his tongue delicately brushed her clitoris, less could me more. As she drifted off to sleep in his arms, her last conscious experience was of hearing an owl hoot far away across the fields.

Emma had breakfast with David the following morning and then drove back to the Angel to pick up her things. As she climbed the stairs to her room, she experienced the same pleasurably guilty sensations she had known coming back from an all-night teenage party. The tingling in her pussy, the lack of sleep, the need to get a change of clothes, the overwhelming sense of having done something the night before that none of the others around her had. It felt good, that same slinky purring feeling that, in their different ways, Billie Holiday and Bonnie Raitt knew about and sang about. She had their tapes in the car – she played them all the time, because in their congruity of feeling and shared emotion, they reminded her of who she was too. She showered quickly and from her travelling bag got out clean jeans and a sweatshirt. On an impulse, she chose black lace bikini pants and a matching underwired bra – not the kind of thing she would always wear on a working day but, what the hell, that's what she felt like wearing. After scouting out a couple of locations, she was meeting David for lunch and a girl needed to be ready for anything that might happen.

# Chapter 2

David was busy in the kitchen at the cottage. Even while he was still lingering over breakfast with Emma, he'd already decided what to give her for lunch. A big green salad of rocket and radiccio – not yet entirely out of fashion, at least not in this part of the world – with chopped eggs and anchovies and croutons. For pudding, strawberries and cream – what else? Some cheese afterwards? Vignotte? Cambozola? He still had some wonderful Cuban coffee left over from a trip to the big Intermarché outside Dieppe a couple of months ago, and he remembered to get it out of the larder. He knew they wouldn't want to feel too stuffed at that time of day, so he didn't go too far overboard. Nevertheless, he walked down to the restaurant later in the morning and – carefully avoiding the other members of staff who were around at that hour – borrowed a nice-looking wedge of Vignotte, whose absence Louis would later go spare about. Back at home, the wine was already chilling nicely in the bottom of the fridge.

He felt good, no two ways about it. He couldn't remember the last time he had felt so relaxed and assured in the company of a woman, barely hours after meeting her. And, moreover, he and Emma had seemed to gell together right from the very start. She was good to look at, interesting to talk to, had an independence about her that had immediately attracted him. Physically, she was pretty hot stuff. Some women were screamers, others were slow burners, but with Emma the balance seemed just about right for him. Last night's sex had been especially good. It left him with a deep feeling of contentment, as though through their passion some profound inner stillness had been reached in him. The encounter in the cornfield had been as explosive as any he had known and it had taken him a good half-hour that morning to put the bathroom back in shape – towels in the most unlikely places, the mats still soaked, the mirrors streaked with splash-marks. Once in bed, in a far less urgent manner, they had made love again before sleep finally overtook them. His foreskin area felt distinctly raw this morning.

He got the impression that Emma was kind of straight-ahead in terms of what she wanted. He wasn't just thinking about sex, or about her attitude to her work, though he got the feeling from talking to her that she was the kind of person you could ask to do something and leave them to get on with it in their own way, knowing that they'd deliver, with interest, at the end of the day. But despite himself, he found his mind drifting back to the way they'd made love. He reckoned you could tell a lot about a woman – practically everything, in fact – from the way she made love. True, they'd not done anything really wild but potentially he sensed it was all there in her, given time and the right circumstances. So many women seemed to hold themselves back from giving him what he really wanted from them. But she was, he knew, the kind who would abandon herself utterly. He was learning about her all the time.

He felt speedy from the lack of sleep but his mood was buoyant and confident. At times he was almost laughing at himself for the way he had responded to Emma's arrival in his comparatively untroubled Cotswold world. He sensed he was acting like a schoolboy with his first girlfriend – it all seemed so new and fresh and exciting, free of the usual complications of adult relationships. He even felt slightly nervous about meeting her again, conscious of the kind of impression everything would make, from the food to his own appearance. To dispel the anxiety – although it wasn't his usual choice for morning music – he played *Tristan und Isolde* at a cracking volume, waiting for the extraordinary moment of consummation in the third and final act when Wagner's music describes a full-blown operatic orgasm. As the tenors thundered he hard-boiled the eggs, picked herbs from the garden, debated making garlic bread and then thought better of it.

It was another stultifyingly hot day, and all the windows in the cottage were thrown open. He knew, as he worked in the kitchen, that there was far more to his meeting with Emma than sheer immediate physical desire. There was something else there, intangible, immaterial, but none the less real for him. In the normal course of events, after a quick screw or a one-night stand, the overheated conversation of the evening would be flagging into strained politenesses by morning – and long before then, sometimes. He was usually only too glad to get away or to embroider some half-truth that would see his latest conquest off with a promise, unfortunately only rarely honoured, to call her one day soon. This time, however, it was different and he was glad of it. He was palpably looking forward to seeing her again, and it wasn't just for the chance to go to bed with her. Though she'd said not to expect her much before twelve-thirty or one, if then, he found himself impatiently looking at his watch, taking unnecessary care over the food he was preparing for her. Passing through the bedroom, he caught a whiff of her perfume and a small, warm tremor of excitement passed quickly through his heart.

He made himself a pot of coffee and sat out in the garden. They would eat out here, he decided, making a mental note to wipe off the birdshit that had accumulated on the table and chairs since they'd last been used. It wasn't a big garden, by any means, but it was well sheltered from the wind and the shade from the old rowan tree was a welcome antidote to the summer heat. Nor was it necessarily the tidiest garden in the village. It was handsome rather than pretty, of more than passing interest to anyone who knew about plants but, like Guy the Gorilla who was fast asleep at his feet, kind of shaggy round the edges – or at least he liked to think about it that way. He let his plants get on with life, rather than worrying them to death with hoe and secateurs. He wondered what Emma would think of it. She hadn't seen much of it that morning, being in a hurry to be off while the light was still good.

He had already had one caller that morning. One Sunday each year, for charity, quite a few of the people in the village where he lived threw open their gardens for visitors – of which there were many, for Hemstead was 'sought after'. The organisers had for two or three years now been trying to persuade him to put his own garden on the itinerary – in fact it was Mrs Masters, the chairwoman of the committee (there were no 'chairs' or even 'chairpersons' in this neck of the woods), who had dropped in on him earlier in the day. There were a lot of interesting and unusual herbs in David's garden – many of which eventually found their way on to the table at The Ancient House – and he had become quite famous for them.

In declining the invitation, which by now she must surely have realised was customary with him, his powers of invention had been tested to the full. 'I'm just so incredibly busy with the restaurant,' he said, trying to assume a beseeching expression. But Mrs Masters would not be fobbed off so easily. She tried praise and then, when that failed, she tried to arouse feelings of guilt within him. Neither worked.

'It would take me a couple of days at least to get this place even tidied up,' he protested with the elegance and impeccable logic of a born evader.

'I'll get some of the village boys to help, if you like,' she had countered.

'But we're right in the middle of staff holidays, which means I'm working twice as hard as usual. Yesterday, I was even peeling spuds. You can bet Mossiman doesn't peel his own potatoes. In any case, the open gardens weekend is one of our busiest at the restaurant,' he went on, improvising wildly. 'I can't be in two places at once.'

'Surely you can get someone to stand in for you,' said Mrs Masters, her downy moustache glistening slightly in the summer sunlight.

Being honest with himself – if not with Mrs Masters – David basically didn't like the thought of several hundred people trooping around his property all afternoon with their kids, dogs and ice creams. He nurtured his privacy, and begrudged the amount of effort that would be needed to bring his little patch of England up to scratch, or at least to pass muster before the basilisk gaze of Mrs Masters. In the company of neighbouring lawns and cottage gardens that were so lovingly tended each day by retired gentlefolk and other like-minded obsessives, it could only seem second-best. Not many would see it for what it really was.

But then David had an inspiration. The cottage was, after all, a fair way from the true heart of the village. It would be difficult for some of the older visitors to walk so far, because parking in the lane was very difficult during the day, with tractors needing to get in and out of the neighbouring fields. Trying not to sound too triumphant, he pointed out that his narrow gate and uneven paths would make things very tricky, if not downright impossible, for wheelchairs. Having come so far to see his garden, it would be terribly disappointing for any disabled visitors who turned up. Mrs Masters conceded defeat, and went in search of other volunteers. Later on, David telephoned her with an offer of bundles of herbs which he would cut from his garden to be sold to the visitors, all proceeds to go to the common fund. She seemed mollified, and faces were saved.

Living a little way out of the village had other advantages for David. In the first six months that he and Jim McDowell had run The Ancient House, he'd actually lived on the premises. They had fashioned quite a comfortable apartment for him on the upper floor. Thursday evenings (they didn't open on Sunday and Monday) he normally had off but as often as not – especially in winter, when there was little incentive to get out and about – he'd have been upstairs doing things on his own, maybe entertaining friends or just quietly enjoying himself. A couple of times an evening, at least, there'd be a tap on the door and Hannah or someone else would be asking him why the laundry still hadn't been paid, or if it was OK for a guest to pay in US dollar traveller's cheques, or what they should do now that table three, a booking for six at nine o'clock, had turned up at eight with twelve of them on a particularly busy night. He had got quite sick of it in the end. It was all right for Jim, who lived ten miles away – he could enjoy the privacy of his own evenings off in peace. People seemed to think that David's being on-site for the best part of twenty-four hours a day gave them carte blanche to assault him with all manner of trivia. When the cottage came up for sale three years ago, he had snapped it up and now his evenings were truly his own once more. He could get up to all manner of mischief if he wanted to and no one would be any the wiser. The former flat was halfway through conversion into a second dining room, to cope with the ever-burgeoning reputation of The Ancient House.

Finishing his coffee, he went back inside, got the vegetables and things for lunch out of the fridge and was just about to start on the salad dressing when the doorbell jangled. He looked at his watch – 11.20. It couldn't be? Emma, not entirely sure of how long her work would take her that morning, had alluded vaguely to 'somewhere between twelve and one.' Great, he thought nevertheless, she's early. Again he felt that little skipping nervousness in his heart as he pushed his way through the cluttered living room to the front door. But it wasn't Emma. It was Gabrielle, Jim's wife, dressed to kill in a Guy Laroche silk suit and a hat festooned with roses.

'Hello David,' she said cheerily. 'I've come to screw you.'

Gabrielle McDowell meant something more to him – considerably more – than her merely being the wife of his former partner in The Ancient House. She had a small but very far from insignificant part in David's tangled personal history. Three years ago, Jim and Gabrielle had first begun to experience serious problems in their marriage. These had led, ultimately but perhaps indirectly, to Jim's decision to pull out of the restaurant altogether. The main difficulty between them, though David rather suspected that Jim never even had an inkling of it, was the fact that he and Gabrielle had been having a passionate fling. It had all blown over and things, for a while at least, seemed to get back on an even keel, at least as far as David could see. But he knew the cracks had been merely papered over. He knew Gabrielle was dissatisfied with her marriage – she had told him so, often enough, as they lay in bed in some hotel (they never made love at the restaurant flat or in her own home). Jim was unhappy with the way things were working out too but could never bring himself finally to sever the ties that bind. Changes, though, were obviously necessary and long overdue.

Gabrielle had seemed oddly indecisive about the whole business. David, to her, represented what might be. She sometimes said that she often found herself wondering why Jim couldn't be more like him, so relaxed, easy-going, less inclined to take the worries of the world on his shoulders. While she wasn't fool enough to think they could ever possibly make it as a couple (their relationship, as both knew, deep down, was physical rather than personal) she didn't seem to have the willpower to go out and make something of her own life. Always, it seemed, there had to be a man in it. Without someone hovering there, paying court, she didn't feel she could exist as a woman. Jim's route out of the mess – a pretty strange one, David had always felt – was to give up The Ancient House. He had gone a long way down the road of appraisal and evaluation and the general mood of self-analysis had led to him deciding to move on. He needed to do something to break up the log-jam but he could never quite figure out what. In pursuit of this elusive but critical element of change, he and David had some long, boozy discussions that simply went round in circles – Jim wasn't the kind of guy who was able to open up about how he really felt about things, even to someone as close to him as David. If he'd known his partner was screwing his wife, there was no telling what he might do. He decided to make changes and The pulling out of Ancient House seemed the most obvious thing.

Nowadays, and probably still none the wiser about his personal demons, he ran a computer software company in the Thames valley. By all accounts, he was doing pretty well. He and Gabrielle had lived apart for six months or so but they'd got back together again not long after Christmas. Jim had seemed pretty positive about the way things were going whenever he spoke about it but David – who admittedly had only met her a couple of times in the interim – never felt really sure about what Gabrielle thought about it all. As Jim ruefully admitted, she wanted novelty and excitement and Jim – a self-confessed workaholic – seemed the least likely candidate to provide those qualities in her life. The best he could do, albeit unwittingly, was to provide her with what she wanted from life, in material terms at least. As David quickly came to realise, this wasn't the same as giving her an opportunity to try and find out who she really was. Having shared a bed with her, on and off, for a number of years, he didn't know and he was damn sure Gabrielle didn't either.

David was one of several partners in the curious games Gabrielle played with herself. Through becoming a player, David had begun to find out a little about what made himself tick. Six years ago – though it seemed longer – he had come back from Australia with his life in tatters. He had no job and very little money, and extremely limited prospects of making any. But more important to him at that stage in his life – he was then in his late twenties – had been the break-up of his relationship with Abbie Kaufmann. He had met her in the States when she was a law student at UCLA and he was working at one of the Lappa Valley vineyards. It had, if there is such a thing, been love at first sight for both of them. They very quickly found themselves living together and in due course, having accumulated a fair bit of working capital, they set off to see something of the world. They travelled by way of Latin America, Japan and the Pacific Islands until they ended up, after an eventful year and a half, in Sydney. At first, it had gone well. Abbie, a specialist in company law, had joined a fashionable practice while he took a job restoring antique furniture in a harbourside warehouse. Through one of their regular clients he received the offer of a job managing a vineyard in Western Australia with a growing reputation. After a lot of discussion that went on well into the small hours he and Abbie had decided to give it a go. She arranged a transfer to her firm's small Perth office – although a lot of her work could be done from home – and they bought a run-down place out on the Parrawarra River with the intention of doing it up and, what the hell, maybe starting their own vineyard. The whole business had been an unmitigated disaster.

It wasn't just that the vineyard where he worked was taken over and he found himself eased out of a job. Despite the blow to his self-esteem, he simply moved on, to another vineyard, for half as much again as he had previously been pulling in. There turned out to be big structural problems with the house – not, to a practical guy like David, insurmountable ones, but not the kind of things he'd want to face after a tough week. But the big problem was Abbie herself – or at least, in his relationship with her. Until now, she had been – or at least David had assumed she had been – the kind of person who was content to move on, stop a while and move again. After a year living among sawn beams, floorboards and dust, she began to emerge more and more as a city person. Perth she found distinctly provincial. Sydney was far more her scene, LA all the more so. She liked city lights, city culture, city people – lawyers, media types, professionals. 'All that hippy shit, David,' she said to him one dreadful thundery night, 'I've just grown past it. It was fun while it lasted but that's all it was, a phase.'

She was no longer, he had to admit, the same woman he had met four years earlier. She was more mature, more controlled, more sure of the direction she wanted her own life to move in – and it wasn't the same as his. He was growing up and changing in his own way, but he didn't want things quite so cut-and-dried – and still didn't, for that matter. What they both realised was that they were neither of them on the same bus any more.

45

Three weeks later she announced she was going back to California and, while she was happy for them to remain friends, for her their partnership was as good as over.

He knew, deep down, she was right. But the parting still hurt, and subsequently the long nights of loneliness, the drinking, the string of casual affairs – at times his life seemed like it was being acted out of a script from some country and western song. He was amazed, catching an FM station from time to time on the car radio, how in such a highly charged emotional atmosphere the words of even the most banal song could strike deep and resonant chords within him. It was a period about which he could remember very little in later years. At the end of it, though, he'd grown up. Six months after he saw her drive off down the dusty road for the last time, he had sold the house and was on a long-haul 747 back to England.

Jim McDowell was an old friend from London days. He was heavily into computers but had got bored with it and had decided what he really wanted to do was to open a restaurant. He had found something suitable outside Oxford and, over dinner and a lot of wine one night, he casually asked if David would be interested in joining him in the venture. David had the know-how and the temperament, and he liked the idea right from the very start. Jim knew he was, in many ways, an ideal partner, even if he couldn't put any money into it. They shook hands on it, and Jim's wife Gabrielle kissed him warmly.

Things started to happen between them fairly quickly. David wasn't by nature a womaniser – that side of his personality only began to emerge by degrees much later – and he was certainly not the kind of guy to sleep with a friend's wife for the hell of it. But Gabrielle made it plain she was available to him if he wanted her, and want her he did. He liked her shiny exterior, the stylistic flair, the carefully presented sexuality. She was all so very different to anyone else in his own experience – she was, in some ways, like something out of *Dallas* – but he still fancied her. He was fond of her too – there was a person underneath the lip-gloss and padded shoulders – but it was her body rather than her heart and mind that he really wanted. He loved the attention she paid him – he liked being given little treats by her, a shirt or a bottle of wine, the feeling that he was important to someone. Once, when she was off with Jim on one of his endless trips abroad, she Fedexed him a lock of her pubic hair. What worried him, though, and what made him always keep her slightly at arm's length, was the suggestion – never overtly stated – that she wanted more from him than he was prepared to give in return. He knew this, but had not the moral courage to face her with it. He was happy to go for discreet meals with her, to feel valued by her and to screw her – but he didn't want any more from their relationship. She did, he knew, but she cared too much for him to risk everything by saying so, at least directly. And so she made herself available for him.

They had sex in cars, in hotels, in David's Oxford flat, but never at Gabrielle and Jim's house. It was never a full-time relationship either but it smoothed off many of the rough edges of his parting with Abbie and it had carried on, episodically (each, by now, had had other lovers) when they moved to The Ancient House four years back. On the whole it was a purely sexual chemistry between them – at least as far as David viewed it. He had never really got her to say much about her deeper feelings for him, if indeed there were any (if he had suspected her of getting in too deep, it would probably have ended the relationship there and then). But this intimacy had made them into friends too, after a fashion. There was no question of their being anything more profound – certainly not on David's side. When her marriage hit major difficulties eighteen months back, it seemed to signify a cooling-off period in their relationship, rather than the intensification that David might have expected. They hadn't slept together for a year or more now but quite often, under certain circumstances, David found himself thinking back to those earlier encounters.

All of this – or at least its essence, distilled and refined over many months of considered weighing-up in David's mind – passed before him as they stood face to face in the summer heat. A bee settled on the sunflower by the door, an empty milk-float whined down the lane; and still they stood there looking at each other, as though waiting for one of them to say something.

'Well,' said Gabrielle at length. 'Aren't you going to ask me in?'

Full consciousness returned in a rush. 'I'm sorry,' he said, temporarily grasping for words. 'How extraordinary . . . come in, come in. What on earth brings you here?'

He kissed her on the cheek. She'd changed the heavy Opium she used to wear for something lighter and fruitier. It smelled good on her. Her hand brushed his arm and she went through into the living room.

'I'm down at Dulvercote for a wedding,' she said as she took off her spectacular hat and tossed it casually on to the sofa. 'Or at least the reception afterwards. Julia de Glanville, she's a good friend of mine, I don't know if you ever met her? I don't think they came to the restaurant. Very grand people, small chapel in the grounds, just immediate family. I don't have to be there till one. As you're practically on my way, I thought I'd call in.'

'You look stunning,' said David, with total honesty. The simple peach-coloured silk seemed moulded to her body, clinging where it needed to cling and swinging elegantly loose where it didn't. She didn't reply. She knew it. Those heavy, uplifted breasts, with the deep cleavage designed to excite, had been prepared for him that very morning.

'You don't look so bad yourself.' He was wearing a plain blue T-shirt and ripped-off denim shorts that showed his powerful legs, already brown from the summer sun. He smiled, his slow lazy reptile smile that so many women had found irresistible.

They looked at each other in silence. The nervousness he had been feeling about Emma's impending arrival reappeared in a flash. He didn't really want these two women to meet – it didn't feel right to him, not at this stage anyway, or in these circumstances.

'Would you like a . . .' he ventured. Gabrielle had always enjoyed a drink.

'No thanks. A bit early, even for me. But can I use your loo?'

Jesus, he thought to himself after she'd disappeared upstairs. He found himself feeling slightly faint, and the room seemed unnaturally hot. He was, he realised, quite strongly aroused even by her presence and the feeling was compounded, moreover, by the difficulty of the situation. Under normal conditions he'd have been more than happy to have a surprise visit from an obviously randy Gabrielle. But with Emma due round almost at any minute it gave an unwelcome edge of complexity to his mood. He ducked into the kitchen, sloshed down a glass of chilled white wine and was grateful for the intoxicating rush of bubbles to his head. When he came back into the living room, Gabrielle was standing by the empty hearth in her underwear.

'I've come to screw you, David,' she repeated. 'We've got an hour. How would you like me?'

Lust shot through him like the motion of an express lift. Gabrielle had always had this power over him, the ability to direct his thoughts unerringly towards the carnal, to feel commonsense and necessity slipping away from him like cast-off clothing. At that moment, the impending lunch and even Emma herself simply ceased to exist for him, and whatever desire he had been feeling for her during the morning was focused instead on his visitor.

For a few tantalising seconds he stood there transfixed, just looking at her. Gabrielle was quite tall, five feet eight or nine, and with her hair up it made her look even taller. She stood there on the hearthrug in ridiculously high heels – she can't have driven down from Marlow in those, he found himself thinking. She must have changed them before parking the car.

Her silk French knickers were the same shade of pale peach as her Laroche suit. Her underwired bra was a froth of lace at the front where her breasts hung heavy and full. She wore matching suspenders and sheer, glossy stockings in smoky grey. In a room like David's, with it antiques and books and mellowed furniture, the summer sunlight drifting in through the heavily leaded windows, the effect was like a photo-spread from one of the upmarket lingerie catalogues that were advertised in the Sunday broadsheets.

The suddenness of his erection surprised even him.

Without consciously thinking about it, as much a slave as ever to his bodily desires, he quickly crossed the room and took her in his arms, crushing to him her fleshy body in its sheaths of warm silk. Her tongue sought his, tracing its way over his neck, her hands all the while pushing up under his T-shirt.

Blood roared through his head as they paused for breath and then kissed again, with ferocious intensity. Time stood still. Fifteen miles away, had he but known it, Emma Hadleigh finished studying the last of the Polaroids she had taken on location and decided it was time for lunch.

Gabrielle slithered to her knees and pressed her head against his groin, with its burgeoning erection. Oh Christ, he thought. He had all but forgotten the extraordinary skills she could display with her mouth and tongue. She was one of the few women he had ever met who enjoyed having him come in her mouth.

Then she was busy with his zip, roughly yanking his shorts down as he pulled his T-shirt off and over his head. His cock lolled there, stiff and ready. She took hold of it in one hand, gently stroking it as she licked around the top of his thighs, her cheeks brushing against his thick pubic hair. Then her lips closed over it and he felt himself transported into another realm.

He opened his eyes to see Gabrielle looking up at him, a wicked twinkle playing around her features. She nibbled around the tip of his glans, her tongue gently playing with the slit at the end of his cock, before swooping down and taking as much of him as she could into her mouth. She did this repeatedly, an exercise calculated to tease him into madness, the pause after each deep suck becoming an aching void of anticipation

51

that was immediately gratified.

He glanced down at her deep cleavage vanishing into a mysterious fleshy darkness, her breasts swelling full and ripe, her nipples pressed hard against the thin gauze of peachy lace. God, he wanted to suck her, to press his cock against the warm fullness that seemed to invite him to nestle there. He could see how tautly her suspenders were stretched against her thighs, the legs slightly parted so that her knickers were moulded tight against the fleshy lips of a pussy that he had sucked and fucked so many times in the past. He took hold of her shoulders, urging her on, thrusting his cock into her mouth. She liked her men to be forceful and dominant with her.

Her hand slipped down between her thighs, behind the silk, seeking out her own private pleasure-places. This was what she had liked to do so often in the past, to suck David as she played with herself, secure in the knowledge of her desirability. Later they would fuck, slowly and deliciously. Men needed spunking first, she had once explained as they lay panting before an open window in a hotel overlooking a Dorset cove – to draw out the overflow of tension in them. Only then could they screw her the way she liked. She had not slept with David for a good year at least now – had not even seen him for six months or more – and yet immediately she seemed to be as free and uninhibited with him as she had been even in the wildest days of their affair.

And David too, for his part, sensed something quite different to the emotions of the previous evening with Emma. There had been an inevitability about their coupling but there was also a faint nervousness, an unsureness that was completely lacking here with

Gabrielle. It was the difference between something new and exciting and something comfortable and familiar, the difference between the known and the unknown. Both had their place, both were sensations he could handle. Here in this sunlit room, with birdsong in the garden and a heavy sultriness in the air, he abandoned himself to the realm of the senses.

As he felt his seed rising within him he took hold of her head with both hands. Her cheeks were engorged, her heavily made-up eyes closed as though she were dreaming. There was a wildness in him now, a red mist that seemed to be descending on him, a delicious lewdness of thought giving way to a total surrender to the sensations of his body. He caught sight of her buttocks straining against the silk, her high-heeled shoes, her breasts swinging as she leaned forward. Here he was, being sucked off in his own living room at twelve in the morning with someone due to be coming for lunch at any minute – and he didn't care. He let out his pent-up breath, made a sound that was half-groan, half a cry of triumph, and then his seed boiled over into Gabrielle's mouth in thick, succulent pulses of pleasure.

Almost at the same time he could sense her tensing up. As though she had been waiting for his signal, he was aware of the movement of her hand between her legs becoming more urgent, more insistent, more immediate, as her swollen clitoris responded to her own expert touch and she moved back and away from him, letting his cock flop from her mouth. As she did so, he saw a little dash of semen overflowing on to the perfectly applied lipstick. With her free hand she grasped him round the buttocks, pressed herself forcefully against his muscular thighs and came in shuddering waves of sighs.

'I think I'll have that drink now,' said Gabrielle at length, when she had had time to compose herself.

Slowly normality began to return to David's mind. 'Right,' he said, and went through to the kitchen. His legs were trembling – man, he long ago decided, was not designed to have orgasms while standing up. As he poured out the wine, the phone rang. He picked up the portable phone that was lying on the worktop.

'Hi!' came Emma's voice, calling from her car. Why did he feel that momentary pang of guilt so strongly? 'Look, I'm going to be a little later than I'd said. The studio is sending me a fax to the Angel and I have to drive over there and pick it up. I'll be with you in an hour.'

'You could use the fax at the restaurant,' he ventured. The Angel was in the opposite direction, giving him even more precious time. He felt a cocktail of emotions, confused and vaguely anxious and at the same time strangely elated. It had always been like this with Gabrielle, wondering what was going to happen next, the fear of imminent discovery even when they had known Jim was far away.

'Yes,' she said, 'but I didn't know the number. Anyway I'm on my way now. I'll see you soon.'

Inwardly, David was relieved. He put the phone down and carried the drinks through to the living room. With his immediate lust for Gabrielle slaked and Emma letting him off the hook, he could think more clearly. Emma could not be with him for an hour at the earliest, by which time Gabrielle would have to be at her reception. There was a pattern there somewhere, he reckoned. It would be OK. Things were looking good. His whole body seemed to glow in the sunlight. He wanted more sex.

Gabrielle was now as naked as himself. They sipped

their wine, lips nibbling at each other, making small talk.

'How's Jim?' he asked, glad of the soothing effect of the Chardonnay.

'He's fine. He's in LA at the moment. That's why I'm going to Julia's wedding on my own. Aren't you lucky?' she added, her hands with their elegant nails caressing his cock. Already he felt the faint stirrings of renewed desire.

'And how are things?'

'Between us, you mean? OK, we rub along. I do my things, he does his.'

'Does he know about us?'

'Does it matter? No, I don't think he does. Christ, he didn't guess back then, so why should he suspect anything now? In any case, I think he respects you too much to even consider it as a possibility. He knows that I've not always been the dutiful wife but then he's not always been the dutiful husband either.'

Gabrielle had never had a career as such, not since she met Jim at any rate. Despite the film-star ambience that surrounded her, she was an intelligent woman with a gift for organisation. She had, no doubt, carefully worked out what time to leave home so she could be with David in time for an hour's sex before going on to her wedding reception, allowing a good fifteen minutes or so for freshening up and re-applying her makeup. But she had never put her skills to any practical use, at least as far as he could see. She had helped with the restaurant, keeping track of invoices, chasing suppliers and that kind of behind-the-scenes stuff. The filofax and the planners on the wall were just so much surface, though, he was sure. She was a sensualist at heart, seemingly content to be a kept woman, with her friends and fitness clubs to keep her busy during the day and a steady round of socialising during the evenings and at weekends. If that entailed a few discreet dalliances, then that was par for course, especially in the comfortably-off Thames valley milieu that she and Jim now frequented. No doubt Jim felt the same about these things. He was far from dumb.

Slowly, almost languidly, they found themselves in each other's arms again. This time the kisses were longer, richer, less frenetic. Guy the Gorilla shuffled in, roused from his morning nap. He glanced at the entwined couple, registered the look on David's face, and shuffled out again. With the practised ease of the familiar lover he had once been, David's hand snaked down towards the warm slickness of Gabrielle's sex, the outer lips already engorged and puffy, her clitoris aroused by his touch.

'God, you know how to do that to me, don't you, you bastard,' she breathed. He licked her neck slowly and sensually. She liked that, he remembered. She liked him to tongue her ear, too, until she squealed and wriggled like a schoolgirl. That was another bond between them. Once, driving along the Oxford by-pass years back, she had seen him gazing in the rear-view mirror at a bunch of sixth-form girls at a bus stop. The following weekend, with Jim away in London, she had dressed herself up in the complete St Trinian's outfit and invited him over for the afternoon. His balls were still aching the following evening. There were other games she enjoyed, too.

Her hands moved up and down his flanks, across his chest, down his back. She proffered him her breasts and he licked hungrily at the plump raspberry nipples – she had never had children – and the dusky aureolae.

'More slowly,' she breathed. 'I like it slow.'

He did as he was bid, his tongue moving in gentle flicks, his fingers continuing to caress her pussy. Almost without effort the two of them moved off the sofa and on to the floor, the polished wood cold and hard against naked flesh, the smell of dog hairs and the old woollen rugs mingling in their nostrils with the muskier scents of sex.

She nudged him with her hips and then he was on top of her, his cock perhaps not entirely erect as yet but sufficiently hard enough to penetrate her easily. She gasped slightly as he slid inside her. His cock, she had once told him, was bigger than Jim's. He had never been particularly sure that he wanted to know that, but it gave him a confidence of sorts. Despite his desire for Gabrielle's warm, soft, accommodating body, he had come three times the previous night with Emma and he wasn't sure just how much staying power he had left.

He needn't have worried. Though he was on top, it was Gabrielle who, quite unselfconsciously, was doing most of the work. Her hips ground against his in slow, sensuous circles, flesh pressing flesh, her big bare nipples brushing the hair on his chest. She nipped his shoulder with her teeth, licked his own nipples with the tip of her tongue in a way that made his cock stiffen appreciably and then he was away, falling into rhythm with hers, intoxicated with the mixture of perfume and sweat that rose up from her gorgeous body.

She looked up at him, big eyes wide, the makeup smudged now, an unmistakable flush of colour in her cheeks that was not entirely due to the summer heat. His hand slipped under her buttocks, slightly lifting her up as he forced himself into her. She spread her legs more, bringing them round and up over the backs of his thighs.

'Fuck me, David,' she breathed. 'I love you inside me.'

David liked a woman who talked during sex. Gabrielle did, more than most. What she was doing, what she wanted to do, what she had done in the past – it all blurred into one long, deliciously pornographic monologue.

'That's good. Oh, God, I can really feel that. Squeeze my tits – don't you like them? I used to love it when you came all over my tits. I love to lick your spunk, David. I want your spunk all the time. I want it all over me.'

Locked in a rhythm that seemed as familiar now as it had done when they had been lovers on a regular basis. David slowly and surely brought her to orgasm. She came with quiet, almost sobbing yelps, her long polished nails digging into his back, her eyes squeezed tight shut, her mouth open. She didn't notice that he hadn't made it himself, not that he especially wanted to. This time the sex with Gabrielle was warm and comforting, not the wild odyssey of earlier days, or even of earlier that morning, with Emma. As he rolled off her and lay looking up at the cobwebs on the ceiling, he felt a contentment and an appealing sense of security.

Both had taken – and given – exactly what they wanted, nothing more and nothing less. Afterwards, as he watched her make herself ready to face the world once again, he was aware of the contradictions in Gabrielle's character. Back on, a striptease in reverse, went the stockings, the silk underwear, the Laroche suit, the heels. Out came the makeup bag and mirror. The adjustments were carefully made, the mask was back in place, the hat at just the right angle. It was like she was armouring herself against the world. He saw her glancing from time to time at her watch as though for assurance. Ten minutes, and she was bright as steel again. This was a woman on whose voluptuous body men erected their fantasies, a vehicle for other people's ideas. Who or what she really was didn't enter into the equation. Half an hour ago, however, and David knew she was feral, a woman in the thrall of her own senses, sure and certain of her own sexuality and heedless of how she felt she ought to appear in the eyes of others.

David knew well enough the version he had liked best over all the years he had known her. That was why he still felt himself seduced by her, intoxicated by her natural vitality. And it was precisely because he, almost alone of the men she had known, brought that side of her out, that Gabrielle had come to David's cottage that morning. The sports-car salesmen and army officers, the property developers and doctors who were her casual lovers in the usual run of things, they were all a bunch of tossers, really. They didn't see beyond the surface, the lip gloss and the expensive hair, a woman who preferred to wear sexy stockings rather than tights and would even keep them on during intercourse. They didn't know, didn't want to know, what was actually there, deep inside her. And so she prepared an image of herself for their consumption. As they were both well aware – though whether consciously or not was no matter – David knew what she was really like, and could unleash her from the shell. It came out in the way he talked to her, the comfortable silences, the way their bodies moved together. And she could never, ever, have him for her own. That was her big regret and, at the same time, her addiction, the reason she would always come back for him. He knew all this, without having to be told. She drove off, smack on time, and now that the longed-for moment had gone he knew that she would be feeling curiously empty and unfulfilled once more.

'Hi!' said Emma, smiling on the doorstep. 'Sorry I'm late. Here, this is for you.' She kissed him and handed over a bottle of locally made cider vinegar.

'Last night's wine wasn't that bad, was it?'

'There wasn't much of a selection in the local shop so I bought this instead. You can have it with your fish and chips.'

'I think I'll lay it down instead. It's a good year. Let's sit in the garden, shall we? Lunch is almost ready.'

A sensitive nose could probably detect the last faint molecules of Gabrielle's fruity perfume in the living-room air and David had decided not to risk it. Inwardly enjoying the role of the charming and elegant host, he steered her through to the back of the house where the table and chairs stood invitingly in the shade.

'This is all very civilised,' said Emma. 'Do you do this every day?'

'Most days I'm down at the restaurant until early afternoon,' he said. 'You would be amazed just how much has to be done. Next week we have the VAT inspector coming and I tell you, I am not looking forward to that one little bit.' He noticed that his heart was palpitating slightly. He was surprised at how oddly forced and stilted his conversation sounded.

'I've not had the privilege,' Emma admitted, accepting a glass of wine. 'I only became VAT registered last year. Don't they usually give you a couple of years to hang yourself before they come to get you?'

'They're pretty fair, actually,' said David. 'Banks and tax people want to screw you into the ground but I've always had the impression that the VAT man is honestly trying to help. I guess I'm just not that into figures and things, so I just play it straight. I don't know how to fiddle things.' Christ, he thought. There must be something more interesting than that I can say. Talk about the weather, the wine – anything.

'Tell me a bit about yourself,' he said, smiling his crooked-teeth smile. 'Go back a few years, when you were a kid and all that.'

'I was born in Malvern. Daddy was in local government in the 1950s and 60s and we moved to London not long after I was born. They moved back there six or seven years ago. To Cheltenham, in fact.'

'Where did you go to college?'

'I did a foundation course at Kingston and then I did post-grad stuff at the Royal College of Art.'

He seemed impressed. She mentioned the names of a few contemporaries and was pleasantly surprised that he had actually met a couple of them, even if nowadays they probably wouldn't know him from Adam. 'How about you?' she asked.

He gave her a brief synopsis as he brought the luncheon things out – born in Somerset, educated at a minor and not very good public school, an art college course, then bumming round the world until landing up – and on his feet – in Oxford with Jim McDowell. Only the briefest mention, and he hoped she would not have noticed, of his childhood and only the most noncommittal remarks concerning his family background.

Lunch, as Emma was only too ready to admit, was superb – as simple things so often are. There was nothing particularly ornate about it, but the quality of the ingredients made elaboration unnecessary. The well-worn table, the heavy wineglasses, the plates and cutlery that didn't match – it wasn't the kind of imagery she would ever have used in a still-life advertising photograph but it would, she said, have made a brilliant watercolour. A guy she had gone out with at college made a very handsome living nowadays doing just that kind of thing. You saw his stuff on book jackets, in the glossies, all over the place. David knew who she meant but he couldn't put a name to the illustrations.

Afterwards she nibbled a piece of Vignotte, bit into an apple. The wine and the heady scent of the summer flowers seemed to have made her drowsy and content. There was scarcely a breath of wind to ruffle the leaves of the rowan tree, in whose shade Guy the Gorilla was sprawled, panting. It seemed the most natural thing in the world when David, as much by gesture as by any spoken word, discreetly ushered her indoors and up to the bedroom where they had spent the long night together.

This time he undressed her slowly, the loose-fitting Pineapple top, the lycra leggings, the tight black underwear. She unbuttoned his shirt for him and licked his nipples in slow, sensuous circles. They were big for a man's, more like a girl's at the onset of puberty. She knew he was the oral type, as her head slid down his slim brown torso.

His cock tasted fresh and inviting, and she told him so. The following week, had she but known it, David would finally get the shower installed in the bathroom, after his frantic attempts at an all-over wash to remove any vestiges of the morning's encounter with Gabrielle

– there had been no time for a bath. The night before, even in the restaurant, she had noticed and liked the clean way he smelled. Later she was pleased to discover how good he tasted. No nasty aftershave and only the vaguest hint of soap and deodorant – his natural body smell was more than enough to arouse her senses. Fresh manly sweat she found a real turn-on at such times – stale perspiration and sweet inspiration just didn't go together. All this she told him, quite unself-consciously.

At first, their love-making was long and slow. They had all afternoon for each other – she didn't need to be back in town until that evening (the lab in Covent Garden where she had all her transparency processing done would be closed by the time she got back, anyway). There was no point in rushing things, even though he was still in his Casanova mode. It had been some little while since he had had two women on the same day – about fifteen years, being honest with himself. In his student days he could – and did – manage it four or five times a night but that was years ago and these days, ploughing steadily on into his early thirties, he was happy with once a night and a repeat performance, if required, before breakfast.

He needn't have worried. At the first ministration of Emma's tongue, he felt the old fires beginning to kindle up inside him. By the time she climbed on top of him and unceremoniously guided his penis into her, his cock felt like it was hard as iron. The curious thing was that, though he had known Emma for less than twenty-four hours, he was already starting to feel as much at home with her sexually as he did with Gabrielle, a woman whom he had been screwing, on and off, for the best part of six years. It hadn't felt that way on the living-room floor in the morning. On top of that was the rare, keening thrill of unfamiliarity, the excitement engendered by her taut buttocks and the luscious, pear-like form of her breasts. He was aware both of the sense of danger involved in a journey into the unknown and also the accompanying and deeply reassuring confidence of the born traveller. He had never noticed before just how important a part of her physical attraction was the sensuous curve of her mouth.

Her pussy was as tight as her leggings, deliciously so. And as if this were not enough, she had ways of moving her inner muscles so that it squeezed and cajoled him almost to the point of delirium. Once, after a particularly rowdy night at the old place near Oxford, he had ended up in bed with a famously glamorous TV newsreader who had been eating there. Intercourse with the great lady, he later confided to Jim – he was not usually the type to talk much, if at all, about his conquests, but then Jim was a great fan of hers and had been more than usually persistent in his questioning – had borne more than a passing resemblance to lobbing a carton of yoghurt down Broad Street. He told this later to Emma. She roared with laughter.

When he finally came in her, he was surprised by the violence of his orgasm. His seed seemed to boil out of him as if after a month of abstinence, his mind intoxicated by novelty and excitement rather than the raw sexual appetite that, though he scarcely registered it, had been sated hours ago. Above all he liked being able to see her as they made love, with the afternoon sun filtering through the old window glass in its various pale shades of green and purple. He came loudly and tumultuously –

Emma had already climaxed a couple of times, he was sure – and within seconds they were wrapped around each other, curled up together like spoons as his sperm slowly seeped out of her and the gentle sound of her breathing was echoed by the wind, high away across the fields in the distant poplars.

He awoke, not with a start, but in a kind of gentle upward curve into consciousness. He had been dreaming about his garden, and people wandering about in it, and as his senses gradually returned he could smell the scent of the nicotianas that grew against the south-facing back wall of the cottage. Emma lay apart from him across the bed, breathing gently, evidently soundly asleep. Still with his eyes closed, he reached out and drew a hand across her shoulders, down her back, across her hips, as though to reassure himself that she still existed. She sighed and seemed to murmur something.

He opened his eyes and looked at her, the soft blonde hair, the sun-browned skin of her shoulders. It was warm in the bedroom but he instinctively drew the covers up over her bare shoulders. His watch, hung on the wooden stand that he had made at school a quarter of a century ago, told him that it was a quarter to six. Must feed Guy, he thought, and then take him for a walk. I'll make a pot of tea for us both.

He got up with exaggerated caution, decided to ignore his shameful old dressing gown that had been almost as faithful a friend as Guy for many years now, pulled on a pair of jeans instead and went downstairs in his bare feet. The border collie stood in the kitchen with his tongue lolling, bright-eyed and bushy tailed. David studied his eyes carefully – he knew what was going on.

'How can you eat this muck?' David asked as he spooned out the dog food, but Guy didn't seem to mind.

The kettle boiled and he made the tea. He thought about making something for them to eat in bed but decided that would be a little over the top – what would she expect, crumpets and home-made jam? He would have to be at the restaurant in an hour, but it didn't really matter if he was late. These days the place could virtually run itself – he had realised this almost as soon as he had moved away from The Ancient House – to the extent that he could sometimes take several days off at a time and leave it to Hannah and Louis and the others to proceed under their own steam. In a few weeks he would close the place down for the annual summer break – this year, he certainly felt like he needed it – and then he was going to take a fortnight off, maybe go to Portugal where friends had for ages been pestering him to come and stay in their villa.

Would things be different now that Emma had come into his life? He knew, already, that this wasn't a one-night stand. She was still here, after all, almost twenty-four hours later. But he didn't know enough about her to make any kind of judgements, not yet, anyway. For the time being he was happy to let things progress of their own volition. It was good karma to let things happen.

As he picked up the tray of tea things he heard a movement and turned round. It was Emma, sleepy-eyed, wrapped up in his tatty old dressing gown. She looked absolutely gorgeous.

'Hi!' she said drowsily. 'I'll do anything for a cup of tea.'

He gave her his practised reptile smile with the crooked

teeth. 'You may live to regret that,' he said, and put the tray down with exaggerated caution. Underneath the gown, of course, she was naked.

# Chapter 3

'Well, what do you think?'

Emma's inquisitor was Martin Churchward of the prestigious West End design consultancy, Collet Churchward Hawksworth Dean. They were standing at the huge, unpolished oak table in the room used by the agency for meetings with important clients. The space was quiet, subdued, air-conditioned; almost all vestige of colour had been leached from the room's fixtures and fittings until everything was a cool monochrome, focusing attention on the pile of scatter proofs laid out on the table before them.

They were looking at the first sheets of the annual report CCHD had designed for Land Investments, a blue-chip property development consortium with a City profile a good deal higher than the Monument. It was the first time they'd worked for the company, and Martin was anxious to impress. Ever the perfectionist, he'd nevertheless made an extra effort with the design of the annual report. On the finance pages, everything was sober, restrained, factual, the lines of small type, beautifully designed, set amid rolling acres of clear white space. On the introductory pages, however, where the Chairman's message to the shareholders prefaced a review of the company's operations, there were eight stunning pages of black-and-white photographs that he had commissioned from Emma. Grainy seascapes alternated with soft Suffolk vistas, while city spires rose above empty fields in which drifted the grey mists of dawn that were only slowly beginning to clear.

The report was, in short, making reassuring messages to investors that their beloved English landscape was in safe hands. Of course, the kind of prime real estate that Land Investments was primarily interested in wasn't at all the sort of rural idyll suggested by those exquisite images, so beautifully printed (at the shareholders' expense) on sleek art paper. From a business point of view, Land Investments was more concerned with the kind of property on which they might want to build a shopping mall, a cinema complex, a hi-tech office block. Their annual report, therefore, was window-dressing at its most sophisticated. It showed their operations perhaps less as they were, but more as they would like them to be seen – they were caring, sophisticated and committed people as well as shrewd financiers.

'Brilliant,' Emma said simply. 'I think they've come out really well. I can't fault them.'

'Good,' replied Martin. 'I think Land Investments are going to love it. If they don't, we're up shit creek.'

He laughed. Producing glossy annual reports and other corporate literature was big business for a company like his. Gone were the days when such documents were dull, bland and deeply conservative. The FTSE front-runners knew that presentation was the way to impress their shareholders and City competitors these days and they weren't afraid to splash out big bucks on production budgets. Companies like Land Investments treated their corporate statements much as a car manufacturer would use a television commercial – as a way of suggesting class, charisma, success. No one actually read the reports, of course, except to check out the Chairman's salary (£295,000 in the present instance). The rest was achingly expensive PR for the company. Hence the use of a photographer like Emma, who would cost them deep in the purse, and of companies like CCHD, whose bottom lime was sometimes mistaken for their fax number. But to Martin, and to Emma for that matter, a client like Land Investments could be worth a lot of money over a long period. Get the annual report right, Martin had said at the start of the project, and you can soon start pitching for other work from them – a new corporate identity, for a start. He could sense the Testarosso was nearly in the bag, the design industry awards just waiting to be plucked off the table. All it needed was the right kind of noises from Liam Forbes-Chalmers of Land Investments, and he was due at any minute.

Emma and Martin waited for his arrival with no small anxiety. 'I think it's best that he meets you as well,' Martin had said when he invited her to the studio for the presentation. 'They're not peasants – they're into the arts in a big way. It's all part of their corporate policy. You should see some of the stuff they have hanging on the walls in their head office. There's an Epstein bronze in reception and a couple of Hockneys in the boardroom. They like to feel they're involved with the arts. They see themselves as patrons of excellence. I've not seen anything like it outside Saatchis.'

Martin's ponytail and Armani suit made their own quiet statement about the age in which he lived and worked. A couple of minutes passed, during which time, he mused, Liam Forbes-Chalmers had probably snapped up enough of Essex or the east Midlands to build half-a-dozen out-of-town supermarkets, and all from the back seat of an XJ6 purring through the London traffic. His father, old Tom Forbes-Chalmers (who was still involved with the company he had founded in the post-war property boom) was said to have been one of the first men in Britain to have a car phone.

Emma was smiling at Martin's off-the-cuff remarks when the receptionist ushered in their client. They made instant and slightly unnerving eye contact. As he shook hands, first with Martin and then with herself (firm and dry, she noted, and held for exactly the right length of time) she noticed something unusual about Liam Forbes-Chalmers. It was not just his strong physical resemblance to David, but also the charismatic aura that seemed to surround him. Here was a man who commanded respect and obedience even before he spoke, before he did anything at all. He was tall, with the same slightly windblown features and dark wavy hair that David had, and he carried himself with a similarly easy confidence. He looked thirty-eight or thirty-nine but was probably older. Whereas David's clothes were as subtly shaped and faded as a length of driftwood, this guy was languid elegance personified.

Emma could not deny his erotic appeal. She had always felt pleasantly surprised, turned on even, by seeing someone in an unexpected context – her first 'serious' boyfriend, the one who had taken her virginity at seventeen, forsaking his sprayed-on jeans and trainers for an unashamedly gallant suit for a family wedding; another, later boyfriend in cricket gear (a couple of weeks later, nevertheless, she'd ditched him for the team captain at the club disco); her own father, even, shedding twenty years by simply stripping down to a pair of shorts on holiday in the Algarve. This time, it was like seeing David after a chat-show makeover. It was a big turn-on.

'So, this is it, then?' murmured Liam, once the introductions and preliminary inconsequences were over and he could turn his attention to the proofs in which he had invested so much time and capital. His voice was understated but nevertheless commanding. Emma knew he would not need to raise it to get what he wanted. For a long time, in silence, he looked at the scatter of sheets on the table, as Emma and Martin exchanged wordless glances. From CCHD's standpoint, a lot of work had gone into the Land Investments job, and Emma could feel that Martin was on tenterhooks. So much, she knew, was riding on the outcome. Emma's part had been comparatively straightforward, but the finance pages had been written and rewritten, chopped and changed so many times that they had practically blown the design budget out of the window. Driven by old Tom Forbes-Chalmers's curious whims about typography and layout – areas in which he knew about as much as Emma did about property investment – Martin and his assistant had been involved in so many late-night sessions that their eyes had begun to assume the dimensions of an Apple Mac screen. In the circumstances, it was a miracle that they had come anywhere close to the deadline.

'The paper seems slightly glossier than the samples you showed me,' Liam said at length.

'That's just the paper it's been proofed on,' said Martin, moving quickly to allay suspicions. 'The finished version will be just like the paper you saw.'

Another pause. 'You don't think these graphs are

maybe just a little on the bright side?'

'Again, that's probably because of the kind of paper. We can tone them down if you want to.'

'No, not at all, I don't think that's necessary. I'm sure you're right. They stand out very well.'

Having examined the crisp columns of figures, the pie-charts and graphics, he turned his attention to Emma's photographs.

'I like the way they break up all that boring text,' he remarked. 'I wrote most of it, so I know how dreary it is. I like the way each is on a page of its own.'

'They wouldn't have worked half so well if they'd have been set into the text,' said Martin.

'That's how I saw it originally,' Liam admitted, 'but I'm glad now that you persuaded me this was the best way to do it.'

These remarks were addressed to Martin but it was Emma with whom he had the eye contact. She liked the way he could concede a point when necessary. She hated the stubborn, macho type.

'This one,' he said, gesturing to her at the sheet in front of him. 'This is the Somerset Levels, isn't it?'

'That's right,' said Emma. 'It's near Curry Rivel, if you know that part of the world. My boyfriend was born nearby.'

She realised, almost immediately, that it was the first time she'd ever referred to David as her boyfriend. It felt strange and curiously exciting, even though she'd known him not much longer than a fortnight. She was looking forward to going down to the cottage again that weekend.

'Isn't that interesting?' said Liam Forbes-Chalmers. 'I had an aunt there, and we often spent summer holidays with her. It brings back lots of memories.'

'Would you like to have the original print?' said Emma, acting on an impulse.

'Could I?' said Liam, slightly taken aback. 'I'd be happy to pay you for it. I just love those dark clouds, the glimmer of the water beyond the reed beds. It's very moody. Yes, that would be very kind. Tell me how much.'

'It's a gift,' said Emma. 'I've really enjoyed working on this job. And Martin's been generous with the fee, so I think we can stretch to a freebie or two.'

'That's very kind,' said Liam. 'I wish more of the people I worked with were as open-hearted.' And then he was back discussing technicalities with Martin, querying this, quibbling over that. He's certainly good as a details man, thought Emma after he had hurried away to his next appointment, but he's got a shrewd grasp of the basics as well. No doubt he's an absolute whizz with the counting beads and abacus – he wouldn't be able to afford that suit and those shoes if he weren't – but he seems to have got a bit of soul too.

Martin caught her abstracted gaze. She felt, though she could not be entirely certain, that there was a slight caution in his eyes.

'He liked it,' she told David when she called him from the studio that afternoon. 'In fact he wanted a print of one of the shots.'

'Hope you stung him for it,' David murmured, sounding ever so slightly jealous. He'd rather wanted a print of the photograph in question for himself. 'You gave it to him – are you made of money? Even if he'd bought it, a guy like that would probably write it off against tax anyway. You get his sort in here all the time, and they never leave much of a tip. That's how they get where they are. What was he like, anyway?'

'He was OK,' said Emma. 'I think even you would have liked him. He reminded me of you.'

David ignored this. 'You're still coming down this weekend?' he asked, again with that slight dismissiveness in his voice. She knew better than to take the bait.

'Of course,' she said, laughing. 'I'm really looking forward to it. Hopefully I can get down on Friday evening. I still have to do a couple of still-life shots in the studio for that Sainsbury's thing. God, that one seems to drag on and on.'

'Think of the money,' he said. She could hear a woman's voice in the background. 'Look,' he said suddenly, 'the rep from the wine merchant's arrived, I've got to go. We usually manage a little tasting around this time. You needn't be jealous – she's married. See you Friday, then.'

'See you.' She put the phone down. No doubt about it, meeting David had made a big impression on her life. In the few weeks she'd known him she'd spent as much time as she could down in the Cotswolds. It was the perfect balance for her busy professional life. Not really a born wanderer, she had become adjusted to the need to have to shoot off anywhere at a moment's notice, and she felt envious sometimes of his stability and his willingness to stay in one place for long periods. They'd had some great times, though, and that moonlit session in the cornfield had been only the beginning. Only last week – Monday evening, David's regular night off when the restaurant was closed – they had scaled new heights of experience. They had driven out towards Marlborough and a simple, unpretentious pub that served the most amazing seafood. Were shellfish really an aphrodisiac?

This was the question that entertained them as they mulled over their meal in the pub garden, as the locals played darts in the adjacent public bar and the sun went down over the rolling downs. She said they were, he said they weren't. On top of a couple of cold beers that settled the dust in her throat while they ordered – they'd driven down in the old Light 15 with all the windows down – she'd had oysters for a starter and most of a bottle of Pouilly Fuissé to herself. David, however, didn't like to drink more than a couple of glasses, at most, when he was driving, and he kept himself in check. They'd rubbed legs together under the table repeatedly. By the time the meal was over, she was fairly swimming and they were hungry for each other.

As they drove back, the breeze playing through her hair, she absently stroked his leg. Slowly, teasingly, her fingers had moved higher. She could feel the burgeoning stiffness of his erection through his jeans. She leaned across to tongue his ear.

'That was a lovely meal,' she purred.

'You didn't want a pudding,' he recalled.

'Your cock will have to do,' she said. 'I wanted to get home and into bed with you.'

'I'm driving as fast as I can. It's difficult enough on these roads without a half-naked woman sprawled across you, with her tongue doing naughty things.'

'I don't think it's naughty,' she said. 'I think it's nice. Perhaps there are other things we can do.'

She gave his cock a squeeze. It had grown significantly harder. She slipped her hand in between the tops of his thighs. It came on to rain, at first in a gentle spray and then in big, warm drops that hit the windscreen like night insects. She wound the window up in a hurry.

They drove on in this manner for miles, the tyres swishing along the wet roads, she nestling against him, stroking the sensitive inner thighs and his heavy, bulbous testicles. What curious things men's balls were, she had often thought. They intrigued her. She and David didn't speak, and there was no need to, not even when she deftly unzipped him and exposed his cock. The wiper blades beat time. Though the car windows were closed she could still smell the night above the leathery smells of the old car.

'Sod this,' she said, unclipping her seat belt. She held his stiffness in her right hand while, with the fingertips of her left, she traced little abstract patterns of touch across his sensitive glans. His cock felt particularly hard – perhaps it was the evident novelty of the situation. It was also surprisingly cool, although its tip was warm and spongy. To her it was like the most delicious of playthings, a toy capable of giving infinite pleasure. To many women a cock was a cock but to Emma it was an object almost of veneration and affection, whoever owned it.

She formed her fingers into an O-shape and began to rub gently up and down his shaft. She sensed a change in his breathing. On the cassette player Ry Cooder was steppin' out with his customary mixture of sensitivity and raunch. Emma felt excited, as the trees flashed past in the headlights, the broken lines on the road echoing the rhythms of the music and the movements of her hand. David concentrated as best he could on the road.

He gasped softly when she took him in her mouth, her tongue swirling at first around the tip before she took in as much of him as she could. A distant voice told her that it was actually bloody uncomfortable down there, half-kneeling on the floor, the gear shift pressed against her breast. She felt vaguely car-sick too, but she no longer cared. She loved David's cock and she wanted it inside her. She sucked until she could sense she really would be sick and then she slid back into her seat.

Again, she pumped him up and down with her fingers formed into a ring. She was almost surprised when he came so quickly, his semen flooding out over her hand. He gripped the steering wheel, eased up on the accelerator, and gave in to the inevitable. She glanced around and reckoned the guy in the car behind must have been quite taken aback, watching the old Citroen alternately slowing down and speeding up for no apparent reason. David, on the other hand, was hardly aware of the car pushing up close behind him, even though he hated being tailgated. The souped-up Ford swept past in a blaze of lights and a thump of dance music and they had the long straight descent into Brampton to themselves.

But that was last week. Finding it difficult to concentrate on looking at contact sheets in her studio, she wished the weekend would come round. She recalled how that same evening, still fired by her thirst for experimentation, he had taken her inside her tight, puckered anus. It was the first time she had ever done this with anyone and she had asked him for it specifically. It was her idea, not his. It was so very different to how things had been with Vinnie, the guy she'd lived with for two years or so. She'd been younger then, and less sure of herself. She didn't have the confidence to say what she really wanted. She let him make the decisions, went along with what he dictated because she thought it was expected of her. Now she was starting to come out of that phase, to assert herself much more. But even with Vinnie, she had never gone so far as she had with David. She felt so much freer and looser with him.

She had, to be truthful with herself, found the anal sex excruciatingly painful, at least at first, but at the time – almost insane with sexual excitement – it was the idea of reaching out and grabbing the forbidden fruit that appealed most. Still, she'd done it now, and maybe it wouldn't be so bad later. They might try it again the coming weekend, if David fancied it. In a way, she had told him the following morning, it had been like banging your head against a wall – the real pleasure came when you stopped doing it. 'I enjoyed it,' he had said, 'but I'm not sure whether you did.' She admired him for his honesty.

Her reverie was interrupted by the ringing of the phone. She took it herself – Sasha, her assistant, was off coaxing an extra effort from the lab that did most of their colour processing. It was Liam Forbes-Chalmers and she was not in the least surprised to hear from him.

'Look,' he said after they'd exchanged the initial pleasantries and he'd said how pleased he'd been with the way the annual report had turned out. 'There is something else I'd like to discuss with you, something that you might be interested in. How busy are you at the moment?'

She had a stock answer to this question. Clients liked to know you were busy – if you weren't, it might have negative connotations – but at the same time they liked you to be able to make time for them. 'I've got quite a lot on,' she said, 'but there's a couple of things hanging fire, so I have a bit of leeway.'

'Can you make lunch with me on Thursday? Do you

know Macaulay's, just off Ludgate Hill? I was wondering
if you might be able to meet me there if you can spare the
time. There's something I'd like to discuss with you and
I hate talking business on the phone.'

Liar, she thought. You must do it all the time. You just
want to chat me up. Of course she knew the restaurant.
Macaulay's was a lovely old place with a lot of character;
the food was excellent but best of all was its evocation of
a vanished era. Emma had never been there but it was
occasionally featured in the Sundays. Even David, not
always an admirer of London eating habits, had spoken
highly of it. Good, simple food, beautifully cooked, he
had said. People go there to eat, not to be seen.

'Yes,' she said without a moment's hesitation. 'Do you
want to tell me what this is about?'

'Not now, Emma. But it's a business thing and I think
it could be good for both of us. Can you make 12.30?'

'12.30 would be fine. I'll try and bring that print I
promised you.'

Professing thanks, he rang off.

What was that all about? she immediately found
herself wondering. Is he trying to pick me up? It was all
very intriguing.

Macaulay's was one of those deeply old-fashioned
restaurants of a kind which, in London at least, had been
hunted down by food-writers and other curiosity-seekers
almost to the point of extinction. Off Ludgate Hill,
between Fleet Street and the City, it hid itself away from
the gaze of the inquisitive down an unpromisingly grubby
narrow street.

To those in on the secret, however, Macaulay's was a
gem. No one knew with any certainty when it had been

founded – some time in the Regency, was the best guess. It was a dark and labyrinthine place, the ground floor still resembling the coffee-house it must surely once have been, the basement a rabbit-warren of small rooms and tables in unexpected places. Even its crisp white tablecloths were the stuff of legend, as were the long white linen aprons worn by the waiters. All of them were men, and all of them looked as though they had been working there since Neville Chamberlain's day. The maitre d' wore, of all things, a tail coat. Such traditions, however, were greatly valued at Macaulay's. This wasn't Disneyland, this was the real thing – you couldn't fake that patina of authenticity, Emma decided as they were shown to their table.

In deference to the correct way of doing things, Emma wore a simple dress of cream linen with matching jacket and a row of red beads that went perfectly with her lipstick. She and Liam Forbes-Chalmers were tucked away by themselves in a small alcove (they could hardly call it a room) below street level. The coolness was a welcome respite from the baking noonday sun. Through a basement area window, they could see hurrying footsteps above them but of their fellow-diners, there was no sign. Though other people were eating barely a few feet away, all they were aware of was the discreet hum of conversation and the occasional clink of glasses. Securing a table here was never easy, even a week in advance – Liam must have moved mountains to get a booking at such short notice. Interestingly, though both upstairs and downstairs were full as usual, the table next to theirs – the only other one in their little chamber – remained obstinately empty, despite the prominent 'reserved' notice.

'Someone's missing out,' said Emma, nodding at the empty table. It was nearly half-past one, and the maitre d' didn't take kindly to latecomers.

'A no-show by now, I should think,' said Liam. 'How's your pheasant?'

'Delicious,' replied Emma between mouthfuls. 'I've never tasted nicer.'

As befitted its old-money ambience, the menu at Macaulay's was heavily biased towards traditional game and fish. The venison, in season, was legendary; the rabbit pie an institution. The trout they had had for starters had been perfection in itself, the flesh flaking away into nothingness, with that slightly earthy flavour that no farm-bred fish could ever hope to emulate.

Liam, delighted with the print she had brought for him, had come to the point fairly quickly, almost as soon as they'd ordered. He said what he meant, and Emma liked to know where she was. That was one of the things she liked most about David, too – Vinnie could be so wishy-washy.

'As you might know from Martin, Land Investments is quite heavily involved in arts sponsorship,' he began. 'OK, hand on heart, it does save us quite a sum in company tax but it also helps increase our profile. We do like to feel we have a commitment towards creative work in all its forms.'

'Martin said you'd sponsored the "New Artists" exhibition at the Serpentine last year.'

'That's right. It was very successful. Next month we're sponsoring an exhibition of work by Klaus Bohm at the Minories Gallery. Martin's been working on the programme for us. Do you know Klaus Bohm's stuff? He's very fashionable in Europe but he's not quite so well known here. Not yet, anyway. It's all arranged but the posters aren't going to be out for a couple of weeks. After Christmas, we'll be putting a lot of money into a Paul Nash retrospective at the Tate. We are also going to be involved, for the first time, with next year's summer season at Covent Garden.'

'That must cost you a packet,' said Emma.

'The big stuff, like Nash and the opera, we can't possibly afford to put on by ourselves. The amount of money involved is just incredible, so other companies have to have a part too. But the smaller exhibitions, like Klaus Bohm, are more manageable when we're the sole sponsors. It also gives us much more exposure, when our logo is the only one you see on the poster. We've done three of four now at the Minories and they're beginning to reap dividends, not just for ourselves in terms of the exposure and the value people place on our name, but also for the artists concerned. OK, so Bohm is hardly an unknown but it's certainly done his prospects no harm, in this country at least. A place like the Minories has a fully international audience.'

'Where do I fit into all this?' asked Emma, feeling puzzled.

'I knew you'd ask that,' he said, his eyes twinkling. She was struck by the perfect symmetry of his face when it broke into a smile. 'What I'm driving at is to sound you out about the possibility of you being involved with us for next year's show at the Minories. It needn't actually involve you a great deal in terms of time. We can take care of all the organisation. All it needs is access to your work – although, in the past, we and the gallery people have usually been happy to go along with what the artist selects for showing. And, of course, you'll need to show up at the launch and be on hand for the press if they show an interest. I know this is very much off the top of my head for the moment but I was wondering how all this might sound.'

Emma paused for a moment, trying to suppress her mounting excitement. Four years ago she'd been doing publicity photographs for a swimwear catalogue and now she was about to have a major exhibition of her own work. She could hardly believe it. Her fingertips traced a pattern in the condensation on her glass.

'I think it sounds bloody wonderful, to be honest,' she said. 'Obviously, you'll need to speak to my agent as well. But in broad principle – yes, it's fine. It's almost too good to be true.'

'Well that's good,' said Liam. 'I'm very pleased. We can talk about it again nearer the time. Do you know Dastor, who owns the Minories? Talk to him if you like. He's very good.'

And that was it. They hardly referred to it again, for the rest of the meal. He had got what he wanted and she had something she could hardly have bargained for. For the most part, they talked about travel, holidays, that kind of noncommittal thing. The service, like her escort, was discretion itself. Emma looked at him as he complimented the waiter who came to clear their plates. How uncannily like David he is, she found herself thinking – and not for the first time. The same kind of eyes, a similar sort of hair. His features, though, were more elegantly balanced – David's face had an appealing lopsidedness, the two halves almost but not quite matching, as though two portraits of the same man by different artists had been spliced together. It was one of the things she liked most about him, and it was responsible for a lot of his character.

The perfectly poised Liam Forbes-Chalmers ordered lemon sorbets for them both, and coffee, and a fine old brandy. It was with no small surprise, then, that she felt his ankle against hers. At first it had seemed accidental, but then it had happened at increasing intervals. So what, she found herself thinking. I like him. He is very good-looking. I am a woman of twenty-six.

It had certainly been a memorable meal but the curious thing, Emma noticed when they tried to resume their conversation after Liam had excused himself and gone to call his secretary, was that she could hardly recall what they had been talking about. Still, she reflected, he had been excellent company, the perfect gentleman, undemonstrative and witty in a very English way. She liked him, she had to admit. The idea of the exhibition really thrilled her. She could hardly wait to tell David.

Somewhat to her surprise, he offered her a cigarette.

'Not for me,' she said. 'But go ahead. I kind of like the smell of fresh tobacco smoke.'

Impulsively she struck a match and held it out for him. His hand brushed hers as he inhaled. They looked at each other, a questioning glance. The glow was there, all right. The go-ahead.

They had more coffee, another cognac. And then she felt his hand under the table, on her knee, moving up her thigh.

She looked at him. 'Ought we to be doing this? Here?'

'I think we should,' he replied with effortless charm.

She sipped her brandy. Now his hand was under the hem of her dress, feeling the soft flesh of her legs, gliding smoothly back and forth but moving inexorably towards the sensitive skin of her upper thighs.

'It's a bit public, don't you think?' she murmured, fear of discovery rising in her conscience.

'All the more exciting for us,' said Liam. 'Besides, the waiter won't be back until we're ready to leave.'

He certainly has magic fingers, Emma thought to herself. She sensed her breasts thickening and the nipples hardening with desire. She wanted to go to the loo, but didn't feel she could break off. He would be terribly offended and, besides, she needed him. For the exhibition, in the long term, and more immediately to satisfy her own burgeoning bodily lusts.

His hand was at the top of her thighs, brushing against her panties. Half of her wanted him to stop, the other half to go on. The urge to pee was becoming stronger with her growing arousal. His fingers caressed her sex gently through the cream silk, catching and stroking a stray wisp of pubic hair, outlining the unseen shape of her lips. She was aware of a growing dampness in her crotch.

She moved slightly on her chair and allowed his fingers to enter her vagina. She couldn't, at this stage, look at him directly. He was talking about Crete, or at least she thought he was talking about Crete. She saw his other hand resting on the tablecloth, the cigarette smoke curling upwards. For the first time she noticed he was wearing a wedding ring, a thick and expensive band of white gold. I might have known, she found herself thinking. Still, she was in a relationship too, and she didn't feel she was being unfaithful in any way. She was a free woman, after all.

Nevertheless, despite Liam's ministrations, she couldn't get her thoughts away from David. Her mind drifted back to the night coming home in the car. She thought of David's cock, strong and hard in her mouth. She looked at Liam. He smiled, but there seemed to be little warmth in his eyes. I like you, she said to herself, but I don't want to suck your cock. You can put it in me, though, if you like.

He had three fingers in her vagina now, and she felt full and stretched. The pressure against her bladder was becoming almost unbearable. And yet despite herself she parted her legs more to accommodate him, leaned backwards in the chair, thrusting out her pelvis. I just hope I don't wet myself, she thought.

She was surprised when he suddenly crushed out his cigarette and withdrew his fingers. He held them up to his face, wet and glistening with her secretions, inhaling deeply and appreciatively. He licked the tip of his index finger, the one that had been doing all the work on her clitoris. Then he offered the finger to her. She licked it too, tentatively at first and then drawing it deeper into her mouth, holding his palm as she did so. It tasted salty and musky, a bit like anchovies. But I'm still not sucking your cock, she said silently.

He stood up and drew her to him. But instead of the anticipated kiss – and she hated kissing men who smoked, they smelled like a saloon bar carpet – he turned her round, pushing her face forwards on to the table. Solidly built from two-hundred-year-old English oak, it scarcely trembled. He drew her dress up around her hips and his hands caressed the silken globes of her buttocks. There was a pause, a hesitancy – was someone coming? she wondered with a stab of alarm. In the excitement and novelty of the situation, she had all but forgotten where she was.

She realised he was putting on a condom. What must

he think? she asked herself. But at the same time she realised what an incredibly cool thing it was to do, in the middle of a restaurant on a busy lunchtime.

And then he was inside her, pushing and thrusting, forcing her down until her breasts were crushed flat against the tablecloth. His penis felt big within her sheath but she knew that she was not yet fully aroused, that her own vagina was still tight and tense. It was never like that with David, with whom she wondered sometimes if she might be too wet, that he might find it embarrassing even. She caught a whiff of Liam's expensive cologne, subtle and unobtrusive, and saw smoke rising from his crushed cigarette as it smouldered in the ashtray.

Her own passion smouldered too, without ever quite catching fire. She felt no guilt about what she was doing – the urge to go to the loo, allied to her very real fear of discovery, were uppermost in her conscious mind, almost but not quite quenching the flames of desire. But that smell of cologne triggered her subconscious, and she thought of David's own distinctive body aroma, clean and fresh, and of David himself, his muscles and his mind, and she thought of what they meant to each other. And suddenly it wasn't Liam making love to her at all any more, it was David. It was David who was inside her, David's balls brushing against the backs of her thighs, David's hips pressed against her backside. She closed her eyes and in a moment she was miles away, back in a Cotswold garden, in a cornfield, giving him oral sex in the bathtub, in his car, in his bed. All the dozens of fragmented memories went spinning round in her mind like a whirligig and she came, quietly but powerfully, a woman in control of her body and her mind. She didn't even notice whether Liam had finished or not. Men usually did, in her experience.

At least no one had disturbed them, she reflected, as she quickly excused herself and, with no small difficulty – for Macaulay's was less than generous in its provision of facilities for its female guests – found the ladies, inside which she locked herself with feelings of considerable relief. When she got back to their table, it had been cleared of all the remains of their meal, and Liam was acting as though nothing at all untoward could possibly have happened. You're a cool one, she found herself thinking, as he asked her if she had ever been to Tashkent.

When she saw David that Friday evening, she told him all about the exhibition plans. He was, if anything, even more excited about it than she was. Naturally enough she didn't mention the episode at Macaulay's but later that weekend she was to wonder what, if anything, he would have made of it, even had he known all its precise details.

They had been watching a video of *Fatal Attraction*, and the talk got on to the subject of jealousy.

'I think she was a fool to get involved with him in the first place,' she said. 'She must have known he'd never leave his wife and the kids for her.'

'Maybe that's not what she started out thinking. Maybe it was just a chemical thing, at first. A one-off, followed by another one-off. Maybe she got out of her depth.'

'You could be right. But then why not pack him in, if he wouldn't continue the relationship on her terms?'

'I guess that's what the film's all about – that deadly obsession. For him, she was just a bit on the side.'

'I think there was more to it than that.'

'Do you? Well, you could be right.'

'I wonder about us, sometimes.'

'Do you? How?'

'Well, we've never really spoken about it, have we? About what we mean to each other.'

'I'd have thought it was fairly obvious. I don't think it needs analysing quite like that. For me, it just is. I don't try and put any meaning on it, I just accept it for what it is.'

She found herself in agreement with him. 'You mean, what happens here is what happens here, and outside that isn't really our concern.'

She knew about Gabrielle, though not about the incident when she had turned up unexpectedly just as David was preparing lunch for Emma. He didn't want to embarrass her, and there was no real reason why she should have known. He'd told her about Abbie, too, and a couple of other women with whom he'd been involved in the last few years. Likewise, David knew about Vinnie, but not about the character of the relationship beyond the fact that now she was very dismissive of him. Jeremy and Alun, her MP, were for herself. She couldn't help but like David a lot, but she certainly didn't think it was any of his business knowing about Liam Forbes-Chalmers.

'You're probably right,' he said. 'I don't want to exercise any kind of control over you. I don't want anything from you that you're not prepared to give naturally. So there's no point getting jealous. If there's something you won't give me, or that I can't give you, then we're not meant to have it. Otherwise we'd probably have it already. Does that make sense?'

'I think so,' she said. This was so different to Vinnie. Where are you going? Who are you seeing? His attempts at controlling her were what had really finished them off. But she had to ask him.

'Are you screwing someone else?'

'No, I'm not,' he said, and she knew he was speaking truthfully. 'But people need friends and lovers for different reasons. Like there might be someone you can know as a friend but you don't fancy them at all. And then again, you might have a sexual relationship with someone who you might actually find it difficult to talk to on any intelligent level. Maybe there's one person you can get all of this with and maybe there isn't. You must know what I mean.'

She avoided the question and turned it round on him. 'Are you trying to tell me something? Is this something that's happened to you?'

'I think it happens sooner or later to everyone, in a way. Yes, I have had girlfriends who have been good fun and all that but as for anything more, forget it. And women who I value as friends where the sex just hasn't worked out for one reason or another. Don't you feel the same?'

'I guess I do. I suppose we each of us want the perfect relationship but, until we can find it, we take a bit from here and a bit from there.'

'Sounds like Frankenstein's monster.'

'Sounds like every boyfriend I've ever had – something, but not everything.'

She lay awake long after they had made love that night. Was he saying she didn't matter that much to him? She knew that couldn't be true. Or, more likely, was he not saying, as she felt in her heart, that they had no claims on each other, that each should have and cherish a sense of freedom? That certainly mirrored her own feelings. With Vinnie she had had a mutually dependent relationship that, in the end, had proved stifling. Sure, she fancied him – probably fancied him still – but he allowed her no space, no chance to be herself. He only saw her through his own eyes, not as an individual with rights and a personality of her own. David was strikingly different. He seemed only to be interested in her for what she actually was – he didn't seem to have any preconceptions about what she ought to be. It was, she realised, a relationship that was totally and incredibly free of guilt, of the sense of expectation. He might not want to be told that she'd screwed Liam only a couple of days before but, what the hell, he should be able to accept it. She fell asleep feeling good about him, and the two of them. She liked the way they lay together.

One evening the following week, back at her London flat, Emma unexpectedly took a call from Liam Forbes-Chalmers. She had absolutely no idea where he'd got her home number from. She certainly hadn't given it to him.

'I'm sorry to call you at such an hour,' he said. 'I tried your studio but you were out all day.'

'I've been out on a shoot, actually,' she replied. 'I only got back half an hour ago. I'm just about to have a shower.'

'I wouldn't have been so persistent but it's quite important. Look, the crux of the matter is that it looks like the Klaus Bohm thing is off.'

'That's bad news,' said Emma, wondering what the crisis had to do with her. 'Why is that?'

'A lot of his most important stuff is with a gallery in Frankfurt and they are placing the most ridiculous demands on us about insurance. Dastor says they're talking out of their arses but they are being incredibly tough about it. I've spoken to our own insurers and they say we'd be out of our minds to go along with what they're asking for.'

'What are they saying?'

'They say we should cancel. I spent most of the day on the phone trying to sort it out one way or the other and I think I've achieved absolutely bugger all. Frankfurt are being completely intractable. What I want to know is – and I realise what short notice it must be – if you could let us bring your exhibition forward a whole twelve months.'

'You mean to next month?'

'Well, it's the end of next month.'

'That's six and a half weeks.'

'That's still plenty of time, surely. I mean, we've already agreed that you wouldn't necessarily need to shoot any new stuff.'

'It's a good job we did. It's not impossible, Liam, but – I don't know, I feel so rushed about it.'

'Are you too busy?'

'I'm not actually. But can I think about it and call you back in the morning?'

'You could, but I have to fly to Paris. I need to leave here by seven. Look, there's no great risk in any of this. You said you had plenty of stuff that would be suitable. In any case, we might still get Klaus Bohm. What I don't want is to have all this machinery in place and an empty gallery waiting for us. The last thing I want is for you to think you're our second choice.'

'Of course not. You couldn't have foreseen this happening and, anyway, I'd already agreed to do a show next year.'

'You seem to be making positive noises.'

'Well, I am – but I'd still like to sleep on it.'

'Sure, I can appreciate that. But look, surely you know in your own mind – intuition and that kind of thing. I mean, surely there's a voice saying you want to do the exhibition if the chance arises, right?'

'Of course you're right. I'd be a fool to turn it down.'

'So it's happening sooner than you'd expected, that's all. Next year, who knows, you might have different plans. Maybe the exhibition will make a big difference to how things pan out for you work-wise. Why wait twelve months when you could get things moving right now?'

He is a persuasive bastard, she admitted to herself. That's why he's got where he is. She could feel herself giving way.

'Well OK then.'

'You mean you'll do it?'

'Yes – but there are one or two things I'm still uneasy about.'

'Don't worry about it. We can talk about it another time. All you need now is to start sorting out some pictures. Go and see Dastor if you like – he can answer any questions for you while I'm away. There is one other thing, though.'

'What's that?'

'Talking to you, just hearing your voice, gives me the most incredible hard-on.'

Emma felt like she'd just dropped out of a window fifteen floors up. Her arms and legs suddenly seemed very prickly.

'Is that right?' she said, hoping he would mistake her breathlessness for something else.

'Sure. I mean, I just keep going back over that afternoon

in the restaurant. I keep thinking about you bending over the table, you know, and me pulling your dress up. I really liked your knickers, Emma. I wish I could rub my cock against them now. Cream silk. I wish I could lick you, down there, you know.'

'Yes I know. I know what you mean.' Oh Christ, she thought. But she could begin to see the funny side of it.

'Would you like that? Would you like me licking you down there?'

'Yes, sure. Tell me what you'd like to do.'

'I'd like to kneel down behind you and lick you through your knickers. Lick your bum, too, all over. What kind of knickers are you wearing now?'

'French knickers,' she replied quickly. 'Black lace French knickers. And a matching bra.' Actually, she was wearing white cotton bikinis, but she didn't want to spoil his fun. Besides, she was rather enjoying this.

'Why don't you put your hand inside your knickers, Emma?' he suggested. She was doodling on the pad by the telephone.

'Sure,' she said. 'That feels nice. What are you doing?'

'I'm holding my cock. Jesus, it feels big, you know, really hard and stiff.'

'I know.'

'So I'm kneeling down behind you with this incredible hard-on and licking you out. God, I can really smell your pussy. It smells good, your pussy. Does my cock smell good to you?'

'A nice clean cock always smells really good.'

'Now I want to pull your pants down, down to your knees. Can you feel the silk sliding over your thighs? Do you dare guess what I'm going to do?'

No, she thought, but I've an idea you're going to tell me.

'When I've finished licking you I'm going to make you rub your knickers all over my cock. And then I want you to suck me, while you're rubbing that creamy silk against me – against my balls, against my backside. And I want my cock right deep down in your throat. Have you ever done that, Emma? Lots of women say it makes them gag but I know you can do it right, Emma. You're the type who likes a guy deep down in the back of your throat, aren't you?'

'Sure I am,' she said. 'A nice big one.' But not yours, buddy. David's, maybe.

'How's your pussy feel, Emma?'

'Hot and horny. I like the way you talk.'

'I thought you would. It's good to talk, isn't it? So we know what we want.'

'What do you want me to do next?'

'I want you to bend over, like you did over the table. Then I want to shove it right up you, really hard, you know. Can you feel me moving about inside you?'

'Yes, I can. You really know what you're doing, Liam. Are you holding your cock right now?'

'Damn right I am. But I'm imagining it's your pussy and we're moving in and out, in and out. That's how it goes, isn't it, in and out, in and out.'

'Yes – in and out, up and down, in and out.'

'You can feel the rhythm, now, can't you Emma? You can feel my big dick right up you. And I can see your bare arse, 'cause you aren't wearing pants anymore, are you? And I can smell you – sexy and sweet, and nice to lick.'

She had to admit, it had been quite a turn-on to taste her own juices, back in the restaurant. But right now she wanted to be in her own fantasies, not in his. You could do this face to face with a lover, each lost in their own world, but it was kind of impossible on the phone to someone. She'd better hurry him along. It was time for her to seize the initiative.

'I'm licking it now, while you talk to me,' she lied. 'Tasting it, every little drop. Mmm, my fingers are all sticky.'

'I bet they are. I wish I was licking them too. And I'm thrusting into you all the time, really hard now, and there's your arse, and I'm going to slap it for you, even while I'm fucking you. You like that, don't you?'

'Yes – slap my bum. Slap me hard. But keep fucking me. Don't stop. Keep your cock up me.'

'God, yes, I'm so big, I just wish I could see you, see my cock going in and out of you from behind, right up there now. Christ, it's so wet, and there's your bum there and—'

'And what?'

'And now I'm up your bum. Easy now, oh that's right. That's just so tight, Emma. I'm squeezing my cock now, just like it's up your bum. Just a little push now, I don't want to hurt you. Just a push, and a push and—'

She'd expected odd grunts and gasps as Liam came but there was nothing, only a brief silence over which she could hear the static on the line. There was a rasping sound, which she guessed was a big bunch of tissues being pulled from a box.

'Was that good?' she said softly after a while.

'Really good. You give good phone sex, Emma.'

Perhaps I should do it for a living, she thought to herself.

'We should do this again, yes?' Liam said. 'Look, I have to fly out early tomorrow. Maybe I'll call you in a couple of days when I get back? Or maybe we can have lunch again? What do you think?'

'Yes, sure. Look Liam, I have to go. My shower's running.'

She was lying, of course. But he'd already hung up.

Emma half-considered a drink, thought better of it, and went into the bathroom. How absolutely extraordinary, she found herself thinking – but she couldn't deny that she was aroused, not necessarily by Liam or by what he had said but by the situation itself. She'd had – what name did you give them – obscene callers before, but that was years ago when she lived with Vinnie and she'd been quite shocked about it. This time it was very different, because she was so much stronger. In a strange kind of way, it put her in a good mood.

She switched on the shower taps. Liam was a very sexy man, unquestionably, but Emma had to admit she found him shallow. There was that beautiful, symmetrical face, the effortless grace – it was more than just good manners – and the ability to get what he wanted. But somehow she sensed there wasn't all that much more to Liam Forbes-Chalmers. A year ago, six months ago even, she might have been utterly bowled over by him. But now – well, a lot had changed in the past few weeks, and she didn't feel the same any more about men. Apart from one.

She knew now she was in love with David. She knew, also, that what she had thought was love in the past – with Vinnie, and with one or two others, most notably her MP – was actually nothing of the kind. It was a dependence, a wish to be the little girl, to be looked after, to be cherished. That was what she'd liked most about those guys, the way they'd adopted an almost paternal role with her. The sex actually hadn't mattered all that much to her, when she really looked hard at it.

David made her feel like herself. She remembered something that a girlfriend had once said. They'd been talking about drugs, but it wasn't men's dope-talk. That seemed to be just another power-trip, as if dope were a form of base-jumping for the mind. This was women talking between themselves. Emma's friend had said the same thing that she felt about David, but this time it was cocaine that made her feel like herself. The other drugs made her feel like she was someone else. Coke gave her back her identity. And that was how it was, for Emma, with David. She'd never thought of that before. He gave her back her identity.

She slipped out of her clothes and showered slowly and luxuriously, rubbing the gel all over her body, feeling the warm cascading water. She towelled herself dry – that would be her Desert Island luxury, a huge, soft bath towel – and went into her bedroom. The conversation with Liam Forbes-Chalmers was already forgotten.

She dimmed the lights, took out a small bottle of fragrant oil, tipped it into a burner. As the gentle, soothing smell of rosewood filled the room, she sat quietly on the edge of her bed for quite a while. Then she opened the big old pine dresser, moved some clothes aside, took out a package from the back of the drawer. Carefully she folded back the layers of tissue paper and took out her prize.

It was a nightdress, in oyster silk and lace, from Janet Reger's shop in Beauchamp Place. It weighed next to nothing and it had swallowed up a large part of her fee from her first big advertising job, a series of fairly explicit shots for a jeans ad. She had bought it for herself

– in fact she had never been with anyone while wearing it. It was for special occasions, for her alone. She pulled it over her head and the shimmering folds dropped from her shoulders. At one side it was slashed from hem to the waist and the lace caressed her long legs as she moved barefoot across the thick rug.

She lay back on the bed, eyes closed, breathing flatly and evenly. She allowed her mind to empty of thoughts. Work, the book, the exhibition, even David, all seemed to drift away like autumn leaves. She felt calm and serene. Nothing could trouble her here, in her secret place. She loved the smell of rosewood, the oils from her bath making her skin smooth and rich to the touch.

She lay like this for some while – maybe fifteen minutes, maybe as much as half an hour – her breathing slow and regular, her eyes gently closed, alive to nothing apart from the sensations of her own body. There was no sound, even from the street outside, but a wind chime tinkled softly from time to time in the updraught from the hall.

When she finally felt at peace with herself she reached out for the soft velvet bag on the bed beside her. She took out a vibrator, black, smooth, elegant – a grown-up's love toy, not the cheap tat advertised in the back pages of dubious magazines. She ran her fingers over its complex curves, tracing a line down its length. She touched its tip against her upper arms, her thigh, her cheek.

Again she lay back, eyes closed, stroking herself. She ran it over her breasts and in between them, squeezing them gently together with her hands until they enfolded the vibrator. Then she turned it on – the hum was barely audible – and pressed the tip against her nipple.

A tingling ran quickly through her, setting up a

resonance deep within her body. With her other hand she stroked her thigh where the nightdress had fallen back. Her senses felt alive, alert, active. Nothing could trouble her. She deserved this. She needed it. It was her release.

She scooped her breast from the oyster lace and held it tenderly while she moved the vibrator across the aureolae and against the nipple, which hardened perceptibly until it was firm and succulent. Then she turned on to her side and caressed her other breast. Soft waves of pleasure seemed to flow right through her, and her body was floating in a sea of sensation. There was no thought now, only feeling.

And everything was done so slowly, with such tender care. Emma made love to herself with a finesse that even David had only rarely glimpsed. There was no hurry, no need to do anything but let things take their natural course, to do what she and she alone wanted. And that was the secret.

Until finally, her hands moved to her groin, playing with the soft hair, running the vibrator gently over it and down into the soft, welcoming folds of her labia, the soft puffy lips waiting there in welcome. She didn't need to think about what she was doing – everything was instinctive now. The rhythm hardly altered.

And then she had inserted the vibrator into her vagina itself – but only part way, so the sensitive nerve-endings at its mouth responded most fully to this shimmer of sensation. She lay back on the bed, her legs wide apart but not stretched, and ran her fingertips over the ultra-sensitive flesh at the tops of her thighs, the vibrator still inside her, doing its work silently and subtly.

Again the breathing, but it had a more ragged edge

now, and she felt herself drawing closer to the edge. Her mouth was open, the slow steady pumping of her lungs turned into a gentle pant. With extreme tenderness she drew the vibrator out of her vagina and applied it to her clitoris. It was done with the delicacy of a butterfly's wings fluttering but the effect was almost transcendental. The slow, rhythmic tingling that had been coursing through her loins like a slow-running river became a heedless, headlong urge.

And then she was shooting through the rapids, the white water foaming all around her, hurled from side to side by forces over which she no longer had any control, hurtling forward oblivious to everything but the ceaseless and irresistible forces of that mighty river. The waterfall came rushing up and she plunged over the rim and out into the universe, free at last.

# Chapter 4

David drove westwards along the M4, bound for the west coast of Wales. It was an unexpected journey to be making but, with things quiet back at the restaurant, Emma hard at work on something or other and a near neighbour more than happy to look after Guy the Gorilla for a few days, it was one that he was perfectly happy to undertake. Besides, he wouldn't be paying a penny for the trip.

Jim McDowell had rung him a few nights earlier. As he had done ever since he had begun his affair with Gabrielle – or rather, since Gabrielle had begun her affair with him – David had felt momentarily anxious on hearing his voice. He had nothing to worry about on that score, however. As usual.

'There's this hotel for sale out in west Wales,' said Jim when he had finally got to the point (he was a great talker, was Jim McDowell). 'I wonder if you'd mind taking a look at it for me?'

'I didn't know you were into hotels,' said David, slightly taken aback. 'I thought you were in computers up to your neck.'

'Still am,' replied Jim, in the manner of someone addressing an inquisitive ten-year-old. 'I just think it's about time I started diversifying – chickens and baskets and all that. I just liked the sound of this place.'

'Go on.'

'Twelve bedrooms, set in its own grounds on the coast – about six acres, I think – and miles from anywhere. Outline planning permission for further developments. It's in a bit of a state but nothing too intimidating from what I can gather, reading between the lines.'

'How much?'

'Two hundred and twenty-five thousand. I could probably get it for under two hundred.'

'Why are they selling?'

'The original owner sold out to a consortium about seven or eight years ago. They had plans for turning it into a conference centre and all this stuff – though God knows who would want to trek out there. But nothing ever came of it and basically it just sat there and rotted. Holiday trade was dropping off at the time, "murder mystery" weekends proved a bit of a damp squib, the place didn't have the cachet to attract the big spenders. It does OK but, as my old schoolmaster would say, could be better. The next step down will be as a DHSS hostel. Well, perhaps not quite that bad.'

'So why are you so interested in it?'

'The potential, dear boy. Revamp it, get the fabric sorted out, bring in a chef, splashy advertising in *Country Life* and so on, and we could be on to a winner.'

'So why don't you go there yourself?'

'Already have. But I don't want to show myself too much – I prefer being a bit of a dark horse. What I'd really like would be if you could go down there, have a look around, stay for a couple of nights and then tell me what you think. Bung me the bill, of course. Is that a tall order?'

'Not at all. I could go midweek when the restaurant is quiet.'

'That would be a big help, David. By the way, Gabrielle said she was glad to see you the other week.'

I bet she was, thought David. Having one's cock sucked by Gabrielle McDowell he knew to be one of life's richer pleasures.

'Yes, it was lovely to see her. Big surprise though. If she'd have rung ahead I could have given her lunch. How was the wedding?'

'It went very well, she told me. Old chum of hers. She's in the Isle of Wight at the moment – gone to see her mother. Anyway, enough of this. If you can get down there and suss the place out, then maybe we can have a word later. By the way, I'm not trying to sound you out to see if you'd like to come in on it. This is very much off my own bat, but if you want to sink a quarter of a million into it, then you're welcome.'

All this had been through David's mind several times before the vintage Citroen crawled over the Severn Bridge. As he sped through South Wales, he slipped Bruce Springsteen in to the cassette player and looked out at the passing scenery. It had been a good few years since he'd last been in this part of the world and the changes were manifest. He had never seen so many demolition sites in his life – acre after acre of flattened rubble where steelworks and heavy engineering plants had stood. The vehicles on the motorway seemed older than those he was used to seeing along the M4 corridor, lots of rusting Toyotas with one door a different colour to the rest, blackened vans belching smoke. Every few miles he'd catch sight of a vacant lot with unwanted trailers parked up, waiting for buyers who never came.

Coming from the peace and prosperity of the Cotswolds, the atmosphere of failed hope reminded him of the tougher parts of Springsteen's New Jersey, or of driving through Eastern Europe in the days of the Warsaw Pact. Whatever South Wales had once been, it certainly wasn't any more.

All this changed, mercifully, when he left the motorway behind after Swansea. Immediately he was plunged into the kind of green womb in which he felt most at home. He liked this part of the world – it had a roughness and spontaneity about it that was lacking in the well-manicured landscape where he lived. No one would (or would dare) build with corrugated iron in the Cotswolds but here it seemed oddly fitting, the blooms of rust in many different shades, the well-weathered blacks and greens already beginning to merge with nature.

When he finally hit the coast road – and with not another car in sight – the vista out over the sea was breathtaking. Not just because it was spectacular, but because it was like entering a secret kingdom. This was not the world of Sunday supplements and colour advertising; it was west Wales going about its everyday business. Everything he saw, was just so bloody natural, totally devoid of artifice.

The hotel nestled in a crook of the road, its grounds sloping down to the sea. It was a solid Victorian kind of structure, bristling with eccentric spires, the fading stucco standing out from the dark trees that surrounded it. David liked it a lot. It was the kind of place where, in period television detective series, wealthy murder victims are wont to have lived.

'I'm David Casserley,' he told the bright girl at reception. 'I have a room.'

'Oh yes, of course,' she said, turning to the book. Through her crisp white blouse he could see wisps of lace, and the darker rings around her nipples. Small in stature, with masses of red hair worn in a French pleat, she reminded David of a girl he had gone out with at art school.

She caught his glance, and her eyes widened.

'Sorry,' he said. 'You remind me of someone I used to know. Actually she was from Wales as well.'

'Oh yes?' she said cheerily, looking up. 'Well, there are a lot of us Welsh about.'

'It's very strange,' he said, knowing she wasn't entirely comfortable with the way he kept looking at her. He felt oddly light-headed, but this girl was much too young.

'I'm sorry. It was a long time ago. You look very like her. But I must be imagining things.'

Her green eyes narrowed. She looked again at the book, and at him.

'David Casserley,' she said. 'David? Were you at the Slade?'

'Yes I was – but that was back in the seventies.'

'I thought the name sounded familiar when I saw it in the book. I'm Jenny's sister—'

Jenny Fenwick. Of course – he couldn't recall her name at first. He remembered she'd been keener on him than he was on her. He'd never slept with her, everything but, though they'd gone out together for a couple of months. She was 'saving herself' – as girls sometimes did in those days.

'So you are—' he furrowed his brow, in a pantomime of deep thought '—you are Kirsty. Gosh, I don't think you were even at school then. How extraordinary – you look so like your sister did when she was your age. How is she?'

109

'She's very well. She's married to a chap in local government, Michael. They have three kids and they live in Northumberland. She used to talk about you – you were a wood engraver, weren't you?'

'I was then. Before that I was a photographer, and now I have a restaurant.'

'Really?' she said. 'Jenny would be surprised. She said you were always a bit of a wild one, never quite knew what you would do next. She still talks about you from time to time.'

They studied each other in silence, he looking back down the years, she looking at big sister's boyfriend whom she had never met, whom she knew only from photographs and reputation.

'Well, here you are now and you'll be wanting your room. Do you need the porter?' He only had a soft overnight bag.

'No, I'm fine, really.'

'Your room's up the stairs, turn right and go to the end of the corridor. I think it's the nicest room in the hotel. You have a lovely view of the bay.'

'Fine,' said David. 'I'll maybe catch you later.'

'I'm off duty at eight,' said Kirsty. 'I'll be here until then. That's when the night porter comes on. Oh, and if you're eating, I wouldn't leave it much later. They're a bit iffy about things like that in the dining room.'

She made a gesture with her hands and wrinkled her snub nose.

'I'll bear it in mind. See you later, Kirsty.'

Bloody hell, he thought as he chucked his bag into a corner and stretched out on the bed. Jenny Fenwick – how long had it been? He worked it out at sixteen years.

110

She was vaguely punky back then. And Kirsty was just like her in so many ways. Extraordinary – perhaps there was something in the ether that had caused this string of surprises. It had been something of a turn-up to find Gabrielle on his doorstep that day back in early summer but theirs had always been the kind of on-off relationship that was as likely to resume unexpectedly as it was to fizzle out. But this kind of coincidence was straight out of the pages of a Thomas Hardy novel. Whatever next, he ruefully reflected. Do I get to meet every girlfriend I've ever met, like a drowning man's life flashing before him? There were a few he would be happy to avoid, given the choice.

Jenny Fenwick. They'd gone to a few gigs together, partied, done the usual student things. He'd even spent the night with her a couple of times – she had a flat in Wimbledon that had seemed an oasis of civilisation compared with the hovel he and bunch of third-year sculptors inhabited – but he'd never had her fully. She had lovely big tits and she was happy to let him nuzzle and play with them to his heart's content. They had writhed naked on the floor when they had the place to themselves and she was, he recalled, the first woman he'd ever brought off with his tongue. But she'd never, how had she put it, 'let him'. Perhaps out of pity more than anything else she would give him a hand job to keep him quiet but for the most part it had been straightforward student sex – messy, amateurish and hugely enjoyable. They had never actually finished with one another, merely drifted apart.

So what was this – a new beginning, or a chance to round things off? He showered, changed and went down for dinner. The food was good but nothing special. The dining room, however, had great possibilities – large, spacious and easy to move around in, with huge windows offering a view of acres of green lawn rolling down through trees to the lead-grey sea. There weren't many diners – just two or three older couples, a family with teenage daughters, a military-looking gent of the kind to be found riding gently at anchor in many establishments of this sort. The staff were efficient but lacked evident enthusiasm for the job. The place, in short, needed a bloody good shake-up of the kind that Jim McDowell was well equipped to provide.

He had coffee in the residents' lounge. Again, a promising room but given over to the beige and the bland. Gabrielle was good on interiors, and a lot of the work on the place they had before The Ancient House had originally been at her instigation. He found himself wondering what kind of a place Emma had – she hardly ever mentioned her place in St John's Wood, other than as somewhere to sleep and have meals. He half-considered a walk but decided against it. Instead, he sat in his room with a can of Guinness brought for precisely that purpose and settled down with *The Long Goodbye*.

He was barely three chapters into it when there was a tap on the door. Late-night courtesy call from the manager? he thought. A surprise visit from Gillian Ford, his first-ever girlfriend from way back in primary school? Dropping the Chandler paperback on the bed, he opened the door cautiously.

It was Kirsty Fenwick. As he told himself later, he might have guessed.

'Hi,' she said with the same brightness she had displayed at the reception desk. 'I just wondered if you fancied a chat.'

'Sure,' he said. 'Come in – I thought you'd gone home at eight.'

'I have a flat in the annexe,' she explained. She'd changed from her regulation-issue crisp white blouse and pencil skirt into leggings and a black Lycra mini. Her boobs, he noticed, had lost none of their prominence in the process.

He offered her the other can of Guinness. 'Thanks,' she said, and settled into an armchair by the window.

'I'm sorry to come barging in on you like this,' she said hesitantly. He politely demurred – the pleasure was entirely his, he said.

'It can get a bit boring out here in the evenings,' she went on, evidently charmed by his smile. 'As you can see—' she indicated their surroundings with a sweep of her hand 'there aren't an awful lot of places to go to round here.'

Sipping Guinness, they talked with a readiness that perhaps surprised both of them – about what each of them was doing, about past history, about life in general. He and Jenny, he now realised, had hardly talked about anything, really – just where they were going, what they were going to do, which albums they were going to buy, who was going out with who. Talking to Kirsty was more like talking to Emma, much more easy and spontaneous.

He was on his own, far from home, and enjoying himself. Their first kiss was as inevitable – and as preordained – as her coming to his room. Like teenagers at a crowded party, he actually took her on his lap in the big armchair, and her tongue felt firm, strong and pointed as it played around his lips (Jenny had been a good kisser, he recalled, in the days when such things were significant). He breathed in her perfume, soft and

113

fruity, with a sensual hint of musk.

He clasped her closely, a burgeoning desire vipering through him. He stroked her shoulders, the soft bare flesh of her upper arms. Her tongue roved around his face, his neck, his ears. He felt her breasts crushed heavily against him, and could feel the warmth rising from her body, bringing with it a muskier edge to her perfume.

Her hair was thick and lustrous as he played with it, their lips pressed together still, their tongues snaking and intertwining. She had, he noticed, incredibly sweet breath, and like his own her teeth had a slightly uneven quality that he found oddly appealing.

She grunted softly and squirmed a little, as if to seat herself better. She reached for his hand and placed it on her breast. Its point was hard with desire. Through the tight Lycra of her minidress he could feel the lacy fabric of her brassiere. He took the weight of her breast as she leaned forward slightly and it seemed to spill over into the palm of his hand. He stroked, pressed, squeezed, cupping it as his tongue again sought hers. His penis was stiff and, with her body on top of him, it felt horribly uncomfortable, like a spring trying desperately to uncoil itself.

She had her hand inside his shirt, running under his arms, across his chest. She raked her long, red fingernails across his nipples and bit his earlobe. 'Come on, lover,' she breathed. 'Let's see what you've got for me.'

They stood up. He felt oddly unsure of what to do next – it was as though he were an impecunious student fumbling still with her sister, not a successful restaurateur of thirty-six who had slaked his appetites with a long and largely satisfactory menu of carnal delights. Sensing his momentary hesitation, she took the initiative.

Kirsty unbuttoned his shirt, running her hands across his chest, cupping his pectorals as though they were female breasts. She was not more than five feet four – David stood six feet tall without shoes – and she needed only to bend her knees a fraction to be able to take his nipples in her mouth by turn. As she did so, he shucked off the shirt, tugging his hands through the cuffs, heedless of the button that sprang off – he never did find it – and tossing the garment aside.

He sat on the bed and kicked off his shoes. Kirsty stood there watching him, her eyes aflame, her chest visibly panting. He was surprised, looking at her this way, how long and colt-like her legs were, accentuated by the spike-heeled ankle boots she wore.

'This is a very nice welcome,' he found himself saying. It seemed a vacuous remark to make, but she smiled warmly and looked him straight in the eye.

'Perhaps you're a very special guest, Mr Casserley,' she responded.

Still not shifting her gaze, she tugged the tight Lycra sheath over her head. Her breasts wobbled noticeably as she did so. They were magnificent, large and full, tantalisingly separated into two luscious globes by an uplift brassiere of intricate black lace that plunged low at the front. She caught his gaze and came over and straddled him, pushing her superb bosom almost into his face.

'Fancy a little suck, David?' she breathed in a husky whisper.

He reached up, slipping his fingertips inside the cups, easing those marvellous tits out into his hands.

Unbounded, they were heavy and pear-shaped, the nipples a delicate raspberry pink, long and inviting. He licked each one in turn, like a wine expert tasting a new vintage. And then with an audible sigh he took as much as he could of her breast deep into his mouth.

His tongue swirled around her nipple just as Kirsty's had with his, nipping and teasing, caressing and cajoling. She threw her head back, her hands steadying herself on his strong shoulders. He released the nipple from his mouth and saw it glistening and swollen to twice the size of the other one. She looked down at him through her mane of red hair and smiled encouragingly.

'The other one,' she murmured.

He repeated the exercise, licking and lapping, feeling her strong back muscles with his hands as she pushed her chest forward towards him. She seemed to be pulling him to her breast like a mother with her baby, urging him to suck, offering him not just pleasure but life itself. He unhooked the bra with practised ease – never a fumbler, even as a teenager, he had always rather fancied himself as a natural with hooks and eyes – and cast it aside. He noticed the red marks on her skin where it had held her flesh at bay.

They rolled over to lie side by side on the bed. She tugged at his belt, unzipped him, and all the while her tongue and lips were hungrily seeking his body. He took over and struggled out of his chinos, pressing his full erection against the softness of her thigh. His hand slid under the waistband of her leggings, under the thin, wispy material beneath, and then his fingers could feel the soft, crinkly fur of her pubic mound and the lips that gaped so invitingly. He closed his eyes, alive only to the experience of touch.

116

She was incredibly wet even before he touched her. Her panties were soaked. He wondered if – it wasn't beyond the bounds of possibility – she had already come. He ran a finger experimentally along the warm, slippery groove of her sex. She moaned softly, and spread her legs more for him. He stroked her gently, fingers delicately exploring the sensitive folds, his knuckle brushing against the erect clitoris.

He opened his eyes and saw she was looking at him again, willing him on. He pushed a finger deep into her vagina, and then another, and her gaze never faltered. Her tongue snaked out and sought his, one arm around his shoulder, the other lying crushed and immobile between them. His hips moved slowly and easily against hers, like a long, low, loping blues rhythm, sensuous and easy. She matched him, note for note, lick for lick. He felt good.

When she came, his fingers still wriggling inside her, it was without obvious display. She sighed, drew in her breath, held him tightly and stopped moving altogether. Her eyes, for the first time, were tight closed. Then she let out a great, shuddering breath and flopped back on the quilt, a smile playing around her lips.

They lay together, soundlessly, for several minutes. Then he got up – acutely aware of his erect penis bobbing up and down – and pulled off first her ankle boots, and then her black leggings. Underneath she was wearing shamelessly transparent panties, so brief as to barely cover her pubic mound, whose curls showed through the gauzy black fabric like whorls of lace. He could smell her vaginal secretions, muskily bitter-sweet. She hooked her thumbs under the filmy garment and lay there as naked as he.

Her pussy, when he entered her, was tight and welcoming. He felt enveloped and embraced at the same time, as though she were urging him ever deeper inside her. Kirsty hiked her legs up over his own and it seemed to draw him in ever further. Slowly he began to move in the familiar rhythm, swaying and sliding, an inaudible beat pulsing through his blood like the deepest of deep bass notes. She matched his every move, pushing up against him, drawing away, her hips pressing up to meet his every urgent thrust.

He drew his penis out almost to the glans and then, with deliberate slowness, slid it all the way back in again.

She cried out. 'Oh yes,' she hissed in his ear. 'Do it like that.'

He pulled out again, and in, each thrust like an entry into her vagina. She raked her fingers across his back, more than playfully – it inflicted a sharp and momentary pain on him that only served to heighten his awareness of the sensations that were running riot through his body.

Slowly, consciousness of everything else began to ebb away. The room, the tangled bedcovers, the bedside light, even the breeze that had played through the open window – all slowly drifted away, unheeded and forgotten, until there was only the two of them, lost in a world of muscle and flesh, of fluid and feelings, wandering alone through the darkness of the senses.

There were no formed images now in his mind – not even of the girl beneath him, her red hair and stupendous breasts. They clung on for a while, bobbing around like drifting branches in a stream, before being swept away by a greater and more irresistible force.

Stripped of any need other than to do what he was doing, his body seemed possessed of inordinate strength. He powered himself up from his elbows, taking the full weight of his torso on to his wrists, and thrust hard into her. She squealed – audibly squealed – but he was almost heedless, driven by his own biological urgency, his senses aflame. Their rhythm built up in intensity, each in turn adding a new twist, a different way of pushing, one's tongue from time to time seeking the other's and then pulling away, trailing across cheek or shoulder, soft wet trails of saliva invisibly mingling with body sweat.

Until, finally, he threw himself forward over the edge of the precipice, gliding freely in flight as he had done so often in his dreams, aware only of the tumult in his loins, the pressing urgency, the contractions and spasms and pulsing outburst of energy that preceded that great and final stillness.

When he awoke it was well after midnight. Kirsty seemed to come round at the same time. She rolled over and kissed him lightly on the forehead.

'That was nice,' she murmured. 'You can do it again sometime.'

He felt sated and content. His penis was still asleep, curled up and sticky.

He moved over and put his arm around her. Their clothes were all over the place and the quilt was tangled up at the foot of the bed.

'What happens now?' he said, realising he was wide awake.

'We go for a walk,' murmured Kirsty.

'A walk?' he said, a note of astonishment in his voice.

But then he thought better of it. In for a penny.

'Yes, why not?' he said.

Kirsty got to her feet and padded over to the window. 'The moon's up,' she said absently. 'It's nearly new. And there's a lovely cool breeze.'

She tugged on her dress. 'Come on,' she urged. 'It's calling us.'

They walked barefoot down the deserted corridor, through the silent reception area, out into the grounds. She took his hand. David felt the wet grass on the soles of his feet, smelt the dew smell of the night. All was silent save for the rustle of leaves in the tree and the distant sound of waves. The moon was so bright it was possible to pick out even the smallest details of their surroundings – a sundial, garden seats, the cars parked by the side of the hotel.

They walked by the edge of the sea. The cuffs of his trousers were soon soaked but he no longer cared. His shirt was open and he was glad of the coolness on his chest.

'I kind of knew it was you,' said Kirsty after a while. 'I didn't register the name at first. They're just names on a list to me – they don't mean real people. Or maybe it did register but I wasn't aware of it. But there was something about the way you looked at me and I knew who you were.

'Jenny had a photo album. Jenny has dozens of photo albums – she's the kind of person who has snaps of every phase of her life. I used to look through them from time to time. When I was a teenager I went through a fat phase and I used to look back to the earlier ones to see what I used to be like, trying to will myself to lose weight.

'You were in there of course. You looked different but not that different. Mostly they were pictures at parties, at college, that kind of thing.'

'I never came down to Wales with Jenny,' said David. 'Pembroke, wasn't it, where you used to live. No, Cardigan – Castle Drive. It's probably in an old address book somewhere.'

'No, I never saw you. But I saw this guy in the pictures – I was like fourteen or fifteen at the time – and I used to imagine what it would be like with you. There were lots of other guys in Jenny's albums but you were the one I always liked best.'

'I'm very flattered,' he said, putting his arms round her shoulders. 'Now I know what it must be like to be in Take That!, with all these delicious young girls lusting at you from a safe distance.'

'You used to wear these really groovy clothes.'

'I think that must have been my all-black phase. I was very into minimalism in those days.'

'You had these leather trousers.'

'Don't remind me – they got incredibly hot and they were maybe a half-size too small, but I knew a girl in the fashion department at St Martin's and she got them for me for a tenner.'

'You haven't still got them, have you? I'd love to see you in them.'

'I think I swapped them for a mohair sweater, or something. Besides, owning a restaurant does curious things to your waistline.'

'Pity. Anyway, shall I tell you something?'

'I have an idea you're going to anyway.'

'I had my first orgasm thinking of you.'

David didn't know what to say. But for the darkness of

the copse through which they were walking, she might have seen him blush. How little control we really have over our lives and our affairs, he found himself thinking. We think we have a rough idea of what's going on and where we are in the scheme of things and then – bingo! – you find that for years you've been a bit-part player in a soap opera that you didn't even know existed.

'I used to touch myself, you know,' she was saying when he came back to earth, 'but I never really did anything. But one night – I must have been about fourteen or fifteen – Mum and Dad were away and I was old enough to stay in without a baby-sitter or anything.

'Jenny had been to a party with the guy she was going out with. It wasn't Michael, her husband, it was the one just before him. Her room was on the floor below mine – we had this big, tall old house and I was right at the top. After they got back she looked in to see if I was asleep and then after a while the lights went out and I could hear them down below in her room.

'You can imagine what that was like for a teenager. I'd had boyfriends, obviously, but nothing very much had happened. Teenage boys aren't randy, I don't think – they're just afraid. Sometimes they seem so scared their hands sweat. Teenage sex with boys is horribly embarrassing. But there was no mistaking what was going on down there – I could hear every word, every movement. I tried to imagine just what was going on. I was still a virgin but I knew pretty well what it was all about.

'I never really fancied the guy Jenny was going with but I tried to imagine what it would be like to be down there, with me instead of Jenny in the bed. All of a sudden this image of you came floating into my head. I don't know why, but it gave me a real jolt and I got terribly excited. I was listening to them with your face and body before me in my imagination and the next thing I knew, I'd come.'

'How did it feel?'

'It felt good. A bit strange, like anything that's so totally new, but good. I was walking on air when I went to school next day. You can imagine how I felt when you turned up in reception ten years later.'

The story had a curious effect on David. What excited him most was the danger, the feeling that there were some aspects of live over which he could have no influence, that must always remain unknown until the times comes for revelation. Certainly the vague fear that Jim McDowell might or might not come for him with a loaded gun had added a certain frisson to his affair with Gabrielle. He took her in her arms and kissed her.

'I think I like being a sex object,' he said. They were back in the hotel grounds again, and he caught a scent in the air.

'Where are we?' he asked Kirsty. 'That lemony smell? I know what that is.'

'It's the herb garden,' she said. 'Do you want to have a look at it? It's terribly pretty but it's got a bit overgrown.'

They strolled, hand in hand in the moonlight, through fragrant clumps of basil and borage, of feverfew and fennel. And then, soundlessly and without obvious intent, they lay down together on a patch of camomile lawn. Kissing, stroking and murmuring, their urgency became apparent. She clambered on top of him, her dress hiked up over her hips, and he eased himself into her from below, his cock thrusting upwards like rising bread.

Intoxicated with the scent of trampled herbs, their

bodies moved powerfully together in the moonlight. He pulled down the front of her dress and there again was the magnificent swaying bosom, the nipples taut and hard with lust. He reached out and tore up a handful of lemon balm and then he crushed it against her, rubbing the bruised, floppy leaves against her flesh, anointing her. And then other, equally pungent herbs, some which he recognised by their scent and others he did not.

In the damp air of early morning their hips and thighs seemed slicker still with the secretions of their bodies, the mingling of sweat and more intimate juices. They changed position and he entered her from behind, her backside white and ghostly against the blue-black foliage.

Gradually the very power of his thrusts seemed to force her from a kneeling position to one where she was lying full-length on that green and fragrant carpet, her legs spread wide, her arms thrown out in abandon until she seemed to assume a cruciform shape. And then he was pumping his seed into her and she called out his name, just once, before they lay down together, shuddering, the sweat soon cold on their bodies, their flesh spattered with leaves and earth.

They got back to his room undetected, too exhausted and sleepy to bother doing anything other than to shed their clothes and pull the covers over them. When he awoke at eight she had already gone, but there was a note on the bedside: 'I'm on duty at twelve. Now I know what a chicken feels like ready for the pot. Love K.' He showered quickly, brushed off the worst of the mess from the sheets, and hoped the chambermaid was in as good a mood as he was.

David spent the next morning driving round the area,

wondering what he could say to Jim. Sure, the place had potential, but where were all the people to come from? Not necessarily from round here, he felt – this was farming country, and farmers don't spray their money around. In time the restaurant side might begin to attract money from Cardiff and the prosperous north bank of the Severn – Monmouth, Chepstow, those places. He knew from his own experience at The Ancient House that, with good motorway access, people were prepared to drive sixty or seventy miles for top-quality food, and to pay prices to suit. No, this place – if it had a future – needed the country-house hotel treatment, the thick pile carpets and the antiques, the sauna, the golf course. But would people want to come to west Wales when they could find the same sort of thing in much more accessible parts of the country? He didn't really think so. He knew what to tell Jim.

Not really fancying what was on offer in the dining-room, he had lunch in a little roadside pub and got back to the hotel just before two. He'd seen pretty well all he wanted to see and, after last night, he could do with a lie-down. Kirsty greeted him with a cheerful smile from behind the desk.

'Hi!' she called. 'Did you have a good morning?'

'Fine, thanks,' he said. 'It's so incredibly quiet round here.'

'Isn't it? By the way, this is Debbie.' The blonde-haired girl tapping the computer keyboard looked up at him and smiled. 'Debbie works on the front desk in the morning. I come on at twelve and we're together until after lunch, then she goes home and I'm on my own.'

David nodded a greeting to the other receptionist. She had cornflower-blue eyes and pretty, bee-stung lips.

'We were wondering,' said Kirsty in a conspiratorial whisper, 'if you'd like to come out for a drink with us tonight? There's a good pub about twenty minutes' drive from here we could go to. They do food.'

'Sure,' said David. In his present buoyant mood, he was game for anything.

'I finish at eight today so shall I see you in reception at, say, eight-thirty?'

'Fine by me.'

'Good.' She winked at him. 'Eight-thirty it is.'

Dozing on the bed, David reflected on the twists and turns of the last few weeks. As a rule, he tended to be less the consistent, monogamous type than the kind of guy who had four or five girls on the go at once. Since the break-up of his long-term relationship with Abbie, he'd tended to go out with women on a pretty casual basis. He's see them twice a week, then not at all for a month. If he got lonely, or horny, or both, he'd give someone else a ring. There was always Gabrielle, of course. Occasionally there'd be a party or something and a one- or two-night stand might result. It was fine with him. With the running of the restaurant occupying an ever-increasing portion of his time – and ever threatening to take up even more – he just didn't have the time for more commitment than that which he already made. Also, he didn't feel he was ready to settle down just yet – or at least he hadn't, until he met Emma.

These last few weeks had been very different. Emma had made a big impact of his life, for sure, but the business with Gabrielle seemed to be on again after a long abeyance and now here he was out in some quietly fading hotel out in the wilds of Wales, screwing the receptionist. When was the last time he'd had three partners in as many weeks? He couldn't remember. There were times when he hadn't had three partners in a year, and he'd felt pretty isolated. Now, with women seemingly falling on him from all directions, he felt noticed and wanted. He enjoyed being the centre of attention, for once in his life.

He was in reception at 8.15 prompt, dressed in jeans and a denim shirt and a pair of Nu-bucks. As he waited for Kirsty he flipped idly through a copy of a National Trust magazine. He looked at the manicured gardens and wished he had more time for his own. He noticed a picture of the herb garden at Sissinghurst and smiled, remembering last night.

With her thick, lustrous hair falling loosely around her shoulders, he almost didn't recognise Kirsty when he caught sight of her near the desk. She made a shush gesture with her fingers and pointed in the direction of the car park. He got the message. Mum's the word, he thought, wondering if the barman through the glass doors on the left had seen anything. Walls have ears. Careless talk. Keep the gossips guessing.

He caught up with her on the terrace by the side of the hotel.

'Sorry about that,' she said, kissing him quickly on the cheek. 'But you know how people talk, especially in a place like this. It's not done to be seen talking to the natives.'

He laughed – he understood. 'My car's over there,' he said.

'Let's take mine, shall we? I know the way.'

'Fine by me,' he said, and followed her towards the staff car park at the rear of the hotel. In all the subterfuge he hadn't really noticed how she was dressed. She was wearing a loose blouson jacket of the softest black kid leather and a skirt of the same material.

'I like the outfit,' he said approvingly. 'It suits you. It looks very expensive.'

'It was,' she said. 'Moschino. Cost me a month's salary but I just had to have it.'

She turned to unlock the flame-red VW Beetle. He looked at her legs, wondering about the high heels – he hoped she could drive all right in them – and catching sight, for the first time, of the black seams of her stockings. Like a man caught in a plummeting elevator, his inner organs immediately dropped down three or four storeys. Stockings often had that effect on him but it seemed a bit much for an evening at the pub.

It was as if Kirsty could read his mind. 'We'd forgotten it was jazz night at the Anchor,' she said in an apologetic tone. 'Do you really fancy that? It's trad jazz, that silent movie stuff.'

There were few forms of music that set David's teeth on edge. Greek bazouki music was certainly one, and winsome Irish balladry was another, but almost as bad was traditional jazz, or at least the kind played by amateurs in country pubs, or by professional musicians – who should know better – at beer festivals. Early Louis Armstrong, King Oliver and even the ODJB were fine by him but 'St James Infirmary' played off key by white musicians who'd never been closer to New Orleans than Haverfordwest – that came very low on his list of Desert Island Discs.

'I could live without it,' he said. 'What shall we do instead?' He noticed that her tight leather skirt had ridden up over her thighs, offering a tantalising glimpse of stocking top. Fishnet tights and things just weren't cricket, he reckoned – it had to be stockings, preferably with suspenders, or nothing. This was the real thing. He felt his head begin to swim.

In her high heels Kirsty drove at alarming speed down the green and leafy lanes. Used to the free-rolling characteristics of his Citroen, the way the Beetle cornered in a flat plane was very disconcerting. They had almost to shout at each other over the throaty roar of the VW's engine.

'We'll go round to Debbie's place and have a drink there. It's a nice place, you'll like it. It's miles from anywhere. There'll just be us.'

'I should have brought a bottle of wine,' protested David, but Kirsty waved his reservations aside. 'I filched a couple from the cellar,' she said with a cheeky grin. 'They'll never miss them. I've got some cheese and pâtés too.'

Pretty soon they turned off the B-road and on to a narrow lane leading between high banks of elder. At the top of a low rise Kirsty turned off along a track that dipped down behind tall sycamore trees and brought up at a small cottage from the chimney of which – despite the season – a lazy wisp of smoke curled its languid way around the slates.

She indicated the cottage door. 'Will you knock?' she said. 'I'll get the wine and goodies out of the back.'

David could hear the distant sound of a stream above the evening birdsong. There was no garden as such in front of the cottage, just an expanse of grass which had recently been cut. A blue Mini, which he took to be Debbie's, was parked under a lean-to at one end of the building. From the back of the cottage, he was sure he could hear hens.

He stood at the door and knocked. Inside, music was playing – J J Cale. He'd not heard this album before but the singing and guitar playing were unmistakable. He knocked again, louder. 'Coming,' he heard a voice call and then the door swung open.

It was Debbie, wearing a sheer white Ghost dress that he could see straight through as if it weren't there. There were white lace panties, white lace basque, white lace stockings. He felt, for a moment, as though he was going to faint. Over the rushing in his ears he hardly heard her say 'Come in' and then she and Kirsty, clutching a carrier bag, had hustled him inside and shut the door.

They certainly didn't hang about, those two little Welsh ponies. They'd scarcely got him inside and poured a couple of glasses of wine down his far from unwilling throat than the two of them were tugging at his belt. And he was far from unhappy to oblige – after all, this was a holiday of sorts for him, and he had no ties or commitments to make him feel guilty.

With David sprawled on a sofa and Debbie evidently happy for the moment just to stand and watch, Kirsty took off her leather jacket to reveal that she was wearing nothing underneath – well, next to nothing anyway, just a skimpy, half-cup bra that left her nipples wantonly exposed. She came over to David and, just as she had done last night, offered him each of them to suck in turn. They were big and succulent and he tongued them greedily, using his lips and teeth to elicit little sharp squeals of desire from her. He loved the way they pointed straight out at him – if he were a woman, he'd have liked to have had nipples like that.

Still half-stooping so that her heavy breasts all but

130

spilled out of that frivolous and hopelessly impractical piece of underclothing, Kirsty undid the zip at the side of her leather skirt and let it fall to the floor. Stepping elegantly out of it – but still in her high-heeled black patent shoes – she straddled him as he lay half slumped on the sofa. His heart pounding, he ran his hands over the silky black nylon of her stockings and the cool, firm flesh at the top of her thighs.

'Do you like me in stockings and suspenders?' she asked. That was an unnecessary question, if David had ever heard one. She looked sensational in them. David felt breathless, as if the front of his trousers were about to explode. She wore a broad, black suspender belt, its edges wickedly trimmed with lace and tiny black ribbons. Her panties were almost non-existent, just a simple black thong of some impossibly sheer material that, like her brassiere, made no serious effort to be a practical item of underclothing. Kirsty, in short, was dressed to thrill – and thrill David she did.

Oblivious to the presence of Debbie, who was watching them from the fireside across the room, he could only groan with pleasure as she covered his face with hot, wet kisses. Christ, he thought, this is just unbelievable. It was the sort of thing that was normally confined to the letters pages of the more downmarket girlie magazines – he had a friend in London, latterly a researcher with LWT who, in more impecunious days, had earned £15 a throw for writing such letters to order for a grateful but unscrupulous editor. Two women was always a perennial favourite (why were they always called Babs and Trish?), two men a popular alternative. And now it seemed to be happening to him, for real, right here in a remote cottage somewhere in Wales. If he still had his friend's address, he'd half a mind to write to him with his true-life experiences. It was worth £15 of anybody's money. Talk about spanking . . .

Kirsty unzipped his trousers and freed his bursting cock. She arched her back to help him shuck off his trousers and then, with him still in his shirt, she slowly impaled herself on him. For a minute or two they more or less just stayed there, hardly moving, but then they began a slow, insidious, unmistakable boogaloo. David was glad of the music – J J Cale seemed to set the tone, funky and down-home, no messin' about. He ground his hips in time to the old master's scratchy blues shuffle.

'No, lie still,' ordered Kirsty. He did as he was told. She raised herself up until only the head of his penis was still enfolded in her vagina. And then, using her pussy muscles alone, she squeezed him as hard as she could.

'There,' she said. 'Can you feel that?'

'Of course I can. That's amazing. How do you do it?'

'Pelvic floor exercises,' she said. 'Mothers do them to strengthen their pussy muscles after they've been stretched giving birth. Otherwise, you go all floppy down there. Do you like it?'

She squeezed him again, and again. The sensation was divine. Then she would slide her hips down until his penis was fully swallowed up within her before once more pulling herself up, her luscious black-laced backside poised in mid-air.

She was still wearing those minuscule panties and the black suspenders. David could see how his cock slipped inside the gauzy fabric, felt the thin nylon brush against his balls. And all the time this alternate pushing and teasing, the delicious squeezing of the most sensitive parts of his anatomy.

'OK,' said Kirsty. 'Now it's Debbie's turn. We've got all night. We don't want to tire each other out too soon, do we?'

Not if it's anything like the last one, thought David as, with elegant grace, Kirsty slid off him and he was able quickly to shed his remaining clothes. He was sure he not going to be fit for anything in the morning. These sleepless nights were wreaking havoc with him.

Debbie quickly took her place. She had taken off the near-transparent white dress with its diaphanous folds, and stood there in her stunning white basque. David, wanting to have her just as she was, reached out and pulled her to him, on top of him, his heart pounding with lust. His hands reached around her waist and grasped her plump bum cheeks, squeezing them through the white lace of her panties.

She moaned, her tongue seeking his. 'We've hardly been introduced,' she said, pulling her underwear to one side and guiding his penis inside her. 'You are such a wicked man.'

She wasn't perhaps quite as tight as Kirsty, or maybe it was the excessive lubrication that filled her pussy, fuelled by desire, fired up by her watching David and Kirsty making love. David felt his penis thrust up deep inside her and then the two of them were pushing away at each other, the hardness of his cock contrasting with the pliant wetness of her pussy, her legs parted around his hips, their thighs together. She must only be eighteen or nineteen, thought David, and she had the blonde hair and bee-stung lips of a young Bardot.

'Why didn't I meet girls like you when I was your age?'

he gasped between thrusts. Girls who looked like Debbie and Kirsty certainly existed, but they could have come from another planet.

'Because girls like us aren't interested in boys our own age,' she said. 'They're so boring – all they're interested in is football and how many pints they can drink. Older men know what a girl wants.'

'Which is?'

'To be fucked senseless. Come on David, screw me hard.'

They slid off the sofa and on to the floor. He rolled over on top of her and she guided his cock into her eager pussy. The close-fitting white lace basque felt scratchy against his naked stomach and chest and her equally tight panties rubbed against his cock. These added sensations only served to increase his desire for this blonde Welsh witch. Pressed up on his elbows with his face among her soft blonde curls, he breathed her heavy, musky perfume, tasted the lipstick on those full, sensual lips. God, she was gorgeous, her face composed of soft, subtle curves, those lovely summer-blue eyes, the small straight nose.

He moved over to one side and, balancing on one elbow while he continued to thrust in and out of her, he ran his hand down her body, grasping the soft creamy flesh at the top of her thighs. Her taut suspenders were rubbing against the back of his hand as he slid the tips of his fingers under her stocking tops. This was the part of a woman that excited him most, the soft, vulnerable area around the interesting bits, the warm flesh of thighs, the muscles with their latent strength. A woman in stockings left just enough of it exposed to fire his desire to explore further.

She reached up and pulled his head down to hers, her tongue protruding, pink and wet, from her Bardot lips. He pulled down the cups of her basque and freed her soft, small breasts, the nipples hard and pointed. She shuffled her hips and wrapped her legs around him, pushing him into her, his cock now thrusting hard and fast against those wet, muscular walls whose every squeeze and movement drove him closer to the edge.

His balls began to contract and then, unable to hold back any longer, he exploded into her, his consciousness shimmering outwards in that familiarly huge, momentary series of pulses for whose brief duration time stood still and the origins of the universe could finally be understood, for a second at least.

Lying full-length on top of Debbie, her arms around his neck, he opened his eyes and studied the tiny silver stud in her ear. Looked at closely – he'd not really had time to notice it before – it showed a couple intertwined, their legs splayed, pleasuring each other with their tongues. Both figures, he noticed, were female.

Debbie pushed him off her and sat up. She took off her panties, soaked as they were with his semen and her own vaginal juices, and tossed them carelessly aside. Her blonde muff was matted and damp.

'Here,' said Kirsty, and a glass of wine was passed to him. He accepted gratefully, though Lambrusco didn't normally rate much higher with him than trad jazz. Still, this was one of the better ones – which wasn't saying much – and at least it was served at the right temperature. Most people masked still further its lack of bite and flavour by serving it at the same temperature as a cold Bud in an American bar.

Kirsty, he noticed, had shed both her panties and that ridiculously impractical bra. She walked across the room – what a sight she made, clad only in her high heels and the black seamed stockings – and came back with a tray of nibbles. David stayed where he was, sitting naked on the floor, eating dry-roast peanuts.

They chatted inconsequentially for some while, listening to the Lemonheads. The log fire fizzed and crackled, and occasionally a spark would shoot out and land on the old rug, its texture already scarred and pocked in places. The room was hot and snug, the scent of the burning logs mingling with incense and, above the perfumes, the unmistakable odour of bodies heated by lust. There wasn't much furniture in there – David guessed it must be a rented cottage – but it was good old stuff and Debbie had made the place look comfortable with rugs and hangings of her own. There were fresh flowers in a vase on the dresser and a long line of different-sized Marmite jars on the mantelpiece. That's clever, he thought, being a born squirreller himself. He used to collect old Oxo tins.

He felt at ease here and yet at the same time excited, driven on by the exotic lure of the unknown, the thrill of illicit desires. Kirsty was sitting on the sofa next to him, so that he could rest his head against her sleek nylon-clad legs. Reinvigorated by more wine, he felt old longings beginning to emerge once more. He put down his glass and began to lick along the length of her stockings, their texture surprisingly rough on the edge of his tongue. Up and up he went, like a cat licking its owner, and when she saw what he wanted she parted her legs for him.

With his tongue he tasted the smooth flesh at the tops of her thighs, ran it along each of the four suspenders in turn. He could smell the scent of her sex, warm and musky and waiting for him. Through her dark bush he could see the pouting pussy lips, pink and swollen. He buried his face between her thighs, seeking out the hidden folds and recesses, and she moved herself to press her pussy against his face, her legs over his shoulders.

David loved to perform oral sex on women – it was one of his great strengths as a lover. Was this what Debbie had meant when she said eighteen-year-old boys hadn't a clue? At eighteen, he certainly hadn't been into cunnilingus and fellatio – it was the sort of thing the guys at school and in the disco clubs where he hung out used to snigger about, but no one ever did it. The very idea, in fact, seemed vaguely distasteful. How wrong they'd been, contemplating their spots.

The flesh of her vagina was smooth and firm to the touch. David ate her out with the appetite and appreciation of a gourmet, aware of her excitement at what he was doing to her and the finesse with which he did it. He tortured her and teased her, withholding his tongue for long, agonising seconds before reapplying it to the secret fold behind which lurked her clitoris. And then he was subtle and tender, even blowing gently on her pussy to bring out the full range of sensual experience that was open to her.

As he sensed Kirsty's orgasm approaching he was aware of Debbie's mouth engulfing his penis. It wasn't the best blow-job he'd ever had – there were far too many bumping teeth for that – but she knew how to suck him hard. He wondered about the ear-stud – maybe she was more into women? He'd known bisexual girls before but he'd never, to his knowledge, slept with one. This might be his chance.

Then he felt Debbie's finger sliding along the crack of his backside, and knew what was coming. Women who were really into sex – really into it – loved to penetrate men, he reckoned. Maybe it was their way of sharing their own experience of being entered – it certainly allowed men, straight men at least, to feel what it was like to be entered themselves. And then he felt the tip of her index finger at the tight, puckered diaphragm of his anus, pushing gently until she gained entry.

He could feel her fingernail rasp against the incredibly tender flesh but this wasn't pain – it was just another sensual experience, as she sucked on his cock and he continued to tongue Kirsty's pussy. He felt it slide into him, past the first knuckle, past the second – and there it stayed, just rocking slightly back and forth as, for the second time that evening, he felt his seed boiling up from deep within him.

As he and Kirsty came, Debbie gagged and spluttered, her apologies mixed with coughs as she spat out his semen. She wiped her mouth with the back of her hand.

'I'm sorry,' she said. 'I wasn't expecting that. I thought you'd be ages before you came. It was a bit of a shock.'

David laughed. It didn't bother him that she hadn't swallowed his seed – not many women did. 'I'm sorry too – I guess I got a bit carried away. You don't mind?'

'No, it was good. Just a bit sudden though. God, men's come is so salty, isn't it? It's worse than crisps.'

'Very fattening too,' murmured Kirsty. 'It has more calories than a pint of full-cream milk.'

'Where'd you find that out?' asked David.

'It was in a Christmas cracker,' said Kirsty, pouring more wine and licking her lips.

Having helped himself to food, David sat back in his

chair, gazing at the flickering firelight. He still couldn't quite get used to the idea of what was happening to him – it had all started out so innocently as a simple business trip, a few days' break from familiar routines. He wondered about Emma and felt a momentary twinge of guilt but then – well, what the hell – they were both adults, and they could do what they liked. It wasn't as though they had any particular claim on each other and he liked a little romp from time to time. He chewed an olive reflectively.

Kirsty and Debbie, meanwhile, seemed to be in a world of their own. They were sprawled together on the floor by the fire, both of them naked now, their clothes scattered at random around the room. He'd never seen two women together before, and like any red-blooded man he was interested to see what would happen. He didn't have long to wait.

Looking her deep in the eye, Kirsty kissed Debbie full on the lips, her pink tongue fluttering. Then they had their arms around one another, sensuously stroking each other's tender flesh. The room felt hot to David and it wasn't just because of the big sputtering log fire. Sitting in an armchair like an emperor watching his concubines at play, he nibbled a piece of cheese and sipped his wine.

Debbie kissed each of Kirsty's full, raspberry-shaped nipples in turn, her tongue lingering over the dusky aureolae, as her friend gently stroked her hair. As if on cue, Kirsty stretched herself out full-length on the rug and held up her arms for Debbie's embrace. She arched her head back, her eyes fixed vacantly on a distant point far beyond the ceiling, legs and arms outstretched, abandoned to her needs and her sure knowledge of

Debbie's longing to meet them.

Debbie climbed on top of her, her hips between Kirsty's parted legs, the soft brown fur of their pubic muffs rubbing together in a slow, slinky, rhythmic movement. They seemed to have all the time in the world for each other, as though they were taking part in some ancient ritual, honed and polished by experience. If it was like anything, David thought, what the two girls were doing was like a dance. What was that Little Feat song? 'Horizontal Mambo' – well, that was what rock 'n' roll was all about, wasn't it? Don't let anyone tell you otherwise, he used to say.

Debbie raised herself up on her elbows, proffering her breasts for Kirsty to lick and suck. Kirsty tongued her slowly and seductively, her eyes open, from time to time catching David's gaze but not once acknowledging his presence in this room with its over-ripe, highly charged atmosphere. It was not as if he weren't there, more that this was the real business of the evening and that he was just a little added spice, an aperitif or appetiser before the main course.

What surprised him was how long the two girls were able to keep up what they were doing. There was absolutely no hurry, no headlong rush to get to the end of the road. They seemed to have all the time in the world for each other. Every languid movement was barely perceptible. Minutes turned into light years as he watched, mesmerised, his wine untasted now.

At times, it was more like aromatherapy than simple sex. Debbie smoothed her hands over Kirsty's body – she had exceptionally fine skin, David had noticed – and rhythmically stroked and massaged her shoulders, back, breasts and belly. Kirsty sighed and David caught a glimpse of the inner serenity in her eyes. Their parted lips sought each other's, tongues touched and explored, breasts pneumatically pressed together, nipples touched and parted, thigh rubbed against thigh, foot against foot. Even when they reversed positions, and began – so very gently – to lick each other's pussies, there was no sense of urgency, no manifest desire for the release that orgasm would ultimately bring. Despite the audible pounding of his heart and the blood that coursed through his veins, he found himself slowing down to their pace, aware of the deep shadows that the fire was casting on their undulating bodies, the ever-changing patterns of arms and legs, the hushed sounds of love-making, the gentle vaginal kisses.

Though his penis was tumescent, David felt no particular desire to join them in the firelight. This was a moment – a soft, endless moment – that they alone were destined to share, and he respected their right to it. Debbie was the first to come, a gentle shudder that quickly seemed to grow into an altogether more powerful feeling. She spread her legs wide, almost forcing Kirsty's head down against her mound. This seemed to trigger Kirsty, who rubbed herself against her friend and let out a series of short, ragged gasps that were quite different to the sounds she had made when she had come with his penis inside her. Then they were still, lying together by the fire, Kirsty's thick hair spread out over Debbie's sleek alabaster thighs.

David quietly got up from his seat and poured himself another drink. After a while, Kirsty and Debbie seemed to rouse themselves from their torpor. They all had something to eat, talking inconsequentially about holidays and cars and suchlike. He looked at his watch and was amazed to discover that it was nearly one in the morning.

Kirsty caught his eye and winked. 'The evening's still young, lover boy,' she said with a throaty chuckle.

And then she and Debbie showed him what they used the Marmite for.

# Chapter 5

From a physical point of view, Jonathan Withers wasn't her type at all. He was slightly above medium height, with floppy fair hair and a collar that looked at least a size too large on his skinny neck. His conspicuous Adam's apple bobbed up and down with, for Emma, an appalling fascination, while large blue-framed glasses gave him the look of a fashionable owl. But he knew a hell of a lot about photography, and photographers, and architecture, and architects, and painting, and painters, and much else besides. In fact, after ten minutes or so of talking to him, it was difficult to discover an area about which he did not know a great deal more than the average kind of bloke. After a monologue on garlic bread, David had given up on him, and gone off to talk with some old friends who had come to the show. Emma was left to do the talking.

The opening of her show at the Minories had, after the many and varied panics that had accompanied its genesis, unquestionably been a huge success. All the right people were there, there was a smattering of influential media types, and above all there was a good atmosphere to the proceedings. David had come up by train that afternoon, leaving The Ancient House to its own devices. At six, the catalogues – designed at breakneck speed by Martin

Churchward – were neatly piled on tables, the buffet laid, the glasses polished. Wine and food were chilling, the gallery owner was looking nervous, the people from Land Investments were cluttering up his fax and talking endlessly into their portable phones to New York, Stockholm, Tokyo. By nine the place was packed and the sound of the chattering classes could be heard halfway down St James's.

Emma had talked non-stop to collectors, curators, cameramen and camerawomen. She had smiled, laughed and been praised to the skies. This was her show and, while she was determinedly modest about it, she certainly didn't find it too difficult to be the centre of attention. It was Dastor, the gallery owner – he didn't seem to have a surname, but she guessed his origins were Indian – who had introduced her to Jonathan Withers, the publisher. Beyond the fact that it didn't pay particularly well, and that much was talked about that never actually happened, Emma didn't know a great deal about the book business. But she knew enough to recall that Jonathan Withers was an *eminence grise* in the field of art books, and that Limited Editions, the company that he had founded a couple of years back, was much discussed and admired by professionals in her own field. *Blueprint, Creative Review* and the other design-world heavies ran regular features on Limited Edition's plans for the future as well as their current output. Even *Fuse* had liked its stuff. There was even talk, said Jonathan, of Melvyn being interested in a doing a *South Bank Show* on the company. Do you know Melvyn, he'd said, and she'd confessed that she didn't but she liked the way his hair fell forward over his forehead. But Jonathan was very pleased that she'd actually bought several of his own publications and he was sufficiently a realist to know that her praise was genuine.

The weather had still not broken. In the surrounding streets, pavement cafes were doing good business until late into the evening, and the smell of food hung heavy over the West End streets. The banks of spotlights in the gallery were making things uncomfortably hot, almost as hot as a television studio, but Emma was in no way flustered by it. On the opening night of her show, she felt confident and secure, flushed with compliments and well-earned praise. Art-world party regulars mingled with her fellow professionals, and the deputation from Land Investments was discreetly conspicuous by its well-cut suits and sober mien. Liam Forbes-Chalmers, as luck would have it, had been struck down with flu, but he had earlier faxed a good-luck message through to her, and two dozen red roses delivered fresh that morning were brightening up her flat.

In a way she was glad he couldn't be there – she wasn't sure just how far David's easy-going attitude to their commitment to one another would have withstood the acid test of actually meeting him. He knew about Liam, of course – there was nothing at all to hide from him in terms of what Land Investments were doing for her career – but she had certainly not mentioned the episode in Macaulay's. It was her business, anyway. He didn't own her, not yet at least or, for that matter, would he ever. It was up to her what she did and likewise, his affairs were his affairs. She half-wondered if there'd been something going on when he went to Wales but then, she reckoned, what was sauce for the goose was sauce for the gander. In any case, their relationship was strong enough to survive the kind of niggling jealousy that had ruined so many partnerships. It had certainly done for her and Vinnie, the graphic designer she'd lived with for the best part of two years. It had got to the stage when she could hardly go to the studio without him asking if she was meeting anyone.

As Emma glanced towards the gallery door, a Daimler purred up. Old Tom Forbes-Chalmers himself hove into view briefly like some great battle-cruiser flagship, accepted a glass of sparkling water, shook hands with the selected few, spoke knowledgeably and with great charm to Emma, and was whisked away by his acolytes. His visit to the event to which his company had lent its name had lasted less than ten minutes. Catching the admiring eye of the handsome, grey-haired man from the *Independent* – her tight, grape-coloured sheath dress, she knew, did rather draw attention to herself – she turned back to Jonathan Withers, who was just brushing through the crowd with fresh drinks for them both. She hoped some of the other guests had noticed this – Martin Churchward and a couple of his colleagues from CCHD certainly had, judging by their winks and knowing looks in her direction. Jonathan, of course, was not the kind of figure who needed to fetch drinks for anyone – people, as a rule, came to him willingly enough, almost begging him for an audience. She didn't particularly like the guy but you didn't get twenty minutes of his time if all he wanted was to get into your panties (and that, apparently, would be a bit unlikely, from what she had heard from Dastor, who had tapped his nose knowingly). Nevertheless, an unsolicited phone call from Jonathan Withers was the ultimate accolade from any aspiring photographer or designer and his overtures here, in the crowded gallery, were far from unambiguous. Emma sensed the surge of her own magnetism, and she enjoyed the feeling it gave her.

'What I was wondering was,' he began (for a man of such obvious power and influence, he was strangely circuitous), 'if you'd had any thoughts about a book.'

'You mean, would I like to do one for you?' Emma asked, direct to the point of bluntness. He seemed to blink without actually blinking, but his eye contact didn't waver.

'In a manner of speaking, yes.'

What on earth did that mean, she asked herself, almost laughing. 'In principle, I think I'd like it very much. But I don't have a vast amount of free time on my hands at the moment. What kind of time-scale do you have in mind?'

'That's the problem – or at least, it might not be a problem.' Here we go again, she thought. Can this man ever say what he thinks? The Adam's apple wobbled again. 'I would really like to get something out for next spring. Yes, I know it sounds horribly soon. You might throw up your hands and say that's going to give you nowhere near enough space to do anything worthwhile. But with the technology we're using, getting a book together doesn't take anything like the time it used to. Ten years ago it would take a year at least from getting in all the material from the author to actually seeing a finished book. We can cut that down to little over two months – ten weeks at the most.'

It certainly sounded tempting. 'Was there any particular theme you had in mind?' she asked. 'Or was it just a selection of my stuff?'

'Well, perhaps I could turn that question back on you.' I thought you might say that, she found herself thinking, taking a drink, trying to slow things down to her own pace, to meet him on her own terms. 'Is there any particular direction you feel the book could take?'

He was, she noticed, already talking about it, not vaguely, but as if it were a guaranteed proposition. It was as if he'd decided in his own mind what was going to happen, and all this was a formality.

'I've done quite a bit of work on what we might call the English,' she began to explain, not wishing to set out too much of her stall. Publishers had a reputation for taking one person's ideas and giving them to someone else to execute, usually for less money and with a proportionate drop in quality. One or two of her friends had some interesting stories to tell in that respect.

'You mean people, portraits of people?'

'Portraits of people in context,' she said. 'Car park attendants in their kiosks. Aristocrats in their stately piles. Miserable-looking joke shop proprietors – there's one guy I know of who'd be perfect for that. An English madame – no, not dear old Cynthia Paine again, unfortunately. Someone like you, perhaps, or the chairman of Land Investments in his boardroom.'

'Don't you think some of the pictures here could fall into that category?'

'That's right,' she said. As it happened, they were standing right next to a powerful shot of a farm worker in the Dorset landscape, a picture that could have come out of the last century were it not for the blackened, twisted remains of a burned-out car in the background. They studied it in silent agreement. Looked at one way, it was a portrait photograph. Change the context, and it was a potent evocation of a corrupted landscape.

'I'm talking of about eighty photographs in all. How

many do you think you already have that might fit the bill?'

'Maybe fifty or sixty that I'm happy with. A lot more that you're welcome to look at.'

'It doesn't matter if they've been used before.'

'Not that many have, actually. This has been a bit of a personal adventure for me.'

'And will there be any copyright problems with your clients, the ones that have been commissioned?'

'No, none whatsoever. I always retain copyright – that's always written into the contract.'

'So you need another twenty, that's about right?' Publishers, she had noticed, were always incredibly good at mental arithmetic. 'Or maybe not even that many. I think photographic books often show too much. You can't possibly take it all in. Give me two or three shorter books every time, rather than one great doorstep.'

He certainly wants me to do it, she found herself thinking. But when am I going to find the time? She had promised herself – not to mention David – that she was going to take most of the next month off. At the end of the summer, she had to go to Japan for three weeks and she certainly wasn't going to miss out on that. The director of one of the most innovative dance groups in the country had asked if she would be their photographer on their upcoming tour of the Far East. The money wasn't brilliant but the opportunity was too good to miss. No, late October-early November time was much better – so far, things were looking ominously quiet for that period – but that would be far too late for Limited Editions. Could she do it in the time in between, put together another fifteen or twenty pictures? It was a tall order.

With the intuition of a natural negotiator, Jonathan

seemed to catch the drift of her thought, and lowered his voice still further. 'I'm sure we could make things very attractive for you,' he murmured, 'if you're worried about the amount of time involved. Obviously, you'll have other commitments. It's just that it would really help us balance out our list to be able to have something for next spring. I'm sure I could find a little something extra in the budget if I looked hard enough.'

They usually can, she reflected. Emma had always tried to be fair about fees. A few years ago, when she was just starting out, unscrupulous art directors had often pleaded a restrictive budget as a means of underpaying her. 'I know it's less than you'd asked for,' they would wheedle, 'but do a good job on this and there's bound to be plenty more in the pipeline. Then we'll be able to adjust things upwards.' Like hell, she thought. They'd simply move on to the next mug willing to do a cut-price job, or they'd complain that she'd been happy to work to that budget in the past, so what was her justification for an increase? So she stuck to her guns, knowing that what she was asking for was the right price for the job, and seven times out of ten she got what she wanted – especially if things were already running late, as they usually were. If they still wanted to fool around, then she'd politely suggest they look elsewhere. She was never short of work.

She turned to Jonathan with a radiant smile. 'Well, look,' she began. 'Can I think about it and give you a call?'

'Of course you can,' he replied. He took out his wallet and a fountain pen. 'Here's my card and here's my home phone number. Call me any time you like.'

\* \* \*

David and Emma spent the night at the Dorchester, courtesy of Land Investments. They'd had a late meal at the Gavroche, no less, with two or three corporate heavies and their wives, the gallery owner, and an extremely powerful woman from the Tate who scarcely said a word all evening. Also in tow was Martin Churchward, and Emma was glad that his stock was evidently rising fast with Land Investments – the annual report had gone down incredibly well and, as he'd hoped, a lot more work was now coming his way from them. David seemed to get on particularly well with him, she noticed, and she felt glad – she hadn't as yet had time to introduce him to many of her friends. The bill, they afterwards reckoned, must have been close to four figures, if not actually over it. A single bottle of the dessert wine alone had cost over £200. Did Emma have any other exhibitions planned? David asked her in the cab back to the hotel. In time, he could grow very accustomed to this style of living.

They were both sleepy, exhilarated and half-drunk, as if they had been drinking champagne on empty stomachs (which, earlier on, they had). They fell on each other not, as might have been expected, as carnal gourmets enjoying a final, exquisitely prepared course to conclude the evening's entertainments, but like hungry animals.

'Watch this,' she said as she stood at the head of the bed on which he was sprawled naked.

Her tight, satin dress had been attracting attention all evening. It had come from Betty Jackson earlier in the week, and was the colour of ripe grapes. It seemed almost sprayed on, moulded to her body as far as her hips, but then flaring sensually outwards. As she'd expected, it had drawn more than the usual number of glances – admiring, innocent and otherwise – from the men and women at the opening. Apart from a first solo run at her flat, this was its first time on – or off – and she was determined to make a show of it, for her own benefit as well as David's.

The dress dropped lazily from her shoulders and fell in a soft heap at her feet. Underneath it she was naked.

David's eyes visibly started.

'You mean . . .' he began, but then words failed him.

'Yes, I wasn't wearing anything under it all evening. I mean, what kind of pants can you wear under something like this? Whatever you put on, it's going to show. So I didn't bother.'

She loved his excited confusion.

'How did you feel?' he said. 'You don't normally go around without knickers – do you?'

'Not since I was about three,' she confessed. 'I felt nervous at first. I was sure everyone could see. But afterwards, I guess I kind of liked the idea. There I was talking to the great and the good, and all there was between me and the outside world was this little slip of fabric. In the end, I got pretty turned on by the idea. Didn't you notice anything?'

'To be honest, no. But I have now.'

In a trice he was on his feet and at her side. He kissed her passionately, hungrily, inflamed by her wickedness. He liked a streak of exhibitionism in women and he didn't think they should go around in purdah all the time. Any of the time, it seemed.

She returned his embrace with interest, caught up in the mood of the moment, the sense of expanding horizons and infinite possibilities. She rubbed her bare pussy against his hard thigh and he could sense the wet trail that it left against his flesh.

'Fuck me now, David,' she breathed. 'Let's not muck about.'

She was like an animal on heat. She all but dragged him to the bed, pulled him on top of her and into her. Her vagina was wet and welcoming, easily absorbing him on his first thrust. Her eyes were open but she hardly seemed to see anything any more, the room with its expensive furnishings, the bed linen – she was aware of the erotic possibilities of fresh clean sheets – even the man who was powering into her. The evening had belonged to Emma and she was determined that it should continue thus as long as was humanly possible. For the moment, the world could serve her.

And serve her David did, sometimes like a bull, sometimes tender and caring – whatever the motions of her body and her words dictated. Sometimes she spoke softly, sometimes she almost snarled. She felt herself floating high over the bed, looking down on their intertwined bodies, seeing his hard, muscular backside pumping down and into her, seeing her arms splayed across the bed, her blonde hair, her long legs.

He turned her over, pushing into her from behind. His hands clasped her thighs, kneading the muscles, sliding up and down the smooth creamy flesh that was already slick with sweat. Even with the air-conditioning, it was still hot in the hotel. His wrists brushed her pubic hair and then his finger was seeking her clitoris, finding it, touching it with a gentleness that contrasted with the violence of his lovemaking. How could he be both things at once, she found herself wondering, the brute and the aesthete, and yet somehow he was.

Emma didn't always like it rough but tonight was one

of those times. After all the considered, elegant conversations at the gallery and the Gavroche, the murmured English understatements, the hints and the innuendoes – here was a chance for her to release herself, to kick and struggle and bite, to suck and whimper, to writhe and claw and shout and swallow. She actually drew blood that night – she would be astonished, looking at them amid tangled sheets in the cold light of day, at the scratch marks she raked across David's back – but for almost the first time in her life she felt herself absolutely free of inhibitions. Floating out of the window went the feelings of restraint and moderation and consideration for others that had for so long ruled her life. She came in a gigantic shuddering climax of epic proportions – it seemed to go on and on and on, until she felt she had absolutely no control over her body any more – and when she finally came round she found herself almost falling out of the bed, with the sheets wrapped round her calves and her body soaked with sweat and David's semen.

But there was no stillness after this storm of emotion. David had fallen asleep almost immediately afterwards, but Emma's mind was racing away, saturated with so much information and experience that it could not digest. Uppermost in her mind was the book deal. She was flattered and she knew the money would be good – Limited Editions were not known for parsimony – but she was deeply troubled by its implications for David. It was a book that had to be put together in two months flat – that was what Jonathan Withers was primarily interested in – and she would unquestionably have liked longer. But that would mean they wouldn't be able to spend as much time as they'd planned together.

More importantly, she began to wonder, what did all this mean for her and David? Even before that fateful summer afternoon when he had first seen her at the edge of the cornfield, she had promised herself some time off. She was, she knew, getting tired and even if her clients didn't seem to be able to detect it in her work, she knew her creative energies were flagging. On the other hand, David had been like a shot in the arm for her, feeding her adrenaline, giving her a new edge. Did she really need the break? For her own sake, probably not, at least not for the time being. But as far as she and David were concerned – and increasingly she found herself thinking of themselves a couple – then she did. She really wanted to spend a couple of weeks with him at the cottage, a change of scene, a different lifestyle, a whole new set of expectations. But that could come later, a voice nagged her. After all, he's not going to be doing anything different. His routines were pretty much as they always were.

In the end, she nudged David awake. 'What is it?' he said. 'You've been tossing and turning for ages.'

'I'm bothered about something,' she whispered. She felt she needed to break it to him gently.

'No, you can't get pregnant that way,' he said. 'Go back to sleep. I'm dreaming about women without knickers.'

He was in a good mood, evidently. 'Look, David,' she ventured. 'There's something I can't get straight.'

He leaned over her and switched on the bedside light. She noticed his penis was erect.

'It's about me coming to stay at the cottage.'

'Your mother wouldn't like it, you mean?'

'It's not that, no.' And then she told him all about

Limited Editions and what Jonathan Withers had said, and how it would mean that instead of spending time together, as they'd promised themselves, she'd have to hit the road to get the final few photographs.

For some little while he studied her in silence, the slightly smudged makeup still on (she normally took it off at night; she hated sleeping in it) and the blonde hair spilling on to bare shoulders. He reached across and pulled her over and on to him, so that her head lay on his chest. She could hear his heart beating.

'I think it's a brilliant idea,' he said at length. 'You can't pass up an opportunity like that.'

'But it's not going to be that much money, for God's sake. I could just about manage without it.'

'But everybody wants to do a book,' he countered. 'And you couldn't hope for a better publisher. I wish our friend with the blue glasses would ask me to do a cookery book. I've already got the title – *Scrapings from a Cotswold Kitchen*.'

'But how do you feel about me going off? We were supposed to spend time together.'

'There'll be other opportunities. Christmas, for instance – nothing much happens till mid-January. We could even go away somewhere. I know a nice little hotel in west Wales.'

'So you're not angry?'

'Of course not. On the one hand, yes I do feel a bit disappointed – but it won't be the only chance we'll ever have to do things together. I think you should do it. I mean, you are a person in your own right, you know. You should listen to what your heart tells you you should do, not what your conscience dictates. And I can come away with you for some of the time, anyway, unless you'd rather not have me there. Carry your bags, set up the lights for you, that kind of thing. Full union rates, though, of course.'

'And what are they?'

'Blow-job followed by woman on top.'

'That's what you'd like, is it?'

'It's not unreasonable?'

'Not at all. OK then, consider this a down-payment.'

Feeling almost weak with the relief of having got the problem sorted out, she slid down under the sheets and her tongue traced a slow, silky path across his belly towards his groin.

Despite his protestations, she used David as one of the first sitters for the new batch of photographs. She took photographs of him in the restaurant among all the antiques and dark alcoves, relaxed, smiling, confident, in the faded denim workshirt he liked so much and wore so often (she later found out he had three of them, all in an identical state of distress).

They had planned the weeks ahead with all the care and attention to detail of a military campaign. Emma wanted to get the maximum number of pictures with the minimum of travelling – but also to spend as much time as she could with David. To this end, he was able to arrange things at the restaurant so as to be able to spend the first four days out on the road with her. She would photograph fishermen on the Yorkshire coast on Monday, then move up the coast to find the redundant miners of the once-flourishing Durham coalfield. On Tuesday, it was shopkeepers (she remembered a small, old-fashioned market town high in the Pennines that would be perfect). On Wednesday, tourists at Hadrian's Wall and then –

having dropped David off at Carlisle to make his way south by train – through the tough, gritty coastal communities of Cumbria, a whole new world for her with its rust-ridden industry, rugby league teams and fierce, unmerciful landscape. Maybe Sellafield too, if she could find anyone willing to let her take pictures. After that, she was on her own, working her way back towards England's heartlands. Liam Forbes-Chalmers had fixed things for her to call on some extremely aristocratic chum of his, at his stately pile in Leicestershire. The place had its own folly, and that clinched it. The follies of the super-rich, she could call it.

Having spent a weekend trawling through her negatives and prints, she worked out that fifteen usable images would be enough. She called in to see Jonathan Withers with details of her arrangements, and to sign the contract his people had drawn up. As she noted with considerable pleasure, a cheque representing the first stage of her payment arrived almost immediately. It made a change from the speed with which her invoices were processed by the advertising agencies and design studios she normally worked for. Two years was the longest she had ever had to wait, despite frequent hassling. And this was from one of the few British companies in that field that could genuinely claim to be a household name.

First thing after lunch on Sunday, they set off in Emma's Volvo. It easily swallowed up their luggage, although Emma always preferred to travel light. She took simple, practical clothes and the minimum of photographic equipment – just what was needed to do the job in hand, with spares in case of equipment failure. Having once been stranded halfway up Ben Nevis with dead batteries, she knew always to be cautious.

David drove most of the way, across country to begin with and then directly northwards on the M1. The big Volvo, with its power steering and driver-friendly design, came as a considerable surprise after the idiosyncratic Citroen he normally drove. He drove quickly but with care, rarely dipping much below eighty in the comparatively sparse Sunday traffic.

By early evening, they were cutting across the Yorkshire wolds, the coast only a few miles away. He had booked a room in a hotel in Whitby – in her name, though, for the sake of the receipts her accountant would ask for. It was a warm day but, by the time they had reached their destination, the temperature had fallen and they were glad of the cool sea breezes. They found their hotel near the Abbey which stood, gaunt and ruined, above the town. They dumped their things and went and found a little Italian place that was still open – already there were signs that the summer season was drawing to a close – and then they walked by the harbour, checking out locations for Emma.

She was surprised by how little they needed to speak to one another. Communication by now seemed to be silent, almost telepathic. They pointed things out to one another, compared their reactions, found they frequently coincided. It could all be done by gesture as much as by word. Climbing back up the hill towards the Abbey, they leaned against the railing with their backs to the sea and watched as the sun went down in the west – it seemed to grow dark so much later in the north.

The Abbey ruins gaped like broken teeth – no wonder Bram Stoker had found it such a compelling location for the arrival of Count Dracula. It seemed to draw them in towards itself, luring them by the promise of the exotic and the darkly forbidden. It was no longer a medieval ruin – it was a symbol of some more powerful force, an appeal to their sense of the dangerous and the romantic.

Like children ducking through a gap in the railings after the park gate has been locked for the night, they gained entry to the grounds without too much difficulty. They had the place to themselves in the gathering dark. Soundlessly they crossed the open ground, hand in hand like the lovers Emma now knew they were. The moon, again, was almost full, just as it had been on that fateful June night when they had first made love.

They passed quickly inside the ruins themselves. Cracked arches reared up against the sky, and thick pillars crouched manfully and took the strain of a roof that was no longer there – just a vast and inky blackness in which a myriad stars twinkled. Emma could smell the stones, thick and moist, somehow alive even seven hundred years after they had been ripped from the earth. She had always been alive to the picturesque, to the seductive spirit of melancholy. It turned her on.

She reached out for David in the darkness and drew him to her. He seemed to have become a part of the structure of the place, tall and lean, his body making shapes and angles that merged with the work of those long-vanished medieval masons. Above her, Gothic arches seemed to spear the sky.

Though they stood on what had once been consecrated ground, this place had little in common with the gentle peace of an English churchyard. To Emma its atmosphere was elemental, pagan almost. Here mankind and nature merged into one simple, indivisible whole. It was about blood and flesh as much as the spirit, because they were all the same. They had found their own temple.

He crushed her against him. She was surprised at the fierceness of his longing, as though he too had shared her unspoken thoughts. Their tongues met, mingled and withdrew. They studied each other in the moonlight, each looking into the blackness of each other's eyes, as if unsure of quite what they had found.

He pressed her back against a gaunt pillar. She liked the roughness of the grit against the bare skin of her shoulders, enjoyed the feeling of the coldness seeping through into warm flesh. The pillar was making its mark on her. Her hands slid under David's waistband, loosening his shirt, and she could feel the power of his hips as they moved gently against her.

They kissed again and suddenly his hands were under her cotton dress and up around her waist. She pressed herself forcefully against him, aware of his muscles and the firmness of his body, how his hard flesh contrasted with the soft roundness of her own.

She moved slightly aside and his hand was inside her panties, seeking her private places, brushing against her pubic mound. He held her pussy as a man might hold a small animal, gently and carefully, his hand cupped and immobile. She bit him on the neck, a tiny fold of flesh between her teeth. She sensed him wince with surprise.

They stood thus for some little while, their bodies swaying against one another's, tongue seeking tongue, hip pressing against hip, pubic bone against pubic bone. He drew her dress right up to her shoulders and her breasts were crushed against his own bared chest. Again she had that familiar tingling as her nipples brushed the dark hair of his body, not crinkly like some men's but straight and fine, like down. She loved the broad line of hair that ran from his chest and down to his navel, before spreading out into his pubic region. It had been one of the first things she had noticed when she saw his naked body.

He pulled at his belt and then she felt his cock against her, hard and insistent. She wanted him now – there would be no more preliminaries. As quickly as she could, she stepped out of her panties and there and then, standing on tiptoe – for he was a good three or four inches taller than her – guided him into her.

He came, much to her surprise, almost immediately, flooding her with his seed. He had hardly even entered her fully. What secret thoughts had he been nurturing, she wondered. Or had he, too, been moved by the aura of the place, reintroduced to his primal nature as she had been? What energies, what elemental forces, had been channelled from those old stones into his flesh, into her flesh, until the two became as one? She clasped him to her, strangely moved, her arms around his shoulders, and gazed up at the sky, at the ruined arches, the stars, the mystery.

And then a marvellous thing happened. A shooting star passed overhead, dipping behind the eyeless windows of the abbey, in a long, slow parabola that held her transfixed. It seemed, she knew not why, as though it had made contact with her, with both of them. It was gone as slowly as it had appeared and she knew now that she could never leave David.

They walked back to their hotel, undressed quickly and fell asleep almost immediately in each others' arms. Emma's alarm woke her a little before six – she wanted to be up early to catch the fishermen on the early-morning boats. She dressed, took a single camera body with a couple of wide-angle lenses with her, and set out for the dock.

David was at the mirror shaving when she returned. 'Did you get what you wanted?' he asked, not turning round.

'I think I did,' she replied. 'In fact I know I did. The light was really good. Once they'd realised I wasn't a snoop from the Ministry of Ag and Fish, they let me go where I wanted. But I don't think I ever want to see another fish looking at me again – all those dead eyes, staring at me. They made me think it was my fault.'

'I suppose this is your fault,' said David, studying himself in the mirror.

'What have I done now?' she asked. She knew when he was having her on.

'This,' he said, pointing to a small bruise on his neck where her teeth had nipped him. 'Or was it that bloke from the Abbey?'

'Which bloke?'

'You know, the pasty-faced guy with the big teeth. He was watching us from behind the arches.'

'Are you serious?'

'Sure I am. Didn't you see him skulking there, with the big black cloak?'

'Oh, him,' she said. 'Count Whatsisname. I went back there later and gave him a blow-job. His willy is much bigger than yours.'

'That's as may be. What I want to know is, what do I do about this bloody great lump you've bitten out of me?'

'It's only a little bite,' she laughed. 'Use some of my blemish cream if you like. Or turn your collar up.'

'I feel like some bloody schoolboy,' he said as they went down to breakfast. 'Actually, if you had a love-bite, we used to try and make sure people could see it. It gave you enormous status in the lower sixth.'

They had breakfast, checked out, loaded the things in the car and had a walk round the town. Emma went into Boots to buy tissues while David waited outside, watching the morning shoppers. When she came out, he nodded at the lingerie shop opposite.

'That looks nice,' he said. In the window was a mannequin wearing an exquisitely elaborate pair of cami-knickers in silk and black lace. Emma could see immediately what he was interested in.

'Do you want to have a look?' she asked, rather pointlessly. She knew what he was thinking.

'Could do, I guess,' he drawled with exaggerated nonchalance. 'They might have your size, you never know.'

Inside, Emma ran her fingers through the racks of underthings with practised ease. David, like all men in lingerie shops, hovered awkwardly at her shoulder, trying to look as though he'd rather be buying a set of spare headlight bulbs at Halford's.

'Is this the one?' she said to him at length. 'This is a size 12.'

'Would you like to try it on?' said the sales lady, a woman in her late thirties well used to the ways of couples like Emma and David. 'The changing room is through the door to your left.'

Pulling the curtain closed behind her, Emma quickly stepped out of her jeans and loose-fitting shirt. She had some difficulty with the poppers that held the gusset of the cami-knickers but eventually mastered them and, pulling the slim, spaghetti straps up over her shoulders, she turned to look at herself in the mirror.

The effect was stunning. It held her body like a long

black glove, cupping her breasts and pushing them forward invitingly. It was cut high up at the waist and, at the front, black lace inserts gave a tantalising glimpse of lovingly pampered flesh. She was sure it would have the desired impact.

'David?' she called.

He must have been hovering just outside. He stood there with the curtain pulled back and she was sure she saw his jaw drop.

'Jesus,' he said quietly when he saw her.

'It's lovely, isn't it? Are you going to buy it for me?'

The sales lady appeared at the doorway. 'Is everything all right?' she called.

'It's fine, thanks,' said Emma. 'The size is just right.'

'There's a matching suspender belt if you'd like,' she said.

Yes you would, she saw David mouth, urgently.

'Please,' called Emma.

'I don't think I've got the right size on the rack but I'm sure we had some in the last delivery. Hold on, and I'll just pop downstairs to the storeroom. Can you wait a few minutes?'

'No hurry,' said Emma, enjoying to the full David's obvious excitement and arousal. She flaunted herself at him, spinning round before his hungry gaze, running her fingers between her breasts, wisps of pubic hair tantalisingly visible at the high-cut crotch.

They heard the sales lady going downstairs. In a second David had her in his arms, running his hands over the tight black bodice. She could feel his erection against her leg.

'Hey, what's this?' she breathed. 'Do I have to give you another bite?'

'It's the sea air,' he said. 'It makes me incredibly randy. Get your knickers off.'

'Not here?'

'Here.'

'Now?'

'Right now.'

'You're mad,' she whispered, but in her heart she felt as aroused as he was. She quickly undid the poppers and then he was inside her, crushing her against the flimsy partition. Somehow he managed to sip his arms down underneath her backside and then, almost incredibly, he pulled her up so that her legs were wrapped around his waist.

To stop herself slipping down she clasped him tightly around his neck. She looked in the mirror on the wall opposite and she could see her bum cheeks spread wide, even the lips of her pussy as they opened to engulf his highly visible penis. The sight excited her and she kissed him, hard and wetly, feeling his cock bulging inside her, feeling the expensive lace against her skin. He buried his face between her uplifted breasts and she threw her head back in a classic gesture of abandon.

Again she looked in the mirror, at David's powerful thighs bulging with the strain, at the patterns of black lace on her back, at the soles of her feet where they were wrapped around his hips. The sight drove her wild – she loved watching herself make love. Several times they'd done it in David's bathroom just so she could see them at it in those old gilt mirrors. At that moment she felt so free, so in control of herself and her life. It was a moment she would never forget. And he, David, was so much a part of it all, that she almost wanted to cry out loud with happiness. Intoxicated with the novelty of the situation, with the sense of daring and the excitement of her own obvious attraction for him, she felt that familiar pulsing tingle stir deep inside her and then they both came, practically simultaneously, their gasps of pleasure filling the cubicle.

She slid down to the ground and quickly wiped away his sperm with the tissues in her bag. Red-faced, David stuffed his shirt back into his trousers and mumbled something unnecessary as he ducked back into the shop. She followed him a moment or two later, hair freshly brushed, the garment over her arm. And not a moment too soon, either, as the shop lady came back up the stairs.

'We have just one left in medium,' she said, holding out the lacy black suspenders for Emma's inspection.

'I'm sure they'll be fine,' she said, fingering the delicate filigree lace.

The woman looked at each of them in turn, smiling as she rang up the till. 'It looks like being a lovely day again,' she said as David signed the credit-card slip.

'It certainly does,' replied Emma. 'Let's hope it stays like this.'

The woman was handing her the expensive-looking carrier bag in which the suspenders and cami-knickers had been neatly folded. Then, impulsively, she seemed to change her mind and gave it to David instead. She gave Emma a second, more secret smile. I envy you, it seemed to say.


Ignoring the more picturesque coast road, they cut across the moors as they drove north. Dropping down towards the wide estuary of the Tees, the whole nature of the land seemed to be changing. Behind them was a wild, untamed landscape where the scrubby bilberry bushes scratched out a living in the sparse soil and curlews circled in the sky. Ahead of them was an equally bleak spectacle but this time it was entirely of man's making. Around the coast the steelworks and chemical plants seemed busy enough but further inland was a despairing kind of dereliction hung over everything. Empty factories and boarded-up shops testified to an area that was scraping along the bottom. There was little hope either in the cracked council estates that lined once-busy roads. Disembowelled cars stood wheel-less on driveways, and a liberal growth of crisp packets and hamburger cartons fruited strangely on the untended privet hedges.

In a small town outside Durham, they bought fish and chips from the most promising of the roadside shops they passed, and ate them in the car. They were good but they made them feel terribly thirsty. A few hundred yards down the road was a pub. Not without feelings of misgiving, Emma accepted David's offer of a drink.

To their surprise, the place was as packed as any city-centre pub at lunchtime. Through a thick haze of tobacco smoke, men could be seen nursing pints almost wall-to-wall. Many were quite young, with cropped hair, moustaches and big muscles. These were the guys who'd been thrown out of work when the pits closed, Emma realised, still drinking away their redundancy money. There were older men, too, with beer-bellies and cheese-cutter caps. There were very few women in the large, single, smoky room but the one serving at their end of the bar greeted them cheerily enough.

David had a pint of Newcastle Brown for himself, Emma a bottle of Guinness. 'Is that a ladies' glass?' the barmaid asked. Emma didn't know what she meant, so she nodded and was served her Guinness in the kind of glass out of which children eat ice-cream sundaes. David smirked, and she kicked him on the ankle.

'Your love-bite's showing,' she hissed.

But there was a warm, beery, smoky conviviality in that pub, the loud hum of conversation all around them, the distant whizz and burp of a fruit machine, the seriously unfashionable music that thumped out above the din. Emma and David relaxed and began to enjoy themselves. She bought him a second bottle of 'broon' and had a tonic water for herself. She got the impression that women didn't often buy rounds of drinks in this place.

They were just thinking about making a move when the music stopped and a howl of applause greeted the arrival of a small, paunchy man on a simple stage at the far end of the room. Lights came on above the makeshift wooden platform and at the same time the lights in the main part of the pub began to dim. A shriek of feedback assaulted their ears as he picked up a microphone, which he tapped and then blew into experimentally, as though afraid it might explode if he made too much noise.

'Gdafternoon lazengenlemen,' he drawled in an accent that certainly wasn't local. 'Very pleased see so many of you back here today. Hope you're all having a real good time.' This last in a lewd whisper that was deafeningly amplified.

Emma and David exchanged glances. What was this? Bingo? Not karaoke, please God.

As if in answer, the man with the paunch gave the audience a conspiratorial leer. 'OK lazengenlemen,' he bawled, winking lewdly as pounding disco music began to thud from roof-hung speakers, 'get your hands out of your neighbour's back pockets and put them together to give a warm, Horse and Groom welcome to our big attraction for today – and boy, do I mean big. Let's hear it please for Candy!'

He slid off the stage just as a tall, blonde-haired woman stepped from behind the spangled curtain behind it. A great cheer went up which she acknowledged with a flashing smile. Emma looked at David, who smiled sheepishly. For herself, Emma thought the whole thing was a hoot.

Candy was maybe getting a bit long in the tooth for a stripper but she certainly knew how to work an audience. She must have been standing there, swaying to the thunderous beat, for a good couple of minutes before her facial expressions told the onlookers the show was about to begin.

She was tall, handsome rather than conventionally beautiful, with a big nose and a mass of reddish-blonde hair. First to go was the long, sequinned gown, tossed casually over a chair at the side of the makeshift stage. She took an absolute age over her gloves but she knew exactly how to time things. Then, again after an aeon of teasing and tantalising, came the bra, not like a real one but more the kind of thing that circus performers wore. Beneath it she wore tasselled pasties – Emma knew what they were called, but couldn't work out how Candy fixed them to her boobs, still less how she managed to get them whirling in opposite directions in the time-honoured manner. There was a heavy-breasted girl at her school who sometimes managed to demonstrate the technique in the changing room after gym but, like watching David's dog after he had been swimming in the river to see how he shook his coat free of water,

Emma could never quite figure it out.

The audience were all eyes, with loud cheers and the stamp of heavy footwear on the floor. David, she noticed, was standing there transfixed, his beer untouched. Typical man, she thought with a wry smile. His brain's in the end of his cock.

Off came the pasties and Candy's big brown nipples drew a ripple of applause and quite a few ribald comments. She caressed them in an exaggerated manner, tossing her head back in mock ecstasy. Then she leaned forward and, with surprising suppleness – for she must have been well into her thirties – licked and sucked each one in turn. The audience went wild, especially when she teasingly proffered her now-swollen nipples to the punters.

'That's a bit rich,' said David, but he had to lean over and practically shout in Emma's ear, and she lost the rest of what he said. It sounded like 'get your tits out for the lads' but she couldn't be sure.

The shoes and stockings came off next, and then – with much teasing and pouting – the high, V-shaped panties. There was a loud, good-natured groan when this florid gesture revealed only a tiny red g-string. Cries of 'Gerremoff' rent the air. Candy turned round, glancing back at the audience as she wiggled her big, dimpled ass at them, licking her lips and wiggling her tongue in a pantomime of lasciviousness. Then she bent down as though to touch the floor and slowly, oh so slowly, began to peel off the flimsy garment inch by tantalising inch. As though these guys had never seen a woman's private parts before, there was a noticeable surge forward in the audience.

With the g-string stretched tautly across her hips,

171

Candy looked back through her legs at the hungry men. 'Go on,' they cried, but she wouldn't be hurried. There was more ass-shaking, more tongue-wiggling. And then finally the g-string came off and she stood there, her fingers touching the floor, her legs wide apart in her gold high-heeled shoes, revealing the crimson sex that twinkled at the audience from a nest of bushy pubic hair.

She stood up, brushed the discarded ballgown off the chair, and lay down on it with her legs wide apart. Emma had rarely seen so luxuriant a bush. Someone next to her knocked her glass over but when she turned round she saw that it was already empty. She didn't want another one, anyway. She noticed that the barmaid was standing polishing glasses, chatting to a colleague, both of them equally unconcerned with the goings-on on the stage.

When Emma turned round, Candy was holding up a paper bag. Whatever next? she found herself wondering, but she didn't have long to wait for an answer. Candy reached inside and pulled out a small red lollipop, which she flourished at the audience like a magician waving his magic wand. Then, with comparable ceremony, she slowly inserted it into her vagina. For ten seconds, maybe fifteen, she seemed to be moving it around inside herself and then she drew it out, licked it and tossed it into the audience. Then another lollipop, green this time, and after that a yellow one. Finally she stood up, blew up the paper bag and burst it with a loud bang. At that precise instant the lights on the stage went out. When the house lights came up again, Candy had gone.

Seconds later, Emma vanished too. She squeezed David's arm, mouthed something incomprehensible above the hearty round of applause that was shaking the room and disappeared for a few minutes. He assumed she'd gone to the loo but when she reappeared about five minutes later, she was carrying a camera bag.

'Come on, get that gobsmacked look off your face,' she said. 'I've got work to do.'

She steered him out of the bar, through a set of double doors and down a corridor. She stopped outside a door marked 'Ladies' and knocked.

'It's Emma,' she called. 'Can I come in?'

'Course you can, pet. I'm just making myself decent.'

She told David to wait for her in the car and then went in, the door swinging pneumatically shut behind her. The stripper, wearing leggings and a Whitney Houston sweatshirt, was brushing her hair in the mirror.

'Hello again,' said the woman cheerfully. She spoke in a surprisingly soft, Geordie accent. A cigarette smouldered in an ashtray and there was a glass with white rum or vodka in it, with a can of coke next to it. 'Actually, my name's not Candy,' she added with a mouthful of hairpins. 'It's Linda. Candy's just the name I use on stage.'

Close to, she seemed smaller and more vulnerable than she had done on stage, but Emma responded to the strength of character she so obviously showed on stage and off. Rummaging in the heavy canvas bag, she took out a camera body, selected a lens. Then she fitted a powerful flash unit and looked through the viewfinder around the cramped space in the ladies' loo that served as the dressing room. If she leaned right over the basin she could just get into shot the cubicle where Candy/Linda's gown was hanging from a hook. That was the one to go for.

'You sure you don't mind?' she asked, but Linda brushed her objections aside.

'Not at all, love. We've both got jobs to do. You go ahead.'

'It won't take long,' Emma added reassuringly, loading film into the camera. She test-fired the flash a few times.

'Take as long as you like. Sometimes I work two or three pubs each dinnertime but this is the only booking I've got today.'

'You were very good,' said Emma, sure that this was the right thing to say.

'Glad you liked it, pet. Sometimes I do a different routine but that's the one they seem to like best.'

'Do you do this a lot? I mean, are you busy?'

'Four or five years back, it was a bit busier then. There was more money around, too. You had a lot of amateurs doing it, girls off the estates and things. They were just doing it for a few bob on the side and it showed. Now things have quietened down and we've more or less got it all to ourselves again. I've got an agent in Newcastle and she looks after things for me. I go all around this area — you don't want to go back to the same place too often.' She tipped the Coke into her glass and sipped.

'And do you enjoy it?' Emma asked cautiously.

'Yes I do, in an odd way. I mean, there's worse ways of making a living. My man walked out three years ago but I'd been supporting us both for years. He was a skilled boilersmith but there's no work for him round here. I doubt if he'll work again, but he doesn't seem that bothered about it, the lazy sod. I'm just glad to see the back of him, to be honest with you. I'm happy being on my own now. It takes some getting used to if that's what you've been brought up to but, to tell the truth, I think I prefer it on my own. I like doing what I want when I want. But you don't want to hear about that, do you?'

Emma was busy taking pictures, but Linda continued to address her. She seemed glad of the opportunity to talk to someone intelligent about her work. 'So do I enjoy it? you were asking. Well, I suppose all women like teasing men, in a manner of speaking. You can tell what they think of you by the way they react. Some of them can be really horrible but if you let them know you're in control, then they soon shut up. That's no problem – if you can control kids, you can control men. Most of them are just big kids anyway. I don't let them give me any trouble, but with other girls it might be different. I guess I must have always been a bit of an exhibitionist, too – that side of things comes into it somewhere. I mean, it's not everyone can stand there in their birthday suit. And I know this sounds daft, but there's a bit of creativity in it as well. I've seen girls get up on stage after they've had a few Bacardis and it's embarrassing, it's like they're getting their clothes off ready for the bath. It's all over in thirty seconds. I like to be a bit different, you know. I'm always working on my routines, trying to make them better. I used to work things out with my husband watching and the curtains drawn so the neighbours couldn't see, but now I do it on my own. That business with the lollipops, that really gets them going.'

Emma took other pictures from different angles but she felt the first were still the best, as they so often were. She signed to Linda that she was through.

'Are you done then, love?' the older woman said as she stuffed stockings and high-heeled shoes into a well travelled sports bag. 'You've got what you wanted?'

Emma smiled and, murmuring her thanks, suggested another drink. She liked Linda, would have liked to talk to her, but the offer was politely refused. She obviously had things to do.

'Well, I'd best be off then.' She looked at her watch as she laced up her trainers. 'Is that the time? My kids'll be out of school in half an hour. I'd best get a move on.'

'Can I give you a lift?' asked Emma. 'The car's just down the road.' But Linda declined. Perhaps she was chary of getting involved with strangers, even another woman.

'No, he has a taxi waiting for me. I want to get me money's worth – forty quid for doing that, it used to be fifty but then we're all having to cut back these days, aren't we? Still, at least it's cash in hand.'

She quickly dabbed perfume behind her ear, checked her make-up again in the mirror, picked up the bag and was gone. Emma wound the exposed film back into the cassette and went off to find David.

# Chapter 6

David had planned the weekend of his party – in the way of these things – long before the news of Emma's book came through, and with it the need for her to go off in search of new material. In many ways it was a shame that she'd be missing it, but that was life. She told him he should enjoy himself just as much as he always did – that was why he had his summer party each year – but he couldn't help wishing she could have been there as well, especially with her going off to Japan only a week later. Things had happened so quickly between them that there were lots of his friends who'd not yet met her, and the party would have been the ideal opportunity.

His end-of-summer parties had become something of an institution in the district (he usually held another a couple of weeks before Christmas). With the restaurant closed for its annual two-week summer break, it gave him a chance to plan an entertainment that was more himself. A lot of people who came to The Ancient House were friends as well as customers, but then again there were any number of regulars whom he'd never dream of inviting to his home. Some of them were, well, a bit sniffy, a bit correct, a bit too middle class for their own good. He could never understand the people of his own age – younger sometimes – who were so straight they seemed to be longing for respectable middle age so they could become even more repressed and intolerant than their parents. David's party was for people who were different.

Not that there was anything particularly special about the way the party was organised. The food was imaginative, there was plenty to drink, and a good crowd turned up in good humour to consume it. There was music, a great deal of shouting and laughter, just as there was at many others. But what, as so many people had told David over the last two or three years, made his parties so different was their atmosphere – a combination of intangibles like the kind of people who came, their willingness to talk and enthuse, the subtle balance of personalities so different they might have been expected to clash. David enjoyed the sometimes bizarre combinations of people who, like amoebae, endlessly formed and reformed themselves into groups through the course of the night – architects and anarchists, boozers and Buddhists, a whole alphabet of possibilities. Some of his guests, with their well-defined obsessions and idiosyncrasies, could unquestionably have been labelled boring but none was ever dull. Understanding the difference between the terms, David would maintain after his third or fourth or fifth glass (he always got famously drunk on such evenings), was one of the essential tenets of civilisation. Few people left David's parties until long after midnight and it was usually past three before the last stragglers swallowed the last dregs of the last few bottles of wine and unsteadily suggested to their exhausted (and sober) driving partners that they finally make tracks for home. If anyone showed signs of wanting to stay on even longer, David just left them to it and went off to bed, alone or otherwise.

The party was fixed for the Saturday. On the Thursday, he had had a postcard from Emma in Blackpool. 'Hell on earth,' she wrote, 'but I think it's wonderful. George Formby on acid, Las Vegas tabloid sleaze. Miss you.' She phoned on Friday lunchtime and they had a long conversation about how things were going – pretty well, by all accounts. 'I'm really sorry I can't make the party,' she had added, 'but there'll be other times. I have to see this guy in Leicestershire on Tuesday and then I have to go back to London to get some things sorted out but I should be with you by Friday for certain. Then that's it. I'm all yours.'

'Sure you are,' he had said, and they rang off.

In the afternoon he did the Sainsbury's run. The ad with Emma's cornfield picture had been in all the Sunday supplements the previous week, and he felt a curious sense of brand loyalty as he wheeled his trolley round the aisles. He remembered to get paper napkins, rennet-free cheese for the veggies, sparkling apple drink for his friend Anna who liked it, succumbed to the temptation of a blueberry cheesecake even though he could just as easily have made one himself, forgot the capers and unsalted butter and, as usual, spent infinitely more than he'd intended. Each year's party was to be the new-look, slimmed-down, economy version, and each year he went as mad as ever. Still, it was worth it to let your hair down once in a while.

He bumped – literally – into Lisa Doulton between the deli counter and the beans and pulses (I must remember the chickpeas, was his last conscious thought). Their groaning trolleys collided as both scanned the shelves for whatever it was they were looking for at that precise instant. He was glad to see her. Though he regarded her as a friend, he had always found Lisa a turn-on, from a safe distance at least. More than once she had featured in his masturbatory fantasies, but he would never dream of doing anything about it. It was fantasy, after all, not wish fulfilment.

Lisa was in her late twenties and had once worked professionally as a dancer. Emma would have liked talking to her – they were both vivacious, and she probably even knew the people she was going to Japan with. Lisa was married – Conor, much older, was a director of a company that made award-winning natural history films – and they had a big, newish house on the development at the other end of the village.

'Hi!' she said with a big, wide-eyed smile. David always thought there was something Egyptian about her appearance, the dark crinkly hair and liquid brown eyes. She had the slightly muscular legs and sturdy ankles of a dancer but her figure was terrific, slender hips and a generous bosom that her tight white top only emphasised still further.

'Hello, Lisa,' he replied. 'I'm just getting a few things for tomorrow.'

She looked intently at his already overloaded trolley. 'Is there a whole regiment coming?' she asked. 'You always go to so much trouble.'

'You're still coming, are you?'

'I am, but Conor's probably going to have to cry off. He's filming cormorants in Cornwall all this week and I don't think he'll be back in time.'

'That's a shame,' said David, and he meant it. Conor Doulton wasn't one of his closest friends but he always found him interesting to talk to. They were good customers of The Ancient House as well, and fitted in well with the local scene. The Friday afternoon shoppers pushed past them as they talked casually of this and that.

'Still, it means I can enjoy myself without him,' Lisa laughed. 'After a while you begin to forget who you are, you know. It's like you get submerged into being a couple, at least in other people's eyes. It's like they can't relate to one without the other, so they have to invite you both. I think it's nice to go out on your own sometimes, to remind your friends who you are. Don't you agree? People sometimes forget each one of you exists as an individual. Anyway, mustn't keep you. I'll see you on Saturday.' She pecked him on the cheek and wheeled her trolley off.

He spent much of the evening getting food ready for the following night's party. He made pizzas with three different toppings, a red onion tart, humous, Lebanese falafel – all stuff that could be eaten by hand off paper plates. The weather had held and he'd be able to barbecue kebabs – monkfish, peppers, courgettes – but they could be grilled on the kitchen stove if necessary. He put all the ingredients into a big Pyrex bowl, tipped over it a marinade made from soy sauce, sesame oil, red wine and whatever herbs and spices came easiest to hand, and put it in the fridge to let the bacteria do their work overnight. All the while he had John Hiatt going full blast on the stereo and most of the leftover half-bottle of wine intended for the cooking ended up in his own glass.

He went to bed about 11.30, feeling pretty tired. Getting ready for a party was different to the restaurant, though, and it was a different sort of fatigue. After the restaurant, he was knackered sometimes. This was different, because he was doing it for himself, for his best friends. It was very satisfying. The following day he would make salads, bake bread. He kept going through it all in his head, despite his tiredness. He was, at heart, as excited as a boy on Christmas Eve, wondering what he'd find under the tree in the morning. Women who didn't know him well used to marvel at him: 'How well you cope, David.' They made him out to be some kind of widower, rather than a single man who actually enjoyed looking after himself, and did it rather well. He knew a girl – Anna, the one who liked the apple drink – who did all her own servicing on her 2CV. He wouldn't have dared make that kind of remark to her, though he did once get her to reset the rotor arm assembly on the Citroen when it had been playing up and the local garage had been closed for the weekend.

But sleep didn't come so easily. Truth to tell, he was missing Emma. He wondered what she was doing right now, how she felt about him. He often found himself thinking about her at odd moments, the kind of preoccupation that hadn't happened since the early days with Abbie on the West Coast. It seemed light years ago, now. He'd done a lot of growing up in the meantime.

He thought of Emma, the night at the Abbey, the episode with the cami-knickers in the lingerie shop. They had stayed in a little B&B in the Cheviot hills while Emma took pictures along Hadrian's Wall and two nights running they had made mad, passionate love on the old, high bed at the top of the house, trying desperately hard to be quiet about it, stifling the sounds of wild lovemaking as best they could.

It was all so different to that night with the two girls in Wales. That had been good too, in its way, and really exciting, but there wasn't much more to it than the sex. Without being snobbish about it, he found them quite difficult to talk to. They were pleasant enough, and they laughed a lot and were sort of bubbly, but there wasn't much that he had in common with them. He wondered what did they make of him – somebody different, perhaps? Sex – especially watching the two of them at it while he got his breath back – had been terrific but these days, he didn't see much point in the kind of relationship that was only concerned with screwing. At one time, he'd thought very differently but now Emma had made him get so much more in touch with his real feelings about things.

Unconsciously his hand strayed to his groin. He enjoyed masturbation – he thought the masturbation jokes were among Woody Allen's best ('I haven't had sex with a woman for eighteen months but I still practise for it every night.') He didn't do it that often but it was an important part of his sexuality, a source of no small pleasure to him and to him alone. He could never understand why other men were so coy about it. Either they got laid, or they had wet dreams, or they brought themselves off.

One of the things he liked best about Emma was the way that she could handle his penis almost as well as he could. Most women, in his experience, were far too rough and unsubtle – perhaps it reflected the roughness and unsubtlety of most men's own sexual attitudes, he sometimes felt. But Emma knew when to be gentle and when to be more forceful, when to tease and cajole and when to be direct. Sometimes, it felt like it was his own hand down there – that time in the car driving back from wherever it was, as a case in point.

His fingers were moving up and down his shaft now, squeezing the glans, his mind slowly emptying of the day's minutiae. Masturbation – he preferred to call it 'self abuse' or 'the sin of Onan' – wasn't about wish fulfilment, it was about knowing yourself, about gaining access to your deeper self, your fantasies and even fears. In his mind he'd screwed all manner of women, had all kinds of sex with them in all kinds of situations. The better ones he returned to time and again. Nevertheless, visions of Emma floated unbidden into his imagination, her breasts, her tongue, the way she came with a half-cry, half-pant and the deep stillness that seemed to fill her afterwards. In his imagination he was back in the Dorchester with her, the silky grape-coloured dress slowly falling to the floor, and then falling again. Like the action replay in television sports, the great thing about holding your own was that you could enjoy the good bits over and over again. He thought of her naked body as she stood there in the expensive hotel room and her obvious pleasure in her own sensuality.

That was what he thought turned him on the most about her – the fact that she seemed to know her own mind, that she knew what she wanted, was ready to ask for it. She didn't depend on him to supply her needs. She existed without him, a sexual animal in her own right. They met in the night, made their inevitable conjunction, and moved on. In his mind's eye he kneeled down behind her and she turned round and smiled, a slow and sensual smile that spoke of her own desire for him, a come-on. He wondered what she was doing now. He wondered if it was him she wanted at that moment to satisfy her needs for her. He loved the feeling of a woman wanting him. He thought of Emma again, glancing over her shoulder at him, urging him into her, and then he arched his back and came spectacularly and abundantly over his own naked stomach.

The party was going well, as David always knew it would. Even by 9.15 there was an excited buzz around the cottage and out in the garden, where the night-scented stocks and nicotianas were heavy in the still summer air. The lane outside was cluttered with cars – some people, like Lisa Doulton and one or two others, had come from the village itself, but most were from the surrounding area. Inside, even the tobacco smoke from the four or five irrevocable addicts who had already lit up was failing dismally to wipe out the exotic mix of perfumes that clung to his living room, the heavy musks mingling with lighter, more fruity scents. David even caught a whiff of an extraordinary coconut perfume. I wonder who's wearing that? he thought.

Music, he admitted, was always a bit of a problem at these affairs. Among his friends were opera buffs and folkies, latter-day headbangers and a surprising proportion of people – who he knew, on the whole, to be far from dead from the neck up – who seemed to have no discernible interest in music at all. It was difficult to keep them all happy so he preferred to play jazz – Zoot, Miles or Bird for preference. To the uninitiated, it gave a superficial night-club atmosphere of warmth and sophistication, if nothing else. Perhaps they could play something noisier later, he reckoned, or something quieter. It was all as the mood of the moment dictated and David was, on the whole, sensitive to these things.

'It amazes me,' he happened to be saying to his friend Chris, who was a dentist by day and played guitar in a remarkably good rock band most weekends, 'how so many people of our kind of age just seem to give up on music when they hit thirty.'

'I know,' replied Chris. 'A month or so back I bumped into a guy on Paddington station I hadn't seen for years. I'd known him pretty well at one time, and he had this fantastic record collection. He had all these American imports, he really knew what was going on. Since then he'd got married and had a kid and he was working for some shipping company, and all this miserable stuff. So I said, what music are you listening to these days? And he said, well, you know, we moved house a year or so back and I haven't really had time to get the stereo sorted out yet. In other words, he didn't listen to anything any more.'

David declined the proffered joint and passed on. John and Linda Somerville were, he noticed, at opposite ends of the room as usual. As soon as they hit a party, they seemed to fragment as a couple, reuniting only in time to leave. You might have suspected trouble in their marriage if you didn't know that both at one time had worked for Relate. Getting away from each other was just their way of recharging the batteries of their relationship, as Lisa had been hinting. From something John had once accidentally let slip, he rather gathered Linda was into 'marital aids'. From the look of her, you'd think butter wouldn't melt in her mouth.

And then there were Ron and Peter, his dear gay friends, always such excellent value for money. He had never known two people who, when they were in form, which they usually were, could keep going so long, who throughout the evening could be so erudite and amusing and generous and genuinely caring – not just for each other (though they had their squabbles) but for their friends as well – in spite of consuming the most enormous quantities of wine. Whereas most couples brought a bottle, Ron and Peter brought a two-litre bottle of dry white each, drank most of it themselves and then started on what was left in the kitchen. Peter was the camp one – if anything, he'd been getting worse in the last couple of years. Ron had once, disastrously, even been married, but he could certainly whoop it up too, and his Italian waiter impression was much sought after. But wherever they were, whoever they were talking to, they could be identified by the great shouts of laughter as yet another outrageous story was wheeled out for popular consumption. Only at the very end would they slip gently into drunkenness, like old battleships being scuttled far out at sea, and one of their friends would drive them home. Their departure always seemed to signal the beginning of the end. Sometimes they stayed over at David's instead and the following morning, with eyes like beetles swimming in tomato soup, they would vehemently deny having the faintest, teensiest trace of a hangover, as their shaking hands lit the first of their pre-breakfast cigarettes.

Lisa Doulton, too, seemed to be drinking like there was no tomorrow and very little of today (though it was, by now, close to midnight, and some old blues shouter that Chris the dentist had picked out of David's record collection was sobbing and moaning his troubles to the world to a raucous backing of saxophones and guitars). As he squeezed past her to get himself another drink – he too had probably had more than usual – she accidentally tipped her plate of food on to the floor.

'Sorry about that,' she said as they picked up stray

pieces of garlic bread and salad. 'That was a great pizza.'

'Have some more,' he invited her. 'There's plenty left.'

They were both kneeling on the rough coir matting in his dining room, where the buffet was laid out. Wearing cut-down denims, it felt rough against his knees. He noticed that Lisa was displaying her spectacular cleavage to maximum advantage.

She caught his eye. 'I'm sure they affect my centre of gravity,' she murmured. 'That's why I fall over.'

'You fall over because you drink too much, my dear,' he laughed, and helped her to her feet. He caught the strong scent of coconut on her.

'So it's you,' he said, surprised. 'The coconut smell. I think it's wonderful. I really like it.'

'Oh good,' she replied. 'It's Body Shop. It doesn't cost much, only a couple of quid for a little plastic bottle. They do all kinds of things, like mangoes and raspberries and grapefruit.'

Maybe Emma would like it, he thought, as he picked up a bottle each of red and white – the house wines from the restaurant – and went off in search of drinks to freshen up.

By two in the morning, David was definitely beginning to feel the pace. He'd been up early, had been cooking and tidying up for most of the day, and he'd been talking so much that his jaws were aching. But it had been a great party, once again. He walked into the garden, where the heat was still coming off the barbecue and a last, lone kebab gently blackened on the grill. He picked off a piece of red pepper – he liked the taste of its scorched flesh – and chewed reflectively. He looked up at the quarter moon and wondered, with a rush of drunken sentiment that he felt immediately embarrassed by, whether Emma were looking at it too.

He felt someone at his shoulder, and then Lisa Doulton put her arms round him.

'Look, David,' she said, and her voice, like her eyes, was distinctly blurry. 'It's been a great party, lovey, but I'm feeling pissed. Would mind taking me home? I think I'm going to crash out any minute. I don't like walking through the village at night – you get those creepy guys hanging out by the Roebuck till all hours.'

'OK,' said David, not without a certain reluctance. But if he didn't walk her home, no one else would.

They went down the narrow path at the side of the house, the rose thorn pricking their bare flesh. Someone – the Somervilles, was it? It looked like their Rover – was just driving off in the other direction. But it was a beautiful, starry night, and the cold air helped freshen David's head a little. He didn't know what it was doing for Lisa; she was talking not a lot of sense about her dancing days. They walked through the village, silent apart from the distant sound of an all-night sprinkler. He became aware of a desperate need to go to the loo but, with Lisa leaning against him and stumbling from time to time in the darkness on her high heels, he had to slow his usually brisk walk to fall in step with her. Only the occasional burglar alarm winked redly at them; apart from the floodlights that played on the church tower, not a single light was on as they walked down the main street, past the pub, the post office, the butcher's shop, the restaurant, all so familiar by daytime, so strange and unearthly now.

A porch light flicked on automatically as they went up the path to her home. She rummaged in her bag, couldn't find the key she was looking for, tipped its contents out and located the key by the metallic chink it made as it hit the step. David handed her her purse and cigarette lighter.

'Do you mind coming in just for a second?' she said as she turned the lock. 'I don't like going into a dark house on my own.'

'Sure,' he said. 'In fact, do you mind if I use your loo?'

When he came back, she was standing in the living room.

'Thanks for bringing me back, David,' she said. 'Look, do you fancy a night-cap?'

He didn't really want another drink but felt it would be churlish to refuse. As he followed her out to the kitchen, he was aware of the slinky way she swung her backside as she walked. All of a sudden, and without him realising quite how or why, they were kissing passionately, her tongue inside his mouth, those stupendous breasts against his chest. You are fucking mad, he told himself, but he couldn't stop himself.

'Let's go back to the lounge, shall we?' she said when they finally disengaged. He felt he ought to go right now, before he got too much into deep water, but he was powerless to resist. He did as he was bid.

Lisa put down a couple of glasses and a three-quarters full bottle of Muscadet on the coffee table. 'It'll be a shame to waste this,' she said. 'I had some before I came out. It won't keep.' She poured him a glass.

As he reached out for it, he noticed a video lying under the table. It was evidently hardcore, the high-booted woman on the front dressed in studs and leather. He picked it up, intrigued. Lisa laughed.

'Oh that,' she said, half-embarrassed. 'Conor got it from one of the guys at work. It's really wild.'

'It looks it,' said David, studying the cover as he sipped his wine. '*High Jinks in Hell* – sounds like a laugh a minute. I didn't know you were into this stuff.'

There was a pause, perhaps a hint of embarrassment in her smile. 'Do you fancy seeing some of it?' asked Lisa.

David looked at his watch. It was half-past two. What the hell? He had nothing to do the following day except tidy up the cottage and the longer he put that off, the better. Besides, he fancied Lisa.

'OK,' he said. 'To tell the truth, I've not seen anything quite like this before. Well, not leather and whips and stuff.'

Lisa slipped the cassette into the video recorder and flicked the remote. An image of a man chatting to two women in a bar came on the screen.

'We've started in the middle,' she said, 'but it doesn't really matter. The storyline is a bit vague.'

She snuggled up closer to him on the sofa, her legs drawn up under her.

'Look, Lisa,' he said in a final twinge of conscience. 'Are you sure we should be doing this? I mean, I've known you and Conor a long time.'

'Don't worry,' she said ambiguously. 'It's all a bit of fun. You know what I told you in the supermarket, about needing to feel I'm being myself sometimes.' She lifted her head and kissed him, took his hand and put it on her breast. The Wonderbra – David could recognise a Wonderbra at forty paces – felt hard and creaky, but her breasts were warm and full.

'You've wanted to do that for a long time, haven't you?' she breathed.

'I suppose I have, yes,' he murmured. 'But what about Conor?'

'Conor is two hundred miles away. Forget it.'

So is Emma, he reflected. But he'd always lusted after Lisa, those fantasies, the cleavage. His inhibitions seeped away like sand in an hourglass.

When he turned his eyes back to the video, the action had moved to a bedroom. One of the women had taken a chiffon scarf from a drawer and was draping it over the bedside lamp, bathing the room in a sultry, sexy glow. She turned round and blew a kiss at her partner, the blonde one with the big hair. Then she walked across the room and kissed her full on the lips. David, his memories stirring of that evening in the cottage in Wales, felt increasingly aroused. The guy in the film sat on the edge of the bed and the two women disappeared off-screen, evidently into a bathroom or something. Were they in a hotel or somewhere? It didn't matter.

When they came back, the dark one caught David's eye first. Her make-up was newly applied, elaborate and whorish, but what really got him going was her black leather thigh boots with their excruciating, six-inch heels. Her hair was back-combed into a smoky cloud, her eyes kohl-rimmed in a face of ghostly paleness. Her lips were painted an uncompromising red, like the gash of a wound. Around her neck she wore a spiked collar of black leather.

The camera lingered over her outfit, a skintight black leather corset – he was reminded of Debbie and her white lace basque – which left her breasts exposed, the nipples rouged into redness. Her sex was exposed too, the sparse black pubic hair standing out against white flesh, the lips clearly visible in close-up.

David wanted to laugh but the guy in the film was starting to look alarmed. The dark-haired one was starting to get aggressive with him, telling him what to do, shaking her balled-up fist at him in a way that looked pretty uncompromising. He couldn't catch what they were saying, the sound was turned down low. The guy took off his clothes and climbed on to the bed, kneeling down, awaiting orders. His penis, David noted, was hugely erect.

When the blonde one came in David was even more startled. Her hair was wild and loose, her lips were curled into a sulky pout and she too wore a new outfit – a catsuit of white lace, transparent as gauze, through which her breasts and buttocks, to say nothing of her labia, were plainly visible. The reason why was not hard to fathom. When she stood in her white patent leather ankle boots with her legs wide apart, he could see that not only was the catsuit open at the crotch, but the woman's pubic hair had been completely shaved off, leaving it bare and visible and vulnerable.

'This is getting interesting,' he said to Lisa. She didn't reply.

The blonde one walked across the room, opened a cabinet and took out two pairs of handcuffs, with which she fastened the guy, still kneeling, to the bedposts by his ankles. Then the other one took hold of a whip. There was a good deal of swishing the air as a warm-up but she didn't use it on his naked arse. Instead, she delicately stroked its wicked-looking tip against the white lace of her friend's catsuit, drawing it with tantalising slowness up the inside of her thigh, until it touched the lips of her exposed sex. At the same time she began to play with her own pussy, easing one, then two, fingers into herself, and then a third, expertly massaging her clitoris with her thumb. David had never seen anything in his life before that remotely compared with this. It seemed to be trawling things from the very back of his imagination, going into areas he had never reached before. He wasn't altogether sure the feeling was a pleasurable one, but from the way she was staring at the screen, the ash on the cigarette in her hand almost burned down to the filter, Lisa seemed to be even more excited than he was.

The blonde woman then lay on the bed until that same bare pussy was only inches from the man's face. It was pretty unambiguous what the dark one was saying now. Even as the first stroke of the lash cut into his buttocks, he began to lick at those close-shaven lips, his tongue lapping against it as though eating an ice-cream. There seemed to be a good deal of shouting going on, as the whip came down again and again and things really began to move on-screen. His penis seemed even more distended than ever. Could it be, David thought, that the guy was actually beginning to enjoy himself. These weren't the usual blue-movie stars, he decided, hamming it up worse than the players in the village-hall panto. These people were in it for real, and the thought gave him a curious thrill.

The way the blonde woman came, with the camera close up on her face, was plainly not acting either. David wondered where it was all going to end. Lisa seemed to be holding her breath as if waiting for something and then the camera panned back to the dark-haired woman, who'd been out of shot for some while.

She had kitted herself out with a huge black strap-on dildo, which bulged out from her groin like some obscene travesty of a penis. She stood there in her black shiny boots, a wicked look on her face, the heavy eye make-up only emphasising the leer in her eyes. She ran her hand up and down the huge length of the dildo, caressing it longingly, maybe even swaggering a little. Christ, thought David, as the camera caught the look of alarm on the man's face. Something like that, right up his bum?

But that wasn't what the script demanded. Instead, he saw the blonde woman spread-eagled over the antique brass bed frame, her creamy white buttocks high in the air, her legs stretched far apart. Again the whip tickled her thighs, her buttocks, her pink exposed sex, again it came down, harder and harder, the dominatrix with her scarlet lips and nipples the very picture of fury, the dildo bobbing up and down with every savage stroke. And then she was pressing it against her friend's soft cheeks, begging for admission, demanding release.

David watched in awe-struck fascination as the camera revealed every detail of that bizarre coupling. The blonde girl's clean-shaven pussy seemed to suck that monstrous black girth in on itself until he began to wonder just how much the woman could take. And then the rhythmic thrusting that seemed to go on indefinitely, the cutaways to ecstatic faces, the bobbing nipples, the dark woman's tongue endlessly licking her lover's neck, the hands cupping breasts, the tight black straps cutting cruelly into flesh, until he could see, could actually see in full, close-up detail the trembling that seemed to course through their bodies, the labia in motion, freeze-framed at last at the very moment of triumph.

'Did you recognise the dark-haired one?' asked Lisa, as she fast-forwarded the video.

'I don't think so, no. Should I? Is she some famous porno queen?'

She stopped the tape, rewound it, let it roll on to the scene with the dildo.

'There, look at her face. Don't you remember her? She used to do the weather forecast.'

David stared for a minute and then realisation dawned. Christ almighty, he thought.

'Does it turn you on?' said Lisa, as she fast-forwarded the video once more.

'It's pretty, how can I put it, uncompromising, isn't it?' he said.

'But did it turn you on?'

Her hand was perilously close to his groin. The question was fairly redundant in the circumstances.

'Yes it did. I've never seen anything like that before.'

'Would you like to do something like that?'

'What?'

'I mean, would you like to play some of those games?'

He realised how incredibly tired he felt, how the effect of the wine had all but worn off. The makings of a first-rank headache were slowly tramping across his right hemisphere like a platoon of soldiers' boots. But something drove him on.

'OK,' he said. In for a penny, in for a pound. 'What do I do?'

'Just lie there,' said Lisa.

She hiked up her dress, unclipped her stockings. Then, with practised ease, she used the gauzy nylons to tie first one wrist to the wooden frame of the sofa, and then the other, until he was spread-eagled on the cushions in a parody of the crucifixion.

'Don't worry,' she said. 'I'm not going to beat you. Not today, anyway.'

She lay down next to him, half on top of him, kissed his face, his neck, his shoulders. David unconsciously tried to reach out and put his arms around her but was restrained by her stockings.

'It's weird,' he said. 'I can't move.'

'You don't have to move, lover. I'll do all the work.'

She slowly unbuttoned his shirt, ran her hands through the soft hair on his chest.

'I like hairy men,' she breathed. 'But not too hairy. You're just about right.' She smiled up at him. Then she began to trace her tongue across his torso, around his pectorals, across his nipples. Despite the amount of alcohol he'd got through, his cock was already rock-hard and straining against the denim. He closed his eyes and surrendered himself to the sensations she induced in his body.

She used her lips, tongue and teeth with practised skill. A long, slow lick would be followed by a sharp bite and then a caress. Her hands stroked his ribs, played with his navel, and then he arched his back for her as she took off his shirt completely and cast it to the floor.

His groin came next. She stroked him over his conspicuous bump, lay her head on his chest, kissed the sensitive flesh of his stomach. Butterfly fingers danced across him, this way and that, to be followed by slowly raking nails that gave him goose bumps. Pleasure and pain, pleasure and pain – she seemed to be setting up a rhythm for them to dance to, except that his duty was to lie still and wait for whatever was to follow.

She pulled down his ragged-edged denim shorts and there was his cock, lying engorged and ready, against his upper thigh. He felt oddly proud of himself. She touched it for the first time with a feather-like delicacy. He wanted her to suck it hard, bring him to orgasm quickly and viciously.

She sat up, took a sip of wine, all the while her

practised fingers running up and down his body. He wished she'd get on with it. She'd very cleverly made him want her – but what did she want from him? The film had made him feel distinctly uneasy.

He smiled at her when she asked how he was enjoying himself. It seemed the best kind of answer to give. He wanted to get back to something he knew more about. It was a bit like having one toke too many.

'Take your dress off,' he murmured.

'You'd like that, would you? Say please?'

'Please.'

She raked her fingernails down his ribs. It made him wince.

'Please.'

'Please,' he said, louder, and then he saw the funny side of it and laughed. She hit him, not very hard, across the face. He wasn't expecting that.

But she stood up all the same, tugged at the zip, and the dress fell in soft black folds at her feet. She took off her underwear and stood gloriously naked in front of him. Her breasts were magnificent. Her pubic hair was thick and abundant, and her labia were fully visible, deeply pink and glistening.

'Do you like me naked, David?' she asked.

'I think you've got a wonderful body. I've always thought so.'

'I thought you did. I've seen you looking at me sometimes. Even this evening.'

He was surprised. He'd been aware of her at his party, but he hadn't particularly been lusting after her.

'I don't always do it naked, though,' she went on. 'I've got all the gear, you know. The pvc and stuff. Maybe I'll wear it for you one day, if you ask me nicely enough. Do you remember the last time we came to eat at your place?'

He did indeed. Lisa and Conor and a whole crowd had come to celebrate her birthday. They stayed until well into the early hours and, to mutual embarrassment, Conor's cheque – for an amount that was far from inconsiderable – had subsequently bounced. He nodded.

'I was wearing leather underneath my dress that night. It was my birthday present. Leather corset, leather pants, leather suspenders.'

'Black,' said David, mesmerised, but Lisa corrected him.

'Red,' she said. 'It was all made for me. I love it. Imagine what my pussy is like when I've been wearing leather pants all evening.'

'Nice and licky.'

'Nice and licky. Would you like to lick me now? Down there, I mean?'

'I'd love to. I've always wanted to lick you.'

She straddled over his chest as he lay there on the sofa, until her pussy was just above his face. He was excited by her musky, vaginal aroma and the sight of the engorged labia that seemed to invite his questing tongue. He licked her tentatively, drawing just the tip of his tongue across the outer labia, exploring the manifold ridges and furrows of this strange flower that seemed to open out before him.

He heard her moan. His nose was buried in the muff of her pubic hair – it really was extraordinarily luxuriant – and he inhaled deeply the unmistakable smell of a woman on heat. And then his tongue began again its probing of her inner recesses until, finally, he opened his mouth wide and sucked in as much of this anemone as he could.

She gasped. 'Suck me, David,' he heard her breath. 'Tongue me out.'

He licked her again, this time his tongue pushing deeper into her vagina. She squatted down on him, his nose engulfed by her liquid folds, threatening to asphyxiate him. Somehow he was able to wriggle his head to one side and breathe more easily, his tongue all the while continuing to flicker and probe.

After two or three minutes of this his jaws were beginning to ache but he kept on at his work, aware of Lisa's obvious enjoyment of what he was doing to her, aware too of a curious distance that he felt was between them. He found her clitoris and teased it so very gently with just the tip of his tongue – she winced, shivered a little, and then pressed her thighs more firmly against the side of his head, urging him on like a rider on horseback.

He licked and played with her, wondering what she looked like in her red leather gear, aware too of the unusual coconut perfume mingled with the scent of her secretions. She was very wet now – no wonder the Victorians had thought that women actually discharged vaginal fluids during orgasm – and he sensed she was very near her climax. He gently nipped the soft flesh at the tops of her thighs with his teeth and it seemed to drive her wild. She ground her pussy against his face and he thrust his tongue, hard and stiff, as far as he could inside her. He sensed rather than felt directly a faint trembling running through her genital area and then she called out something incomprehensible and came right across his face, shuddering and gasping, pushing him away from her as she did so.

'Hey, that was good,' Lisa said as she slid off him,

reaching out for her glass. He was aware of her fluids drying on his face, the smell of her still strong in his nostrils. He tried to sit up but realised he was restrained, and sank back on to the sofa. He didn't want any more wine, anyway.

She looked at him. 'I don't want you to come in me, David,' she said. 'Not now, anyway. Shall I do you? Let's watch another video, shall we?'

David hadn't felt so confused in a sexual situation since the time when, at the age of nineteen, he had failed to get an erection with a pretty young student nurse who had practically dragged him upstairs at a party. What did she want with him? What was he doing here? What did he want out of all this? he found himself asking. His instincts, normally so sure, were muddled and indistinct.

She loaded a new cassette, touched the remote and fast forwarded. The surreal humour of ultra high-speed coupling brought a welcome note of humour to the strange events of the night. Lisa stopped, went back a few frames, and then pressed the play button.

Two women, not the ones he had seen earlier, were in a flat full of antiques. One was tall, with straight dark hair, the other had auburn hair and a full, voluptuous figure. Both were naked apart from high-heeled shoes. A man, fully clothed, sat in an armchair, sipping whisky. He was blindfolded.

Lisa gently took hold of his penis and began to frig it. She half turned on the sofa so she could watch too.

The women kissed each other, ran their hands over each other, touching in an exploratory way. Then the taller girl knelt down and performed oral sex on the voluptuous one, who threw her head back in a pantomime of enjoyment. The blindfolded man continued to sit and sip his whisky. For a blue film, the technical quality was surprisingly good. David had never seen more than a handful of these plotless epics and he had been appalled at how amateurish they had been, all shaky hand-held camerawork, bad cuts and jumpy editing. This one looked like it had been done by a top crew, and the actors and actresses performed like professionals, not porn stars. The movie had, Lisa told him later, been made by a crew at one of the TV companies that had lost its franchise in the great sell-off.

From time to time Lisa would lick his cock, suck it into her mouth, taste it. Then she would continue to move her hand up and down, stroking his sensitive glans, touching the hole at the top with her fingernail. He wanted to reach out and touch her but knew he couldn't become involved, and so he lay back and watched the screen.

Now the women changed places, the tall one sitting on the edge of a chair, the plump one lying at her feet. There was a close-up of vaginal lips and then a tongue flickering, moving expertly along those myriad folds and creases. The tall girl wrapped her long legs around her partner's shoulders. The girl at her feet was stroking and feeling her own breasts. Then an extraordinary thing happened.

The tall girl straightened up, put her legs down and opened her legs wide. The other girl stood up and offered her breasts. The nipples were large, succulent, plump with desire. The dark girl licked them greedily.

And then, amazingly, David saw her partner rub her nipples against her vaginal lips, pressing them into the puffy folds, her breasts between her lover's thighs. And then the nipple, seen in close-up, seemed to be actually inside the vagina, was fucking the girl, was itself being moulded and sucked and shaped by the muscles of her luscious sex.

David glanced down and saw that Lisa's nipples, too, were hard and stiff – this was evidently turning her on too. She looked up at him, smiling dreamily, and almost at the same instant the first jet of his spunk shot out and arced over her breast. She quickly pressed her tits against him, a hard nipple pressed right up against the tip of his penis, and his semen flooded out and over it, silvery-white against the subtle flesh tones of her sunburned body.

He wasn't, he knew, expected to spend the night with her. They parted amicably enough though and, exhausted and three parts drunk, he made his way back through the village. The floodlit tower of the church told him it was a quarter to four. He reached the cottage, let himself in through the back door, found the place deserted and plates, glasses and bottles on every available surface. He left them where they were. A record was still hissing and clicking on his old turntable and he automatically turned it off. Howlin' Wolf – Chris must have put it on. He switched off the lights and went upstairs. On an instinct he checked both spare bedrooms and found them empty – no one was staying over, then. Slightly to his astonishment – it had been a night for surprises, of one sort or another – he saw a purple lace bra under one of the beds. I can't think about it now, he said to himself. He brushed his teeth, drank five or six glasses of water, made his way unsteadily into his own bedroom, lay down fully clothed and within ten seconds was unconscious and snoring heavily.

* * *

David awoke almost immediately. He looked for his watch on the bedroom table, couldn't find it, realised he was still wearing it. It was quarter to ten and he felt absolutely awful. Something had crawled into his mouth during the night and died there. His throat was dry and gnawing pangs of hunger emanated from his stomach. He tried to sleep for a while but his headache demanded something be done, so he got up, threw off yesterday's clothes, pulled on his old dressing gown and went downstairs.

The cottage had that special morning-after feeling too. The smell of stale tobacco was surprisingly strong and the last of the summer wasps had flown in through the open French doors and were picking at the plates of half-eaten food that were scattered around the place. Guy came snuffling round, ready to be fed.

He went to the fridge, took out a carton of orange juice and drank deeply, but it only seemed to make his headache all the more painful. He found a nearly intact slice of pizza and nibbled it absently, and then a wedge of garlic bread – God alone knew what his breath must be like, so he couldn't make it much worse. Already feeling nauseous, he found difficulty swallowing. There was some fruit in a bowl so he ate some of that – an apple and a couple of nectarines – and began to feel a little bit better. The sunlight was a bit much, though.

He showered – grateful, at a time like this, that he had finally had it plumbed in – and got dressed. Then, while the coffee percolated, he tidied up the worst of the mess, emptied ashtrays, shoved the paper plates and their contents into a black plastic rubbish bag that he dragged around with him. He stacked up everything else by the sink, thought about hoovering but decided the noise would be too much. Once this was done, the place didn't look too bad.

Out in the garden, he dragged out a lounger and set it up in the shade of the old rowan tree. He drank several cups of coffee, took aspirin, dozed off in the Sunday-morning stillness. By lunchtime he was beginning to feel almost human. It was time to take stock.

Some curious kind of truth about himself had begun to emerge in the last few days, and had been brought to a head by the events of the previous evening. Even as he had blundered home through the darkness, half-formed thoughts had been floating through his mind.

Just what had he been looking for with Lisa? And, before that, with Kirsty and Debbie from the hotel, and with almost all of the others – except Emma. It wasn't, he now realised, the sex as such that he'd wanted, though that had often been exciting and full-blooded. His needs went much deeper than that, down through the surface of physicality, into another realm altogether.

He realised that what Lisa (and, *ipso facto*, Conor too) were trying to do was to get through to something that had been forbidden them in childhood – a sense of pleasure in themselves, in their bodies, in the functions of their bodies. It wasn't so much what Lisa did that turned her on, it was the idea of what she was doing – being authoritative, saying what she wanted, doing as she pleased. If she wanted to suck a lollipop, she could suck a lollipop. All these hang-ups were having to work themselves out through her sex life. What they did, all the domination and things, it probably had its own excite-ment but it was one that paralleled, rather than was a part of, a true sexuality. The thrills were a substitute for the real thing. Or was he being desperately conservative?

And Kirsty, too – what did she want? She was a nice enough girl but – again, it was this childhood thing – the need for acceptance, the desire to be pleasing in order to win approval. Sex wasn't primarily what she wanted – it was the means, rather than the end. The same thing seemed to have applied to so many of the women that he had known. Gabrielle – there was a classic case for you.

And what about himself? He'd known Emma for two months now and they'd had some great times together. When they weren't together, he drew inspiration from the fact of her existence, from things she had said, from things they were going to do. Why did he need to screw around still? What the fuck was he playing at last night, in Lisa's home, or in that cottage in Wales? Even here, a while back, with Gabrielle.

What he was after, as it finally hit him on that warm, hungover, late Sunday morning, wasn't physical sensation and emotional thrills at all – or at least, not entirely. What he really wanted was affection, a sense of belonging. By making love with someone it seemed, for a while at least, that he was wanted, that his partner needed him not as so much flesh, but as a person.

This was what – if he hadn't been too disgracefully drunk to see it – had been staring him in the face in the early hours of the morning. He had known Lisa for years, thought of her as a friend. When they had sex, it was surprisingly devoid of warmth. It had been the same with Kirsty and Debbie – fun, but not much else. It was all a dance, a psychological game, a part of other games, wheels within wheels, and he'd been too dumb to see any of it, driven by his perceived physical needs like any dumb jock.

They didn't want him, David, the person. They didn't

value his strength, his humour, his kindness. That had something to do with him getting them into bed with him in the first place but basically they just wanted his dick, his tongue, his hands. And when all he took from them was sex, then it became curiously empty, because it was lacking the element that, at heart, he desired the most – their affection and respect. Only Emma gave him that, only Emma had ever given him that. Maybe Abbie had realised that, and maybe she hadn't. Maybe that was why she left him, because he just wasn't on that same wavelength, didn't have that finesse of understanding about people in general and lovers in particular. But not even with Abbie, with whom he had lived for so long, had he even begun to understand about himself so deeply. It had taken Emma to expose the truth to him, to be the catalyst for his awareness of exactly who he was. With the others, he hardly existed. They didn't want him – they wanted what he represented to them, which could be something entirely different, like a father-figure or someone they could bully or whatever it was that kept them from contemplating reality too closely. They were as dumb as he was. Or had been.

At last he felt as though he understood. All those women, all those affairs, all that screwing – what had it all been for? At a purely sexual level, he could have made do with half of it and still been satisfied. But he had to go on, to try and find something that he was too dumb to realise couldn't be found that way. A child gets affection from its parents, in an undiluted and unsubtle form. In adulthood, things tend to shift around and love becomes equated with sex. Women, it was sometimes said (in David's hearing, at any rate) found sex through love. As

far as men were concerned, they found love through sex.
So David had always been led to believe. Now he realised
that things weren't quite so simple. He was trying to find
love through sex, believing that was the way forward.
But instead of the freeway, he found only an endless
succession of cul-de-sacs and avenues, interesting
diversions no doubt but, until Emma had come along,
had got no further along the road than that. In little
more than eight weeks she had made him rethink how
he had lived the whole of his life. Twenty years of male
sexuality had become condensed into one morning, and
then a single moment of intuition and understanding.

He had lunch, slept for a while, woke feeling refreshed.
He went for a long walk with Guy, out into the country,
past the field where he had first met Emma. The corn
had been harvested weeks ago, and now there was only
stubble. He knelt down and picked up a few stray ears
that had survived the slashing flails of the big machine.
He crumbled them in his fingers, watching the grain
spill out. It seemed an oddly prophetic moment but he
could not understand why.

He took the path by the river, avoiding the nettles
that lined the bank, crunching instead through the hard
stubble. It played havoc with his espadrilles but they
were nearly worn out anyway. He found himself thinking
about all manner of things except, curiously, Emma. The
restaurant would be reopening on Friday, the same day
that she would be coming back, and there would be the
new menu to sort out. It usually took a few days before
the waitresses and the kitchen staff got their heads
round it. There was the washing up from last night's
party which still had to be faced. Then there was the
question of what to do about Lisa Doulton – last night

had, in retrospect, been pretty good fun but the implications were creepy. Emma or no, did he really want to get involved in all that? He hoped she would think it was all just a flash in the pan, a drunken romp that had no significance.

He came slowly back down the lane to his cottage, still a little hung over but, on the whole, pretty much at one with the world. He was surprised, therefore, to see a newly-registered BMW on the verge with the hood down. Nobody he knew had a car like that.

There was no sign of the owner as he opened the door of the cottage – he habitually left it unlocked during the daytime – and he wondered whether it might not be someone walking their own dog. They sometimes came down here for a stroll, along the riverside path he had just taken with Guy the Gorilla. Puzzled, he made his way through to the kitchen, guiltily aware that the washing up would not wait another day.

# Chapter 7

The Volvo clung to the tight, dipping roads of the Derbyshire hills like the rock climbers Emma saw from time to time in the distance, negotiating the limestone outcrops. Attracted by their bold, dayglo clothes and equipment, she'd stopped the car at one point and gone off to get pictures of one of the more accessible groups of climbers. They were just about to ascend a sheer face that had been hewn out of the hillside – it must, at one time, have been part of a quarry, forming a deep bowl-shaped scar in the side of the land. She shouted up at them: was it OK to take pictures? Sure, they called back, in ripe Glaswegian. She had been able, without much difficulty, to scramble through the scrubby undergrowth to get to the top of the overhang and was waiting for them when they came up. Half a dozen shots, tightly framed, with the climbers in the foreground and in the background the hills of the Peak District, green scarred with white where the rocks pushed through. A pity all the pictures for the book had to be in black and white, she reflected.

'What will you do now?' she asked one of the climbers when he finally reached the top and took off his helmet, shaking out a mass of curly long hair. Bare-chested in his harness and lycra shorts, he looked like a heavy-metal guitarist.

'Go down and climb it again,' was the laconic reply as he curled up his ropes.

The last few days had, on the whole, been pretty successful. She'd shot off a lot of film all over the north of England, sending the exposed rolls back to the studio by registered post so they could be processed in her absence. The contact sheets would be waiting for her when she got back; there was a lot of stuff that she was excited by, and she couldn't wait to see the results. She was glad she wasn't over-burdened with equipment – it was a drag hauling it into and out of hotel rooms each day. Nevertheless, there'd been a near disaster one day out in the wild fell country near Penrith. She was photographing a hill farmer outside his house – a long, low structure that could have come straight out of medieval England, with the dwelling at one end and the shippen for the animals at the other. Bouncing around their feet, his dog had sent her tripod flying and the camera had crunched into a low stone wall. There didn't seem to be much outward damage to the Nikon – its tank-like body was heavily engineered out of thick brass to withstand this kind of treatment – and after giving it a thorough going over, everything seemed to working much as usual. With other makes, she knew from bitter experience, she might not have been so lucky, but she had been using her back-up cameras for the rest of the shoot, just in case. It was precisely because of situations such as this that she always had spares with her – luck played a big part in photography, but it could move either way. Afterwards, the crisis averted, the farmer had given her a big steaming mug of tea and a thick bacon sandwich – home-cured, fatty and almost black. Out there in the Pennine wilds, with the winds whipping across the bare fells, it had tasted delicious. Anywhere else, and she might not have been so sure.

She'd rung David a couple of times, once from a service area on the M6, and then the previous night from her hotel. Their conversation had been low-key and non-specific – after her call from Liam Forbes-Chalmers, she had begun to realise the implicit erotic possibilities of the telephone – but she was aware of how much she was missing him. Sure, what she was doing was fulfilling and demanded all her time and attention, but being with him – actually being with him, not just thinking about him – gave her life another dimension. She was looking forward to spending at least a couple of days at his cottage – the weekend was coming up, and she knew she'd be through by then – before going back to London and getting her work schedule organised for the trip to Japan. God, it was next week – she couldn't believe how the time had flown. A couple of agencies wanted her to come in on projects as soon as she got back and Collet Churchward Hawksworth Dean – God, what a mouthful that was – were asking her to do something else for Land Investments. And then there was the book – although, once she'd made the prints and handed them over, there wasn't really that much for her to do. It was always like this, either nothing at all or everything at once. There was no in between. You'd no sooner broken the back of one job before the next one was looming up, demanding your attention. If only she could see one right through to completion without constantly having to look over her shoulder.

Yes, she reflected as she negotiated those tortuous roads, a few days with David would be good. If she got through what she had to do quickly enough, maybe she could get there early – on the Thursday even. That would be a lovely surprise for him – she loved giving him surprises, books, CDs, a bottle of wine, her body. The restaurant would be open again by then and she'd love to eat there – maybe she could wear the cami-knickers and suspenders he'd bought her in Whitby. After so many days on the road, she was in need of something imaginative to eat – and she wasn't just thinking of David's body. She'd seen plenty of interesting-looking places en route but somehow she didn't fancy eating alone, and so hotel grills and pub lunches had been the norm for the last little while. She was convinced she'd put on a couple of pounds – her jeans, always a useful barometer of weight loss or gain, were feeling distinctly tight around the waist and her period wasn't anywhere near due. Just as well, she thought, looking forward to the weekend.

There had, however, been one little moment of frisson since she had said goodbye to David on the station platform at Carlisle. Coming off the motorway and heading south through Lancashire, she had become aware of a slight rattle from somewhere in the vicinity of the rear axle. It hadn't affected the way the car drove in any way, but it was annoying and – knowing very little about cars – she was worried in case it might be the beginning of something a bit more serious. After a particularly vicious clatter from the Volvo's back end she had pulled in to a small roadside garage. She needed petrol anyway.

'I wonder if someone could have a look at my car,' she told the woman at the cash desk. 'There's a bit of a rattle and I don't want anything more serious going wrong.'

'Mechanics are all at dinner,' the woman said, evidently

sympathising with the plight of a lone female driver, and a very attractive one at that. 'But I'll have a look round the workshop for you anyway and see if anyone's around.'

A couple of minutes later a young man in greasy overalls came across the forecourt, wiping his hands on a piece of cotton waste.

'What's your problem, love?' he asked in a ripe Lancashire accent. His eyes, amid the smudges of oil on his face, were the bluest and most piercing Emma had ever seen. He was incredibly fine-featured.

Feeling slightly breathless, Emma explained what was wrong. He crouched down on the spillage-stained concrete, peering intently at the underside of the car.

'To be honest, I can't see anything what looks wrong,' he said at length, glancing up at her with those penetrating bedroom eyes. He couldn't be a day over twenty, she reflected. It would be cradle-snatching.

He must have sensed Emma's look of concern. He stood up, and brushed the grit from his knees.

'If you want to run it up on to the ramp,' he said, 'I'll have a look at it for you. It doesn't sound like anything serious.'

She drove round the back of the garage and through the workshop doors. Carefully she parked the Volvo on the hydraulic lift and got out. In seconds, her car was level with her head.

The mechanic used a powerful hand lamp to probe the inner recesses of the big estate car's underside. Killing time, Emma walked around the deserted workshop, with its neat racks of tools and spares and the all-pervasive smell of oil. True to form, there was a girlie calendar hanging from a metal cabinet. Glancing round in a reflex gesture to see nobody was looking, she quickly flipped through it – not that she particularly went one way or the other for tit 'n' bum pictures, merely that it might give her some ideas. It didn't.

After only a couple of minutes, the mechanic called her over, ushering her directly underneath the car.

'This is your problem,' he explained, stabbing at the car's exposed entrails with his lamp. 'There's a clip what secures your exhaust pipe and it's come loose. When the engine's working hard, the exhaust vibrates and it's probably just catching this part of the floor pan.'

'Can you fix it?'

'If I've got a spare clip. If not, I can easily sort something out. It's nothing important.'

He disappeared for a minute and came back looking triumphant, carrying a toolbox. His teeth shone, brilliant and even, in his blackened face.

'I knew we had one,' he said. 'This won't take long.'

'How much do I owe you?' Emma asked when the work was done, but the young mechanic waved her aside.

'Don't worry, love,' he said. 'It'll be under warranty and anyway, it's hardly worth making out a time sheet for a job like that. Mind you, don't tell me boss I said that.'

She smiled, and touched him lightly on the arm as he opened the door for her. 'That's very kind of you,' she said simply. God, his eyes go right through me, she thought. And he's so pretty. A rude mechanical indeed – I could see about that, given half the chance. She started the engine, backed out of the workshop, and with a wave was on her way.

And now she was driving south away from this glorious limestone country and into the greener shire counties, looking for Woolston Hall. The Honourable Philip de la Salle, she had been told, was an aristo among aristos, from a family whose bloodline ran so blue and true that they could trace themselves back to the French nobility of the twelfth century. As well as owning half of Leicestershire he was also, in the way of these things nowadays, something extremely important in the futures market. She had been put in touch with him – or rather, with his secretary – by Liam Forbes-Chalmers, a contact in the City and, it would appear, something of a family friend.

'He's an odd guy in some ways,' Liam had said, 'but an absolute archetype in others. His family all look the same. They have this long gallery full of portraits and they all look like him.'

'Maybe I could do a picture of him in front of one of the portraits,' she had said. She valued first thoughts – they were usually the best ones. 'Perhaps I could do it like a double portrait. Yes, I'll certainly give him a ring. He sounds very interesting.'

Woolston Hall, when she finally found it, was everyone's idea of the English stately home. Having passed the lodge at the one of the side gates – the main entrance, as she found when she first drove up to it, was not used in the normal run of things – she drove through acre upon acre of open parkland, studded with handsome old trees and the occasional wandering deer, neither tidy nor untidy, neither unkempt nor over-manicured.

She parked by the side of the main house which, seen in the flesh, was perhaps smaller than she had been expecting. She'd looked it up in one of David's books on English houses and had seen an imposing, four-square structure in red brick, rising up above a stretch of open water. Of course, she now realised, the lens had distorted the perspective, until the Hall seemed bigger than it really was. It was amazing just how often simple tricks of the trade could deceive even the practised deceiver. Now, having driven through the park, she was surprised by just how suddenly the Jacobean house burst upon the eye. Instead of the gradual approach she had been expecting, there was a dip among the trees and then she suddenly seemed to have emerged through a time tunnel into Shakespeare's England, the warm red of the brick basking in the late afternoon sunshine.

Through Liam's intervention and the de la Salles' kindness, Emma was to spend the night at the Hall. This notion, again, was like something out of another age. Emma didn't know too much about the Jacobean and Elizabethan playwrights but she'd read most of Jane Austen and had always rather fancied the idea of the round of house visits at Northanger Abbey and places like that – even if, in her case, it was to be for one night only. Philip de la Salle had arranged to make the whole of the following morning free for her and, in the meantime, he would be happy for her to have the run of the place, scouting out suitable locations for the pictures.

The sepia tinge was, of course, purely on the surface and, if anything, largely in Emma's imagination. She went first of all to the secretary's office, where all traces of a bygone age of elegance seemed to have been chased away by squads of beaters. Where she had been expecting Adam fireplaces and oak panelling, she found an Apple Mac and fashionable industrial-pattern shelving. But Richard Childs was old-world politeness itself, enquiring of her journey, of the progress of her book, of her plans for the following day.

'I'll have someone show you to your room,' he said, 'and then you can come down and have tea with Mrs de la Salle. Mr de la Salle is attending to some business in Edinburgh this afternoon but he will be back during the course of the evening. No doubt you'll see his helicopter when he arrives. Then I'll arrange for you to be introduced.'

Sonja de la Salle had the fragile beauty of the old china out of which they drank tea. Her cheekbones were high, intensely Slavic, and her hair, cropped very short, was so blonde it was almost white. But she was remarkably comfortable to talk to, a woman at ease with the world of fashion and the arts, a collector herself (of twentieth-century prints and Hans Coper pottery) and something of a traveller. In the drawing room where they were sitting she pointed out old Persian rugs, ceramics from Madagascar, Etruscan stoneware. She had worked, before her marriage, at Sotheby's. She still acted for them occasionally in an advisory capacity. Her brother was Patrick Reynolds, arguably Europe's foremost expert on Islamic art; the family (she didn't mention it, but it rang bells in Emma's mind) were scions of the famous eighteenth-century portraitist.

Before either of them had really realised it, late afternoon had turned to early evening, and a warm glow was stealing over the estate. To what extraordinary places this commission had taken her, Emma reflected. Not long ago she was eating greasy bacon sandwiches with a Cumbrian hill-farmer. Today she was sipping Assam tea out of hundred-year-old cups and nibbling chocolate olivers. In a couple of days she'd be with David in the Cotswolds. The week after, she'd be in Japan. Her own family background had been comfortable, prosperous even, but she was as unfamiliar with the world of Woolston Hall as she was with, say, the still-mysterious East, or of how her car worked under the bonnet. She had a rough idea of how it went, but that was about it. She recalled the mechanic and his baby-blue eyes. Maybe one evening with the vibro, she promised herself.

Later, the two women drank scotch and soda before going for a walk around the grounds. Emma mentioned The Ancient House at Hemstead – the de la Salles had friends in the area, and there was a promise to eat there next time they stayed. There was a folly beyond the lake, a series of arches in emulation of a ruined abbey that had been built by an eccentric forebear in the last century. Emma felt it had possibilities, but still thought the double portrait was her best option. When they got back, Richard Childs told them the master (for so Emma had come to think of him) had been delayed, and would not be back before ten. Sensing Emma's tiredness after her long day, Sonja de la Salle conjured up a light supper for the two of them – omelette *aux fines herbs* with new potatoes and salad – and then gracefully offered her the opportunity to retire. Emma was in the bath when she heard the helicopter arrive. She was thinking about the mechanic, rather than David, and she felt vaguely guilty.

Mind you, he was incredibly good-looking, in a fresh-faced, innocent kind of way. She had to confess that, on the surface at least, he wasn't really her type at all – she went more for tall men with a hint of mystery to them and he was, well, kind of wholesome-looking. Her longing reaffirmed her sense of power over men – not something she had always felt she had – and her hand strayed involuntarily towards her groin.

Did men know that women enjoyed their fantasies

too? she wondered. She sometimes found it difficult to countenance the idea. Alun, the MP she'd had an affair with twelve months back, had always been keen to listen to her lewd imaginings, as she described them to him in bed. Jeremy the obstetrician, on the other hand, had seemed vaguely shocked when she suggested one or two little games they could play – and yet he was a guy who was forever trying out little scenarios on her, like the time in the gondola in Venice. The one-sidedness of his sexuality was one of the prime reasons she'd ditched him in the end.

But that mechanic – well, she didn't even know his name, so that made it even easier. At least he had a face – she never understood why most of the men she fantasised about didn't have faces. She mentioned this to David once and he said it was the same for most of the women he thought about too. 'Do you fantasise about me?' she'd asked him, and he'd said no.

There was a difference between the real world and the fantasy world. She knew that, never in a million years, would she have had real sex with her mechanic. OK, maybe if David weren't around it might have been different but then having David around made a big difference anyway. He satisfied her so much in so many ways that, after the episode with Liam, she felt no need to have anyone else sexually. The desire simply wasn't there, even if the opportunity might be.

But in her imagination, she could do what she liked. Because she valued herself, she valued her privacy as well. It was like her flat in London – she hadn't owned it long but, apart from a few friends who'd been round to dinner, she kept it for herself. None of her boyfriends had ever been there – not even David. She was herself,

221

in her body and in her head. That was why she had such strong feelings for David, because he respected this. He was the same himself in lots of ways.

In the flesh she was content, but in her mind – her private, creative, intimate world – she still roamed free and feral. In her imagination she went back like some prowling animal to the garage with its masculine smells of oil and rubber, and the echoing sound of heavy tools dropping on concrete floors. She imagined giving him the look, the recognition in his narrowed eyes, the furtive glance around.

And then she'd take him in her arms, crush him to her, feeling his cock pressing hard and urgent through his oily overalls against her willing flesh. All the while the fear of discovery, the woman at the cash desk coming out back to check on something, the waiter at that restaurant with Liam, the gondolier. Maybe she wanted them to catch her, to see her displaying herself like some female creature in rut.

She imagined groping him through the coarse fabric, slipping her hand inside, the contrast between the hot ivory smoothness of his penis and the roughness of his clothes. The smell, yes, the male smell strong even over the heavy industrial fug that hung around the workshop. And all the time he would be doing exactly what she wanted, doing it her way, when she said so. She wanted to be spread-eagled over the bonnet of the car, to pull down her jeans for him, to flaunt her naked backside at him and anyone else who might be watching.

And then he'd be inside her, filling her, pushing upwards until she felt she couldn't take any more. She wanted his calloused, oily hands on her breasts, tweaking her pert nipples between thumb and horny forefinger, making her squeal and whimper, camouflaging still further the already hazy border country that lay between pleasure and pain. She wanted him to nibble her shoulders, to feel his breath against her cheek, his stubble roughly rasping against the soft down on the nape of her neck.

He came at the same time as she did and then she opened her eyes and it wasn't the garage workshop, it was a bathroom with mahogany and tiles that she was in, and the water was getting cold.

The session went brilliantly the following morning. Sonja had told her how the long gallery where the family portraits were hung was, before noon, flooded with natural light, and Emma was able to photograph the tall and languid Philip de la Salle against a picture of a seventeenth-century ancestor.

'He was a bit of a rascal, you know,' he observed as Emma was setting up her tripod and positioning the reflectors. Betraying perhaps his distant French origins, Philip had an olive complexion and piercing dark eyes and his hair fell forward across his forehead. He wore an open-necked shirt and heavy cord trousers and even his easy-going manner could not conceal the mannerisms of someone so obviously to the manner born.

'How was that?' asked Emma, relaxed and confident of something she had done so many times in the past that it was almost second nature to her. With the techniques of photography coming to her almost automatically by now, it freed her imagination for the creative work.

'Oh, he had, shall we say, appetites. Mistresses in London, a servant girl in trouble, a bit of a dust-up with a family across the border in Warwickshire. And so did his wife, apparently, have her little foibles. There's a story that two of her children were actually fathered by the Earl of Clare. Both girls, in fact. One died in infancy and the other went mad. Thank heavens the tabloids weren't around in those days.'

'I suppose we all have skeletons in our closet,' she replied. 'Though I don't know anything particularly wicked about my people. My great-grandmother eloped with a surgeon but that's as far as our family scandals go.'

There was a snort of laughter from Philip – she had got used to calling him by his first name – and he settled more comfortably in his chair and stretched out his long legs.

'My great-great-grandmother eloped with a doctor too,' he said. 'I wonder if it was the same man? Perhaps he had a string of mistresses. Did he marry her?'

'Yes,' replied Emma. 'They had six children. He became quite famous in later life.'

'My relative didn't. They brought her back in disgrace from Gibraltar and she later married a cousin who was a bit simple. We have a portrait of her somewhere – she was a very beautiful woman in her day.'

'Who was?' The voice was Sonja's. She had appeared silently at the far end of the gallery. Emma and Philip turned to her. The light caught her short hair, turning it the colour of white gold. Her bone structure seemed even more the work of a gifted sculptor.

'I was just telling Emma about great-great-grandmother Constance,' her husband replied. 'We've been dipping into our family secrets.'

'Not too far, I hope,' said his wife. She looked ravishing

in a crisp white shirt and riding boots. 'I've asked for coffee in the library. Do you want yours now or shall I wait for you?'

'I think we're almost done, aren't we?' said Philip. 'But could I ask you a favour? Would you mind taking a photograph of Sonja for me? Not really for your book, but perhaps as a companion piece to the ones you've just been taking.'

'I'll be happy to. Perhaps here, in front of this picture.' It was, she realised with a start, a Gainsborough portrait of a woman in a blue silk dress.

'That's another lady with a turbulent history,' said Sonja. 'But perhaps we needn't go into that now. We are a family for scandals, aren't we?'

The photograph was quickly arranged and the series of exposures made. Sonja was a natural in front of a camera. Emma would have said she'd have made a perfect model but such a career would quite possibly have been beneath the dignity of such a lady.

Over coffee in the library, the de la Salles tackled Emma about her work. They seemed to know quite a lot about her already – perhaps Liam Forbes-Chalmers had briefed them. The exhibition catalogue was brought out and studied.

'Who do you like as a photographer?' Sonja asked her.

'I like lots of people, for all different reasons,' Emma replied truthfully. 'I like Cartier-Bresson for his spontaneity, for instance, and I like Annie Leibovitz for precisely the opposite reason – you can see the work that's gone into setting it all up. I like pictures that have atmosphere to them – Bill Brandt's portraits, for instance. And again, for very different reasons, I like Helmut Newton – the guy who did *White Women* and all those

225

pictures of women in neck braces and things. I know his stuff is very politically incorrect but you can't deny that there's a real sense of drama in his pictures, that something's going on – even if you can't always tell what it is.'

'I like Helmut Newton,' said Sonja, somewhat surprisingly. 'In fact, I have two signed prints of his work. And Robert Maplethorpe?'

That's a trick question, thought Emma. 'Technically, I thought he was really good,' she said. 'But I thought a lot of it was just upmarket porn.'

Philip and Sonja exchanged glances.

'I think you're right,' said Sonja at length. 'Do you know this woman's work?'

She went to a shelf full of heavy art books and took down a volume of photographs. The pictures were heavily lesbian in content but there was no denying the brooding power of the imagery, the strong feeling of eroticism that came off the page.

'Colette Gifford,' said Emma as she glanced at the cover. 'No, I'm afraid I don't know her stuff at all. But it's brilliant – simple but very evocative. I can't really think of anything I've seen quite like it.'

'It's a private edition,' said Philip. 'A publisher we know in Milan. Your own publisher is Jonathan Withers, I believe?'

'You're in good company,' added Sonja.

'He is very good,' Emma agreed.

'Does he know about the pictures you took for the jeans company? The ones in your brochure?'

These were shots Emma had taken a couple of years ago and she'd got a lot of mileage out of them in the reputation stakes. They were simple black and white images of a good-looking boy and girl in a 1950s coffee bar but there was an undeniable sexuality there, a hidden level of meaning. There had even been complaints.

'I expect he does. Lots of people know I took them.'

'I wonder he hasn't asked you to do something in a similar mould, for a book.'

'Perhaps he might later,' said Philip.

'Would you like to do something like that?'

'I don't know about a whole book,' said Emma, 'but I enjoyed doing the jeans ad. I took some photographs for Bachmann's ice cream but they weren't used – I think perhaps the client felt they came out a little too raunchy.'

'Like Robert Maplethorpe?' said Sonja, laughing.

'I don't think a picture of a guy peeing into another guy's mouth would shift too many cartons of lemon-meringue flavour ice cream, but I take your point.'

'What happened to the pictures?'

'They're in a drawer in my studio.'

'Doesn't the company keep them?'

'Not unless it's specifically written into the contract. I always like to retain the copyright on anything I do. But there have been times when, for one reason or another, I've not retained copyright. It all depends on the client. If they're prepared to pay, then I'll surrender copyright. It's basically just a way of protecting myself from getting ripped off.'

'The pictures you just took of Sonja, then, as a case in point. If we arrived at an appropriate fee and agreed the terms of the contract, you would let us have all rights to them?'

Emma thought for a while. 'In theory, yes,' she said at length. 'It would all depend on whether you thought it was a reasonable deal for you to make. There's not actually a lot of reason why a client should want all rights to the material. But I would have no strong objection in principle.'

Philip considered this point for a while, and then he nodded to his wife.

'We have a proposition to make to you, Emma,' she said at length. 'We like your work, we like the way you work. You make it very easy for people to relax and be themselves. That's one of the reasons why you're successful.

'Philip and I have wanted to have pictures of ourselves to enjoy. A fantasy, if you like. Of course, you will understand that I mean erotic photographs.'

Emma guessed this was coming. She tried to maintain eye contact with Sonja and found it difficult.

'Obviously we're not talking "Readers' Wives" here,' said Philip. 'We are talking about photographs that will celebrate the value that Sonja and I place on this aspect of our lives.'

'The fantasy element. The erotic,' said Sonja, reinforcing what her husband was saying. Emma looked from one to the other in turn. She wasn't in the least embarrassed but it wasn't an easy proposition to take on board.

'And of course we'd need complete discretion and confidentiality,' added Philip. Emma nodded. That went without saying.

'How much do you think a reasonable fee would be?' he went on.

Emma smiled, but her mind was racing. She had always found it incredibly difficult to fix the money side of things, which was one good reason why she had an agent to handle most of the business deals. Back in the

1980s, in the heyday of privatisation sell-offs and power-dressing, the watchword had been to think of the most ludicrous figure you could and then double it. Nowadays, you had to be more careful. She tried to bear in mind what her clients might expect to pay, what they would think was reasonable.

'I'm not sure,' she said at length. 'It largely depends on how much time it would take. I really am incredibly busy at the moment.'

'Say an evening.'

'And when?'

'Tonight.' Emma gaped. She certainly wasn't expecting that. She was expecting, at the very least, a few weeks' grace.

'Well, how much do you think would be reasonable?' she heard herself saying. She couldn't deny the feeling of sexual arousal that was growing in her, occasioned not just by the nature of what she was being asked to do, but also by the power she was evidently able to exert over people who themselves were well used to exercising authority.

'How much did you agree for the jeans ad?'

'Ten thousand pounds,' said Emma. But that had involved over two months' work, she reminded herself. It wasn't the actual shoot that took the time – they'd done that in three sessions, with different models – but all the organisation that went into it, the meetings with clients, the fine-tuning of everybody's expectations.

'Ten thousand pounds, then,' said Philip, looking straight at her.

I don't believe this, said Emma to herself. Pinch me, I'm dreaming. Ten thousand pounds for an evening's work was probably more than Bailey and those people got at the height of their careers.

'OK,' she said as evenly as she could. 'You'd better tell me what's involved.'

'Let's go and have lunch, and then we can talk about it,' said Sonja.

They drove out to an achingly expensive little restaurant in a adjoining village. There was, in fact, to be another couple besides the de la Salles. From the sound of it, the brief was almost impossible – they wanted some pretty hardcore pictures but they wanted them to be creative as well. Over smoked carp on a bed of samphire in vanilla sauce they described the kind of scenes they had in mind. Emma pointed out that she didn't have any lights with her, merely a couple of flash units which, though powerful, were hardly adequate for the job in hand.

'What's the alternative?' asked Philip de la Salle, busy with his fish knife.

'Either I can come back another time—' she saw him nodding his head negatively, '—or I use whatever light's available.'

'And what will the results be like?'

'They should be very good. They'll be quite grainy, and some of the details would be indistinct.'

'But that would add to the atmosphere,' Sonja added, sounding excited. 'Everything is blurred and mysterious. Who are those people, what are they doing? Yes, I like the sound of that.'

'Just one more thing,' said Emma quickly. She'd been plucking up courage to ask them this. 'I don't know quite how to put this, but are you suggesting that I'm to be involved as well.'

Sonja and Philip laughed with surprising warmth.

'That entirely depends on how you feel,' he said. 'You do whatever you like. We certainly don't want to make you feel pressured into anything – I give you my word on that.'

The afternoon passed painfully slowly. Emma walked through the grounds of Woolston Hall, deep in thought about what the evening would offer. She couldn't deny that she was excited by the idea – everyone, whatever they say, has a certain curiosity about erotic imagery – and she had certainly felt a frisson while working on both the jeans ad and, especially, the ice-cream commission, with its impossibly sexy couple locked in each other's arms and licking the rapidly melting confection from various parts of each other's anatomy. That was what the company's marketing people said they wanted and, when they were given what they wanted by the agency that had employed her, they decided they didn't want it after all. That was marketing people for you all the way – assholes with influence, was how Martin Churchward of CCHD described them. This time, it was going to be different.

Alone in the conservatory at the rear of the house she ate a little supper and, untypically for her (for she preferred not to drink while working) she had a couple of glasses of wine with it to steady her nerves. The de la Salles and their mysterious guests were to dine together informally at seven and then the fun would begin. One of the drawing rooms had revealed definite possibilities when she had been shown around the house by Sonja – spacious, not too cluttered, and with plenty of interesting-looking furniture. The room faced west and would be lit the whole time by the setting sun, giving Emma an hour at least in which to work by natural light. For later, the room was well lit, with plenty of table lamps to emphasise the mood. Slowly everything began to fall into place. She sat in the library and waited.

A little before eight the door opened and Sonja de la Salle entered. Emma was astonished by her outfit, a black backless evening dress with a halter neck that was cut impossibly low in front, revealing well-sculpted breasts. She could barely walk on her four-inch heels as she led Emma, in jeans and plain T-shirt, down the corridors of the Hall to the drawing room. Of the servants whom she had seen earlier moving surreptitiously about their business, there was now no sign whatsoever. They evidently had the place to themselves.

Carrying her heavy camera bag, Emma tried to appear unconcerned, though her senses were alive and the adrenaline was pouring from her nerve-endings. Philip stood by the door of the drawing room, smoking a cigarette. He greeted her very civilly, under the circumstances.

'Come in and meet our friends,' he said, holding the door open for her. The woman by the fireplace was tall, in a purple shift dress. Her hair was piled on her head until she resembled a Roman empress. She turned to greet Emma, a smile playing around her lips.

'Hello,' she said, offering her hand with exquisite politeness. Her nails were long and painted the same colour as her dress. 'I'm Ursula Carmody.'

Emma took her hand, murmuring something inconsequential. She declined the offer of a glass of wine – she was here to work, she reminded herself. Enjoyment was necessarily a secondary consideration, for once.

The man she took to be Ursula's partner was silhouetted by the window, wineglass in hand, looking out over the estate. He turned round to greet her and Emma was glad she'd declined the wine, for she would surely have dropped it in her consternation.

It was Liam Forbes-Chalmers.

'Hello, Emma,' he said. Totally unfazed by the situation, it was immediately obvious that he'd set the whole thing up. Emma didn't know what to think, but some residual element of her self-confidence helped carry her through.

'Hello, Liam,' she said as levelly as she could. 'I was wondering who the other couple might be.' And Ursula couldn't possibly be Liam's wife, she said to herself. He was one of the most amoral men she had ever met, but she could not deny his cruel charm. God alone knew what kind of a shark he was in business.

The preliminaries, mercifully, were few.

'Would you massage my shoulders,' said Ursula to Liam. 'You always do it so beautifully to me. It really helps me relax.'

She was sitting on a low gilded chair by the window, her pale features outlined in the soft light of early evening. Liam did as he was asked, expertly kneading the tissue on those elegantly turned bones. Ursula threw her head back and sighed.

'Mmmm, that's so good, you know, Liam,' she breathed. 'You can do this to me all night if you want.'

'I think Philip and Sonja have other ideas for us,' he replied softly, not interrupting the rhythm of his thumbs and fingers.

Across the room, Emma looked through the viewfinder at Ursula's face – the perfect oval shape, the well formed lips, the eyes that were neither green nor grey. She is an extraordinarily beautiful woman, she found herself reflecting. Why is she involved in all this? Her expression spoke of someone abandoning herself slowly to the sensations of her body, feeling Liam's strength and power transmitted through her very bones and muscles, soaking up his energy.

Liam's hand slipped down over her breast, cupping it gently even as, with his other hand, he continued to stroke and knead her shoulders and neck.

She sighed in contentment, putting her head back, ready to be kissed. He stooped down and their lips met briefly, once, twice and then Emma could see her tongue flicker out like a snake's, seeking his.

Ursula Carmody stood up, her long, elegant back turned towards Emma. She saw Liam's hands come round her waist, pulling him to her, smoothing the sensual curves of her back. He seemed, to Emma's surprise, to be entirely oblivious to her own presence, as though making love in company was nothing new to him. Well, it probably wasn't, she reflected. The episode with him that day in Macaulay's restaurant – hadn't that been a form of exhibitionism, a kind of game, designed to test her, to see if she'd join in, to see if she wanted to be a playing partner too? At the time, she didn't know whether she'd passed or failed. After the phone call, she felt differently. Now, it was obvious that she had passed with flying colours. Heaven only knew what Liam had said about her – but the de la Salles were far too polished to let anything slip.

She found herself fascinated by the experience of watching Liam and Ursula through the viewfinder of her camera. She had three with her, in fact, each with a different lens so she could take close-ups, medium and long shots without changing her position. Everything was to be in black and white. She didn't want to disturb her subjects if she could help it. She intended to remain as unobtrusive as possible, a fly on the wall.

She saw Liam's hands reach down under Ursula's long, flowing gown and pull the folds of expensive material up high around her waist. Underneath it she was wearing smoke-grey stockings, ruched pink suspenders, high-cut pink briefs. She closed in on his hands as they squeezed her backside and upper thighs, the supremely pampered flesh that was as firm and smooth as a baby's. Oh Jesus, Emma breathed, feeling herself starting to get damp.

Now Ursula had her hand on Liam's groin, her palms flat against the cool linen, the outline of his erect penis clearly visible. She stood slightly to one side of him, as if to give Emma a better view. She rubbed against him in slow, circular movements, massaging his cock, her blonde hair against his neck and flowing down over his chest. Then deftly she unzipped him and exposed his rampant maleness to the camera's unwavering gaze, holding him in the palm of her hand like a collector with a priceless antique.

She sank to the crouching position, her dress still around her waist so that her suspenders were stretched tightly across her upper thighs. She took Liam's cock into her mouth, tasting it first with the exploratory tip of her tongue before sucking it deep into her mouth, moving back and forth, back and forth with the skill of a practised fellatrix.

Liam rubbed her tousled blonde hair as she sucked him, his eyes gazing out across the parkland of the estate, his face in profile. That's a good one, thought Emma, as the shutter clunked gently – she wasn't using motor drives, they'd have been too noisy. But Liam seemed disinterested, reserved, almost arrogant. He was treating this woman with a distinct coolness even as she sucked his cock, but Emma had little idea of the true nature of what was between them. She was sure, with a woman's intuition, that Liam was not one to form close relationships of any kind. He could be exciting, impulsive, wilful – she knew that from her own experiences with him – but there was an underlying coldness there, a distance, a lack of involvement that seemed so characteristic of his kind and of his class. The image in the viewfinder of her Nikon – it was the one she had dropped, but it seemed to be behaving itself – was very expressive in that respect.

Now Ursula lowered the front of her dress so that her breasts were exposed. They were small and pretty, with delicate pink nipples. She moved to a kneeling position, letting the skirt of her dress fall in a swirl of purple silk across the polished wooden floor, until her breasts were level with Liam's exposed prick. She cupped her bosom tenderly, offering it to him, the nipples engorged and erect. He leaned forward to press his cock against the soft, yielding flesh – Emma, through a telephoto lens, couldn't see a thing – but then he pulled back, allowing Ursula to take hold of his penis and trace its tip around her aureolae and nipples.

Again she licked it, ran her fingernails along its length, sucked it deep into her mouth. All this was plainly visible to Emma. And then she was massaging its ivory firmness against her breasts once more, the purple dome forming a deep dimple in her flesh, cupping them for him, allowing him to slide his considerable length between them. Slowly Liam began to fuck her tits, strongly and rhythmically. He was still fully clothed, of course, but this only added to the strangely impromptu quality of the encounter. This was what would make the image.

He came suddenly and without warning, a copious emission of semen that might almost have caught Emma off guard had she not seen the tell-tale signs on his face of a man approaching his orgasm. The white pearls shot out across her breasts, thick and creamy, as he seemed to consciously spray her with them. Ursula smiled dreamily – Emma was sure she was on something – and, with the tip of an elegant finger, scooped up little dabs of come and anointed each of her nipples in turn.

Emma reckoned this was a good time to change film – she had been shooting steadily throughout. She was aware that Ursula had undressed and was now sitting on a sofa sipping wine, in her classy pink lingerie. Liam, next to her, was still wearing his impeccable linen suit. She assumed it was to be the de la Salle's turn next.

Philip came across to the sofa and took a sachet from the pocket of his Savile Row suit. He sprinkled four lines of cocaine on a Louis XVI table and they took it in turns to snort it. Though she wasn't meant to be involved, he looked across at Emma and raised his eyebrow. She shook her head – not for now, anyway. Once, years ago in her student days, she'd been taking photographs at an outdoor rock festival for one of the music papers when someone in the press area passed her a joint of Congo bush. It had taken the top of her head off and for the next couple of hours, as darkness fell, she was really flying. Somehow, with the camera and flash set on automatic, she managed to keep pressing the shutter. It wasn't till she got into her darkroom that she realised there was no film in the camera. Ever since then, she preferred to keep her head together when she was working. It was unusual even for her to accept a glass of wine.

Sonja, looking slightly glassy eyed, came and sat next to the almost naked Ursula. She put her hand on her knee but Ursula didn't react. Nor did Liam, who was looking at the *Financial Times*. This looks interesting, thought Emma, and she picked up the Nikon in readiness.

It wasn't until Sonja pinched Ursula's small pink nipples into hardness that she seemed to come out of her trance. Soon the two women were tonguing each other's mouths, their hands roving freely over their bodies. They stood up and Ursula stepped out of her panties, revealing a bush of fluffy blonde hair. She helped Sonja with the difficult fastenings of her dress. Emma was hardly prepared for what she was wearing underneath.

Both Sonja's nipples were pierced with slender rings of gold. Between them were a number of thin gold chains, from the centre of which other gold chains ran down her body and disappeared into the folds of her crotch. They must have been rubbing against her labia, her clitoris even, the whole time she was wearing them. Apart from the chains and her gold, impossibly high-heeled shoes, the lady of the manor was entirely naked.

The two women crushed themselves together, tongue seeking tongue, breasts flattened, pubic hair against pubic hair. Liam, still in shot, glanced up at them and went back to reading his paper. Philip was smoking — she sniffed the air. It was a joint, and good stuff by the smell of it. Emma felt curiously detached from all that was going on but at the same time strangely aroused and eager. She was aware of the atmosphere of decadence and indulgence but it didn't seem to seep through to herself. She was glad, in a way, that she was there as an observer and chronicler, and wasn't expected to become involved. She wasn't sure, either, whether this was entirely her scene. Being a voyeur, though, now that was different, something entirely new for her.

Wearing only stockings and suspenders, Ursula bent forward over the back of the sofa. Emma could see her pouting pussy lips, a fringe of blonde curls, the small puckered diaphragm of her anus. Sonja stood behind her, reached out and put her hand between Ursula's legs, stimulating her clitoris until her backside began to move back and forth in a slow, sensual rhythm. Not a word was spoken – there was no need.

Sonja walked across the room, surprisingly elegant in those ridiculous heels, and opened a drawer in a bureau. Ursula looked up and smiled. She spread her legs even more.

Breasts jiggling – they were pear-shaped, well formed and with pert, diminutive nipples – Sonja came and stood behind her friend. Into her anus she inserted a small, smooth ivory plug. Ursula winced at first and then visibly relaxed. Sonja reached round and put metal clamps on to Ursula's nipples. They must, Emma thought, have been excruciatingly painful but Ursula betrayed no obvious signs of discomfort.

Ursula put her hand on Sonja's crotch, her fingers on the folds of her pussy, exploring. Then, from Sonja's vagina, she pulled out the thick, stumpy dildo that was on the end of the gold chains that she wore. She unclipped it, licked it, pushed it into her own vagina alongside the butt-plug. Then Sonja gagged Ursula, who was still kneeling on the sofa, with a yellow silk scarf. It was all evidently part of a well practised ritual, and Emma found herself wondering what was going to happen next. She didn't have long to wait.

Sonja took Ursula by the hand and led her towards the huge ornamental fireplace that dominated one wall of the room. Ursula lay down in front of the flickering logs on the antique hearthrug. Above them, the inhabitants of an eighteenth-century family portrait gazed out as unconcerned as Liam with his *Financial Times*.

Philip de la Salle, Emma now realised, had finally divested himself of his clothing. He stood there, as naked as the day he was born, and his almost hairless body looked in good shape for a man in his mid-forties. But what took Emma most by surprise was the size of his penis. It was incredibly long, easily the longest she had ever seen, and it stood out from his pale flesh with lewd potency. His wife came over and stroked it, running her fingers along its considerable length, a proprietorial glint in her eye. It wasn't a particularly thick cock but Emma reckoned that he could do a lot of damage with it. Anal sex must surely be an impossibility with someone like that.

Then Sonja too lay down on the hearthrug, face up, awaiting her husband. She spread her legs invitingly for him and immediately he was on top of her, that great penis almost instantly vanishing inside her. Ursula lay alongside them, still wearing the yellow gag, occasionally caressing Sonja or tweaking her nipples with their gold rings as her husband screwed her. He would draw himself almost fully out of her and then plunge it back in deep inside her until she gasped and moaned with the feeling of fullness inside her vagina. Sonja reached up and pinched his nipples hard between her red-painted talons, but his face remained oddly impassive. The coke, thought Emma.

Soon it was Ursula's turn. She took out the dildo and butt plug and put them to one side. Philip rolled off his wife and positioned his rampant cock at the entrance to Ursula's love channel. She was evidently less well versed than Sonja in handling something as big as that, holding its great purple dome and carefully guiding it into her until she felt she could take no more. It evidently hurt her – even through the gag, Emma could see her gritting her teeth, could hear her muffled grunts. Perhaps that was why they'd gagged her, to keep her quiet. Jesus, she suddenly realised. He's put it up her bum. But with all the consideration of the true English gentleman that he undoubtedly was, Philip then screwed her with a rare gentleness, slowly and delicately, taking his time, sliding his cock out and then letting her take him in again gently, an inch at a time, until his cock was buried in her up to the hilt. She must, Emma realised, have taken some kind of muscle-relaxant. That was what made her seem so dozy earlier.

He reached round and undid the gag. 'You are so fucking big, Philip,' said Ursula, almost with a sneer. 'I want to swallow you up.'

'You like him up your arse, don't you?' murmured Sonja, so quietly that Emma could hardly catch her words, even though she had moved in close for the pictures.

'I love it,' the other woman replied. The two of them kissed, their tongues flickering in and out of their mouths.

'Let him fuck you from behind,' said Ursula. 'I'd like to see you do it doggie style.'

Liam too was now naked and was standing close to

Emma, drinking champagne, smoking grass. She thought he was maybe going to make a move on her but she was so busy with the cameras, moving from one to the other, changing film as quickly as she could, that he got the message.

Sonja knelt down on the rug, the warm glow of the logs casting a reddish tinge over her flesh, glinting on her chains. The rays of the setting sun stole across the room, bathing it in an exotic tint of peach. The air in the drawing room was heavy with perfume, sweat and the deeper musk of sensuality.

She steadied herself as her husband knelt down behind her and then, once again, he had pushed himself deep into her. It didn't seem to hurt her but her reaction was different now, Emma could tell. She imagined how it would feel to have Philip de la Salle's penis buried inside herself. She wasn't sure whether it was a feeling of pleasure or of pain.

There was something sacrificial about Sonja's behaviour, certainly. On her hands and knees, she seemed to push back at him with an almost haughty grandeur, meeting him thrust for thrust. But soon, where once all had been sighs and murmurs, the two of them were grunting and groaning, more like wild rutting animals than husband and wife.

They were moving faster and harder now, their bodies slick with sweat. Ursula came and stood with Liam, her hand fondling his cock. Discreetly she took off the nipple clamps and dropped them on a table, but her eyes, like Emma's, were glued to the couple on the hearthrug.

Sonja came in a convulsive shudder, her breasts shaking, her breathing ragged. Philip fucked her all the harder with that mighty tool, forcing her downwards with the power of his thrusts until she was face down on the rug, her bare backside in the air. And then, with a great shout, he withdrew his glistening shaft and his seed spurted out all over her back, a white flood that ran in rivulets over her flanks.

Almost immediately Liam was kneeling down behind her in his place. She guided him in between her soaking folds, her vaginal muscles already stretched and pummelled by her husband's savage assault. Where Philip had moved like a powerful locomotive, Liam's rhythm was more stubby and jerky, a series of short, sharp, grunting thrusts that seemed to signal a man already close to orgasm, fired up no doubt by what he had seen. Philip's semen was barely dry on her back before he was pumping his own seed deep into her, drenching her with his vital juices.

After that there was a long pause. Champagne and cocaine were consumed in considerable quantities and then Ursula and Sonja performed oral sex on each other for Emma's benefit, one at a time and then both together, their legs parted, long hair and short hair bobbing up and down. They knew what they were doing – one of her lesbian friends had once told Emma that no one knew better how to go down on a woman than another woman. Ursula gasped as if she was giving birth rather than reaching orgasm, and then she had one after another, a great shuddering multiple climax that left her drained and spent, lying on the floor with her legs apart like an abandoned toy, the lips of her vagina swollen and crimson in the rapidly closing darkness.

Finally, Philip buggered Liam. By this time Emma's head was beginning to swim and she could hardly co-ordinate her hands and eyes. The smell of grass in the room was incredibly strong. Whereas her earlier pictures from that evening had been carefully composed with an eye for light and shape, now she was just shooting what she saw, straight and uncompromising. There was no way she felt able to glamorise it, but then there was nothing especially glamorous – to her eye at least – to the coupling of these two men. Both were handsome, strong and charismatic but by now, to her, they had become just so much meat. Not until afterwards did she wonder about the effect of that great, powerful tool of Philip's on Liam's most sensitive organs, ripped to the tits as he was on coke, grass, champagne and – presumably – the same muscle-relaxant that Ursula was on. Almost from the first time she met him, something had made her think that Liam might be bi-sexual but she'd not really thought about it much. There wasn't, now that she saw him in action, a great deal of finesse to the way he made love.

Both men had poppers ready for when they came, small glass ampoules of amyl nitrate that could be broken immediately before the moment of climax and the vapours inhaled, so that their heart rate momentarily almost doubled. The flood of oxygen to the brain gave a rush that, the aficionados would say, was almost as good as pure uncut smack. All this was recorded by Emma's camera, factually and non-judgmentally, dispassionate and distanced, elegant and yet detached. It was what her clients had asked for, and it was what she had delivered. Sensing the evening was over, she silently packed away her gear and retired to her room. An envelope with a Coutts' cheque for £10,000 was waiting for her in the morning at the breakfast table. The space for the name was blank – she later gave it to the Labour Party. The housekeeper appeared briefly to ask if all was well, and then left her alone. Of her host and hostess, or of Liam Forbes-Chalmers and Ursula Carmody, there was no sign. By eight-thirty Emma's Volvo was crunching down the gravel drive. The first thin mists of early autumn were dispersing from the grounds and the deer roved unconcerned in the park.

On the long drive back into the Cotswolds she thought a lot – less about what had just happened than about what was going to happen. It had, by any rational standards, been a fairly amazing experience and not necessarily one that she was keen to repeat in a hurry. She had found it arousing, extremely so, but she was also aware the whole time of a sense of detachment.

That was what made it all so very different. She felt no great warmth towards any of the protagonists. There was Liam, of course, and she had felt very comfortable with Sonja de la Salle, at least when there was just the two of them. But in a group they seemed cold and remote, untouched by feeling. Sex for them seemed to be all in the head, not in the heart. It was like a ritual, a dance, and yet she could respond strongly, with an artist's eye, to the shapes and patterns of their bodies, to the delicate touch of a finger on a nipple, the form of a breast, the latent strength in a muscle. The setting was fabulous – it was, in many ways, exactly the kind of erotic fantasy she sometimes had herself, the unimaginable wealth, the hint of wickedness, the lure of the forbidden, the siren lure of luxury.

But emotionally it was a million miles away from where she now felt she wanted to be. A year ago, six months ago – she would surely have become so aroused that she would have wanted to be a part of them, to be accepted by them. Now she didn't feel that way. She had her own strengths, her own identity as a person. She didn't need to do things she didn't necessarily want to, just to gain approval and acceptance. She understood the difference now between fantasy and wishful thinking – and she knew that Woolston Hall was firmly in the realms of fantasy. If she thought of it like that, it was a titillation, a diversion, a grand illusion – maybe something to share later with David. She didn't take it seriously because there was nothing there to take seriously – at least, not for her. She wasn't into big dicks and nipple clamps. What she wanted was much harder to find – and she knew now that she had found it.

To say she was looking forward to seeing David again was an understatement in the grand manner. She'd decided to cut out the last day's photography – she felt she'd got more than enough material already. She could go to London, get the film processed – or she could go to his cottage now, a full two days early. It would be lovely and sunny in David's garden and later they could have a meal and make slow, delicious love to one another. She could tell him about Woolston Hall – or maybe she'd save that for later. It didn't take long to make up her mind. There was one last stop she decided to make on the way and by late afternoon she was almost there. She drove past the Angel at Brampton where she had stayed when she first came to the area, past the cornfield and down through the village of Hemstead. There was the restaurant, there was the familiar narrow lane, there was David's house on the left with the Citroen and a BMW outside. She parked her car and, feeling surprisingly calm despite herself, walked down the path. Should she walk right in, or knock? Better to knock, she reasoned.

Some vestige of middle-class etiquette told her it wasn't polite to walk straight into someone's house, even if you were planning to screw them there and then on the doormat.

There was no answer to her knock – the bell didn't seem to be working – and so she went down the path at the side of the house. She guessed he had visitors.

There was a woman lying on a lounger. She had evidently been sunbathing topless, because she looked somewhat surprised by Emma's arrival. She sat up languidly and drew a wrap around herself. With a stab of shock Emma recognised David's ratty old dressing gown but she had no idea who this woman was. It was all very alarming.

'I'm sorry if I startled you,' Emma said hesitantly, 'I was looking for David.'

'He's down at the restaurant,' the woman drawled, smoothing a hand through her tousled hair and fixing Emma with a look of cool appraisal. 'The freezer has broken down and they're ankle-deep in water. I'm Gabrielle McDowell, by the way – I'm an old friend of David's. I'm staying here.'

Staying here? Emma could hardly believe it.

'Have a drink,' said the woman. She'd obviously had several herself – her eyes were bloodshot and she spoke with almost mincing care. She was also angry, Emma realised. 'You know David, then?' she said.

'Yes. It's just that I didn't know that he, you – I've been away, you see.'

'So you're the photographer, are you? David's told me about you. Did he know you were coming?'

Of course he did, said Emma to herself. But they hadn't arranged a definite time or even date – they'd not

spoken for a week. Arriving two days early like this –
well, it was all even more vague. But what the hell was
going on between David and this Gabrielle woman?

'I guess so,' said Emma, feeling confused and even a
little angry herself. It wasn't like David to hide things
from her like this. 'Maybe I will have that drink.'

'David and I have known each other for a long time,'
the woman went on after she'd poured Emma a glass of
something sticky, extremely alcoholic and not very cold.
After the first couple of sips she put it down and left it
untouched. 'We were lovers, you know. Still are, as a
matter of fact. We mean something special to each other,
always have. That's why I'm here now – he asked me to
stay a few days with him.'

Emma could find no words with which to express her
feelings. She was dumbfound. Confused, angry thoughts
whirled around her head. Surely the woman was lying.

'So you're the latest?' Gabrielle went on. 'I don't suppose
you'll be the last, either. He's like that, is David. Always
the charmer. Makes you think you're someone special
and then, when someone else comes along, he'll drop
you. Believe me, honey, I know – I've been through it all.
But that's because I know how to handle him. That's
why I'm here now. The mice will play, and all that—'

Emma's skin felt unbearably tight, as though her
body were trying to burst itself asunder, so violent were
the feelings of pain and outrage that coursed through
her. What the bloody hell was happening? How could she
know if this were true? She wouldn't be sunbathing
topless in his garden if there wasn't something going on.
She could find nothing to say. She wanted to see David –
no, she didn't want to see David.

She felt betrayed. It was like something so very close

to her had been irredeemably violated, like a burglary or a rape. Oh, she knew that something had been going on that time he went down to Wales but they'd had a sort of understanding. It was OK, they were grown-ups, they could handle it. This was different. It was an invasion of her own space, of an area that she thought was shared by she and David alone. All those fine words, and this was what he meant by having freedom – the freedom to screw anyone, any time, anywhere.

With as much dignity as she could muster – for she knew her eyes were brimming – Emma murmured her thanks for her untasted drink and went back to the car. She bumped off the grass verge, narrowly missing the Citroen as the rubber burned on the road. Through the hot, welling tears it was like driving through a rainstorm, and in her heart all was black and empty.

# Chapter 8

At first, David was almost beside himself with fury when he heard what had taken place – at least, the way things had happened according to Gabrielle's version of events. He knew her well enough to be able to read between the lines and find the jealousy and anger and fear that lurked there inside her.

There was, he knew, an explanation that he could give to Emma. It was so innocent it ached, a simple story of how Gabrielle, tearful and distraught, had turned up completely out of the blue on that fateful Sunday evening after the party. But Emma wasn't around any more to hear it.

It had been Gabrielle's car that he had noticed parked outside in the lane. It was new, and that was why he didn't recognise it. She'd let herself in through the French doors at the back of the cottage. He didn't usually leave them locked when he was only going down the road.

It would have been an understatement, then, to have said he was surprised to see Gabrielle standing by the sink, drying-up cloth in her hand. It made him feel uneasy as well.

'Hello, David,' she said, flashing her expensively orthodontured teeth at him. 'I'd forgotten you like to go for a walk on a Sunday afternoon.'

He had found it difficult to speak. He wasn't expecting this.

'You didn't ring, did you?' he said hesitantly. 'We had a party last night and things got a little, you know – I didn't hear the phone, anyway. Where's Jim? You're not going to another wedding, are you?'

'No I'm not,' she said, and suddenly he noticed her eyes were full of tears.

'I've left him, David. I thought we could make a go of it this time, but well, I've had about as much as I can take. I want to come and stay with you for a while. I've nowhere else to go.'

Of course he'd said she could stay – he wasn't so much of a monster that he would hurt someone with whom he had had a relationship stretching back through the whole of the period since he'd come back from Australia. She let it be known that it would only be for a few days, till she got herself together again. At a time like this, she couldn't bear to be with anyone else. She wanted to get away, to be as far away as possible from Jim and all that he represented to her. So he agreed. After all, Emma wasn't due back until Friday at the earliest and Gabrielle had said she was sure she could go to stay for a while with her other friend, the one whose wedding she'd been to earlier in the summer.

It wasn't that he didn't want Emma and Gabrielle to meet. That would probably happen some day, he knew, but he wanted to be ready for it. He wasn't sure how each would respond to the other. They both represented such different aspects of himself. In the company of the two of them, he wasn't sure which version he would come to represent.

So she stayed, for a while at least. He had her word that she'd be out by the weekend. He also made it clear, with as much care and tact as he could, that he wasn't going to sleep with her. When he told her about Emma, he got the impression that she understood. After all, Gabrielle had had plenty of lovers herself over the years. She knew that some were more special than others. She'd seemed reassured by what David told her about the qualities of their own relationship. He didn't tell her that Emma would be coming down for the weekend. It seemed too much like tempting fate.

He went back over the events of those days time and again. Gabrielle hadn't even told him about Emma until they were eating together, that first evening.

'Oh, there's something I'd forgotten,' she had announced as blithely as if she were remembering that a double-glazing company had called. 'There was a girl came to see you. I said you were at the restaurant.'

'A girl?' said David, pouring wine. 'Who was she?'

Gabrielle knew perfectly well, but she was determined to play this one out to the finish.

'I didn't catch her name. She was quite tall, with shoulder-length blonde hair. She seemed to know you.'

David's heart almost stopped beating. He put the bottle down for safety's sake.

'Did she find you?' Gabrielle blandly went on.

Thinking furiously, he made a 'no' gesture. It must have been – but why hadn't she called him? Before or since.

'What did you say to her?' he asked at length.

'I said you were at the restaurant because the freezer had broken down. I said I was a friend of yours and I was staying here for a while. She seemed to take the hump at that. Was it someone you knew? Were you expecting someone? You didn't tell me.'

He left his food untouched and rushed out of the room. He tried to get Emma on the car phone, but there was no reply. He tried her studio, and the flat in St John's Wood, but got no further to her than the answerphone. Hearing her tape-recorded voice, he felt close to panic, and he vented his feelings on Gabrielle. In the end, she cracked before he did.

'Of course I wanted the silly cow to piss off,' she shrieked. 'I don't want her around, David. I just want you. I always have.'

This was what he had been afraid of. Over the years, in her mind at least, their relationship had changed from being a simple sexual thing to – well, a full-scale adult relationship. She wanted him to deliver things that he wasn't prepared to give. But now it seemed that everything that he'd never felt like giving to Gabrielle he had invested in Emma. He could understand why the older woman was so bitter about it. And now – and he could see the bitter sense of injustice that had driven her to do what she did – a vengeful Gabrielle had dealt them a potentially fatal blow.

What must she be thinking now, he thought, as their supper lay untasted on the kitchen table? For the first time since he had quit smoking five years ago, he desperately wanted one of Gabrielle's cigarettes as they sniped and bitched at each other. At the very least, Emma must have thought he was a feckless bastard. What other kind of guy would, as soon as the girl he loved was out of the way, have wheeled in his ex-mistress? Of course, it wasn't like that at all, but what was Emma to make of it? Gabrielle, the vicious bitch, had done her level best to wreck the whole thing. He could just imagine her carefully chosen words, the arch expressions, the cruel teasing, the sense of triumph over an opponent unfairly bested.

Emma must have got back early and have come out to the cottage to surprise him, he guessed. She was like that, always doing little impulsive things. It was one of the things he loved most about her. He could imagine both her mounting, almost child-like excitement and then the bitter pangs of disappointment, the shocked reaction turning to anger, the anger turning to hatred and contempt. Why didn't she ring? he kept asking himself. At least it would give him a chance to explain, to try and make amends. Why the bloody hell should she? a more mature voice told him. She's done nothing wrong. But she thinks you have.

But the phone stayed cruelly silent and that emptiness – because he could only imagine the worst – hurt him more than even the harshest words from Emma ever could. He didn't know how he got through the rest of that evening. He woke the following day thinking that Emma was beside him but it was Gabrielle, who had come and lain down beside him during the night. Not for sex, but for comfort, for the warmth of another body next to hers in the long and lonely night.

In the fresh light of a new day, he tried to look at it from her point of view. In his fury, he'd said some unforgivable things to her the previous night. He'd called her a whore and a leech and a failure who was trying to live her life through other people. He had known all along, of course, that she was lonely and dissatisfied.

He felt sorry for Gabrielle, lying there under the quilt, still asleep in the early morning sunlight. He stroked her shoulder as she lay beside him, glad despite himself of her company in the aching void that had been created by Emma's abrupt arrival and departure. She was a friend, after all, as well as a lover, despite what she'd done.

After a while they got up, made breakfast, read the paper. The post came; with bitter irony, there was a card from Emma, postmarked Buxton. He almost felt like weeping as he read its inconsequential message, now so desperately significant to him. 'Looking forward to the weekend' – oh Christ, he thought, if only it were so. The card was written a couple of days ago. How very different things now looked for all of them.

He was ready for Gabrielle when she made her move. They went for a long walk with Guy the Gorilla – David was sure of his uncomplicated, unconditional love, at any rate – and he told her a little bit more about Emma, not much but enough, he felt, to let her know how things were. All the time a despairing voice kept reminding him, not were but had been.

When they got back to the cottage, she put her arms round him and kissed him, not hard, but full on the mouth. He didn't return it, though he felt a momentary thrill of desire despite himself. He broke free as decently as he could.

'Look, that's not going to help things, is it?' he said, trying to smile. It had all the warmth of a weak winter sun.

'Don't you want me?' she asked, taken aback. 'I mean, I know how you must be feeling and all that—'

He didn't say anything. He could see her cheeks flushing – she was very angry at being rejected. So she thought he'd jump straight out of Emma's bed into hers, did she? It was grotesque.

'You fucker!' she screeched at him. 'You've just been using me, haven't you.'

He could feel the bile mounting in his own throat. 'You went into this with your eyes open, Gabrielle,' he snapped at her. 'How many bloody times have I told you I didn't want any ties?'

'You seemed to get pretty closely involved with her, didn't you?'

'Can't you see that was different? Jesus fucking Christ, not all relationships are the same, you know. What about Jim? You took a hell of a long time to make your mind up about that. I never said, leave Jim and come and live with me, did I? All this has happened in your head.'

Her eyes were red with fury.

'But I wanted you, David.'

'All right, I wanted you too, at the time. But what does "want" mean? And we don't have to do things if we don't want to, you know. You can't force someone to do anything if they don't want to. Look, it worked fine the way it was. Why can't we just leave it at that? Why do you have to try and take it further when I don't want it to go any further with you?'

She stared at him, speechless with rage. She had killed off her rival only for the hero to turn on her. She couldn't believe it – she thought she had the whole thing worked out, like it was on TV. Get rid of that Emma woman and then she'd have David to herself. For good, this time.

'I think you're an absolute fucking shit,' she spat. 'And I thought you were different. Well, you can live without me as well. This is goodbye, David. I hope you're feeling pleased with yourself. I hate your bloody guts.'

She left as soon as she was able to throw her things into a bag. She left a whole pile of cosmetics in the bathroom still, and knickers in the airing cupboard. He found a pair of her shoes under the bed.

After that, David was alone.

Confused by roadworks, still numbed by shock, Emma had taken the wrong turning on to the M4 and found herself heading not for London, but westwards towards Bristol and the Severn Bridge.

'Oh Jesus fucking Christ,' she hissed under her breath and tugged the road atlas from off the back seat. Balancing it on her knees as the heavy lorries thundered past her, she realised there wasn't another turn-off for twenty miles.

But in a flash she realised that she had, after all, taken the right sliproad. It was as if fate had decided her path for her. She would go and see her parents for a few days and try and get herself together, away from all the pressure of David and her work. She saw them only occasionally in the normal run of things and she knew they'd be pleased to see her – even if they'd probably grumble about the lack of notice.

'We've got the man coming to fix the guttering,' she could hear Dad saying, as if that made any difference. She saw the Cheltenham sign and it was like something had been decided for her. She flicked the indicator and moved over into the slow lane.

She didn't want to go to London, back to her empty flat. She didn't want to go to the studio and wait until Sasha had gone home so she could process the films she had shot off at Woolston Hall, because she certainly wasn't going to let anyone else see what she'd been doing there (it was also an integral part of the agreement between herself and the de la Salles).

But most of all, she wanted to get away from David. He'd never even been to her flat but there were reminders of him all over, t-shirts she'd borrowed, photographs, CDs, that kind of thing. She could live without all that. She needed to get her head together, didn't want that kind of intrusion. In less than a week, she had to go to Japan. It was all too much. She wished she could just go to sleep.

A few days with her parents might help her get over the initial surge of anger and the desperate disappointment that she felt about him and the way things had worked out. They would take over as they usually did, making decisions for her, quietly organising her life for her. It wasn't done maliciously – she knew how much they loved her because they made a point of telling her so, even now, and she had never doubted their word for a moment – but, even though she was a grown-up woman now, they couldn't resist giving her advice, telling her to do this or not to do that. It applied as much to what they thought she ought to say to clients as it had done to choosing clothes for her Barbie. 'You'll want this nice sun dress, dear,' she still remembered her mother saying in the toy shop. The fact that seven-year-old Emma thought the violent pink ball-gown with sequins and matching lace trim was absolutely the most exciting thing she had ever seen in her life simply didn't seem to register with her.

Normally she resented that kind of unwarranted intrusion with a vengeance. But with her mental energies, already drained by the long haul around England taking photographs for her book, practically annihilated by

David's cruelty, she felt close to collapse. She wanted to give way to the thick tide of emotions that was churning around inside her, to be loved and be taken care of, not to have to do anything for herself. If she didn't feel she had the strength to be alone at a time like this, her parents were the ideal people to go to. It seemed an opportune time to let someone else do the thinking, to become a dependent, to surrender for a while her much-cherished rights to self-determination. She wanted someone else to take control of her life, for a while at least.

She was too hurt for the moment to feel any real and lasting anger at David's treachery. That would come later, a bitter rage whose vehemence surprised her. She had walked into David's garden with her heart almost bursting and within seconds all her expectations, all her hopes and longings had come crashing down around her head. Seeing Gabrielle in David's tatty dressing gown had immediately told her something was badly wrong. She, Emma, was the only one who ever wore it, after a bath, for breakfast, while making the two of them a post-coital snack. He thought it was beyond redemption, couldn't understand why he hadn't thrown it out long ago. She had seized on it as a child hangs on to an old toy or a blanket, for comfort. And there was that great voluptuous tart wrapping it round herself with a proprietorial air.

She knew about Gabrielle, of course. David had told her about her, and about Abbie, and most of the other significant relationships in his life. It wasn't that she was jealous of him, or even minded him screwing around if he wanted to. They had had a long and detailed conversation – had had several long and detailed conversations, in fact – about themselves and what brought them together and in what ways they still needed to keep a distance from one another. Like a fool, she'd believed what he'd said.

In their relationship they had established that there was freedom – that was what she liked so much about it. It let her get on with her life, let him get on with his. She had her people who she dealt with, he had his. She had a working relationship with her assistant and her clients, he with his restaurant staff and his customers. Neither of them felt any need to interfere in these aspects of each other's lives, so why should they control the other facets? She had the freedom to have it off with Liam Forbes-Chalmers in a London restaurant if she wanted to and there was no way she should feel guilty about it. She now realised, of course, the guy was a total shit but that was her mistake and besides, that wasn't the point either. She had a right to self-determination and that wasn't always something she had known.

She hadn't been sleeping with anyone else since. She knew something had been going on when David shot off to Wales that time but, as far as she could see – and that was some considerable way into David's soul – she knew he by and large hadn't either. It wasn't because she was trying to keep herself pure for him, like some virgin princess on her wedding night. In other circumstances, that blue-eyed mechanic who had fixed her car could have had her in the back seat of her Volvo any time he wanted. That rock-climber too – God, he was all right, and no mistake. It was just that she didn't feel the need to have anyone other than David at the moment. He'd given the impression that he'd felt the same way too, the bastard.

So what the fuck was he playing at? She despaired

sometimes of men, their minds so obviously ruled by their cocks. They were all of them emotional illiterates, she knew that – apart from David. She trusted him, believed in him, loved him even. And yet, as soon as her back was turned, he went back on everything he'd ever said. Men were so duplicitous, so unfeeling, so inconsistent. She felt almost sorry for him, but there was a bitter element of contempt as well.

From what David had said about her and the evidence of her own eyes, she could understand the lure of Gabrielle. Well, she was welcome to him if that was what he wanted. She was sexy and had a powerful aura about her but Emma knew that hard-edged brazenness was all front, probably learned off endless episodes of *Dallas* and *Dynasty*. It all seemed got up somehow, as if she were trying too hard to be every man's idea of the ideal woman. She was the kind of woman who didn't make a lot of sense unless she had a man by her side. On her own, with other women, she would retreat into a shell of platitudes and convention. She couldn't believe that David, if he was half the man she thought he was, had been taken in by her for a moment, and yet there, right before her nose, was the clear evidence that he had been. Saying goodbye on the station platform at Carlisle, he'd gone all soft-eyed and said how he couldn't wait for her to get back to the cottage. And then, as soon as he'd got home, he'd no doubt got straight on the phone to this Gabrielle woman to help fill in the time till she got back. Well fuck you, David Casserley, she said out loud through gritted teeth and she gripped the steering wheel as hard as she could, wishing it were his throat.

Was it only a year ago that she'd finished with Vinnie? God, it seemed like she was a different person then.

Always ready to do what he said, never to say what she wanted. In the manner into which her parents had moulded her, she had gone along with what he wanted, never daring to think that she had a voice of her own. It was really through her work that she'd found out who she was and had realised her own power. These days she could say no if she wanted, or yes, or maybe. She wasn't by nature a stubborn person but she didn't need other people telling her what to do, these days at least. It had taken her years before she had realised she was someone in her own right, and that she had an independence for which other people had a genuine respect. It showed in her work – that was why Martin Churchward put so many jobs her way, because he knew who she was and what she put of herself into her work.

Once she'd grasped this, then her self-confidence had started to come out in her relationship with men. She'd enjoyed them all the more because of that. There was Alun, her MP lover, and Jeremy the obstetrician, both of whom had been taken on board on her terms and then ditched over the side without so much as a backward glance. She'd taken from them what she'd wanted to take, had given them what she wanted to give, and that was it. With Vinnie, things had just dragged on because she was too paralysed by his dominance to do anything about it. With David, however, that decisive moment had come unbidden, ill-timed and unwanted. She knew there was something wrong about the whole thing, but she couldn't put a finger on it. She couldn't bring herself to look at it in any other way than the obvious one. And so her inferences were the obvious ones – and that was where the pain and anger came from.

But there was also a great sadness in her, a feeling of

loss and of promise unfulfilled. It had been so good with him, and could have been so much better in time, of which they seemed to have a great deal. She hadn't wanted it to end this way. She hadn't wanted it to end at all. She found herself crying as she drove along, hot angry tears that scalded her eyes. To distract herself she switched on the radio. The Everly Brothers were singing 'Love Hurts' and she had to pull over to the side of the road and let those great terrible racking sobs wrench themselves free from her heart.

David spent the weekend that promised to have been one of the happiest of his life in a state that swung between paralysis and despair. It was as well that, with the restaurant reopening after its summer break, he had members of staff who could cope with the demands of the business. He certainly couldn't, at least not without the very considerable help of Hannah, Louis and the others. They knew something was badly wrong with David and they suspected it must necessarily be to do with Emma. He wasn't close enough to any of them, really, to talk to them openly about his feelings, but they knew he was going through some deep inner turmoil and they supported him in whatever way they could. They tried not to bother him.

He had tried almost ceaselessly to get through to Emma to explain. But the answerphone seemed to be on permanently, and there was no reply to any of the faxes he sent. Her car phone was dead, suggesting she wasn't using it. He thought of going up to London, to try doorstepping her flat and studio, but realised that was just too hysterical a reaction.

On the Tuesday, of course, she was due to fly to Japan

for three weeks. He wondered how she must be feeling right now – badly hurt, he expected, and justifiably angry with him. If only he could speak to her, he raged, then he could explain everything. But all he got was a resounding silence.

He didn't feel he could call any of her friends and clients on the off-chance that they might have some idea of her whereabouts. He didn't know all their names, but there was the guy at CCHD that she liked and the property developer at Land Investments, and one or two others whose names she had mentioned. But wouldn't they think it a bizarre thing for him to call them speculatively, even if they knew who he was? He discounted the idea pretty quickly.

Each time the phone rang he would leap to answer it, heart pounding. But it would only be someone from the village, or a friend – anyone but Emma. He hardly ever went out except to the restaurant or to walk Guy, for fear that she might phone and he would miss the call. It got so he could sense that the phone would ring a second or two before it did – perhaps by some subliminal noise the instrument made, or was it a heightened perception that had arisen from his overcharged emotional state? He didn't know. He didn't know anything much. A week ago he thought he did, but now all that was blown away.

The weekend dragged on interminably. Somehow he got through the evenings at the restaurant, but the re-opening night had been horrendous. People were being difficult with him – or was it he with them? – and there was a double booking, and then someone reversed into a customer's car and there was an unpleasant scene right outside. He'd not really slept for two nights, and the strain was showing through.

Saturday was a little better. He watched the last match of the cricket season on the television – he wasn't a great admirer of the game, but he hadn't the application to read anything and music was too loaded with emotional meaning – and somehow, with its slow cadences and sudden flurries of activity, that got him through the day. In the evening there was a good crowd at The Ancient House, including old friends who had been at his party last week, like the Somervilles and Conor and Lisa Doulton, looking ravishing in black. Everyone seemed normal and amiable and the simple warmth of friendship did a lot to help soothe his immediate wounds, even if it could never fully heal them. Of course they didn't know – how could they? But it was all tremendously calming, nonetheless. Conor Doulton even asked if he'd like to come to Covent Garden to see *The Magic Flute* the following month with Lisa and himself and some other people they knew. He didn't go much for Mozart's operas – not in his present mood, at any rate – but he'd never been to Covent Garden and he felt it would be churlish to decline. Besides, he told himself, life must go on. He slept well and woke feeling much more positive. He knew he'd been letting himself go, drifting into a dark and treacherous sea of pain. Now was the time to do something about it, to adjust, to accept.

He had Sunday lunch with the Somervilles. Both were trained counsellors – John had a psychology degree – and it seemed they could sense at once that there was something wrong with him. He was normally so relaxed and easy going but today he seemed tense and awkward, even with friends. John usually did the cooking on a Sunday and so it was Linda who asked, with a gentleness that was both professional and personal, if there was anything bothering him.

He knew better than to try and bluff people who had this kind of intuition. So he told her in simple terms, about his relationship with Emma, and what it meant to him, and what had happened on the Wednesday, and about Gabrielle, and about how he himself felt about it all.

'I've got this feeling that I can't cope any more,' he said. 'Which is ridiculous, because until last week things were absolutely fine.'

'Why is it ridiculous?' asked Linda.

'Because I know that I can do these things that I'm finding difficult – like dealing with stroppy customers, and making sure the bills are paid on time, and dealing with suppliers.'

'That's your adult voice speaking. Of course you can cope with these things, David. The Ancient House is incredibly well run. It's the way it is because of what you put into it. Everything about the place reflects you – lots of people say that.'

'Do they?' he said blankly.

'Of course they do. But it's the child in you that says you can't cope. In your present frame of mind, you react to normal adult things as a child would, by panicking. What will go wrong? Why won't anyone help me? It's like a child calling for help. We all feel like that sometimes. But your adult voice says don't be silly, of course you know what to do. Listen to that voice, and forget the screaming kid.'

'It sounds like my parents.'

'What were they like?' asked Linda.

'They were very kind, in their way, but distant. My

dad was an alcoholic and he died a long time ago, my mother lives near Truro. I don't see her as much as I should. I think they wanted me, but they weren't very good at showing their true feelings. Like a lot of people of their generation, I suppose. It wasn't stiff upper lip, exactly, but there was an awkwardness about them when they should have let the warmth show through. They were reticent. They weren't very physical – I mean, I assume they must have been otherwise I wouldn't have been born but what I'm driving at is that they didn't show affection physically. I don't think I ever saw them kiss or even hold hands in public. They were divorced when I was eight and I went to live with my mother. After that, I don't think she very often hugged me or anything – which isn't to say she wasn't kind in other ways. She could be generous, buying me things and stuff, but it always seemed an effort for her.'

'That was her way of showing affection, which she couldn't do physically. How do you think that affected you?'

'Well, it's funny you should ask that question because it was something I was thinking about the other day. For a long time I guess that, maybe to compensate for this denial of physical feelings in childhood, I equated affection with physicality.'

'You mean sex?' said Linda.

'That's right. I think I got the two confused, if that doesn't sound ridiculous.'

'It doesn't sound ridiculous at all. One of the ways in which parents and children show their feelings for each other is by touch, by hugging and stroking and lifting the little ones up in the parents' arms, and all that kind of thing. Adults do it through sex with their partners. If you don't get it as a child, you try and achieve it through sex. In some ways, but not in all, people might try and turn their partners into the parent they wish they'd had.'

'Yes, I think you're right. In fact I know you are. But I think I was taking sex and affection to mean the same thing, which of course they don't. Well, not always, anyway.'

'You mean you would have sex with someone when it was really their affection you wanted?'

'Exactly. Does this make me a mental case?'

'Not at all. I think it's something a great many people are mixed up about.'

He came away from lunch feeling considerably better about things. He knew what the real position was – nothing had changed that. He loved Emma, he was sure of that, and he knew she loved him. The business with Gabrielle was a terrible misunderstanding. Sort that out, and they could be back to where they were. Maybe it was even good that they should spend some time apart for now because, if they were both adults, they must surely both come to the same conclusions about each other.

Over the next few days, he was still up and down a lot, though he was grateful for the help the Somervilles had given him in sorting his emotions out. He tried ringing Emma nevertheless, but always it was the answerphone. He didn't bother leaving a message any more.

On Tuesday, the day she was to fly to Japan, he had a brainwave. He would meet her at Heathrow before her flight. Just five or ten minutes was all he needed to talk to her, then everything would be all right. He rang the airline, found out the departure time (earlier than he had hoped) and realised he might just make it to the check-in counter if he put his foot down. He locked up the cottage and jumped into the old Citroen.

For the first time ever, it refused to start. Afterwards, he felt there was something symbolic about that.

Emma had, of course, spent the weekend at her parents' house near Cheltenham. They had been surprised when she'd rung but pleased to see her nevertheless. She hadn't been down there since Easter, and now that they were getting on a bit her mother and father only rarely came up to London.

It was a comfort to fall back into familiar routines. She still had her own room at their house, with her own things and her own metaphysical space. She suspected her parents knew there was something wrong but she didn't want to burden them with it. They were kind and thoughtful people but their knowledge of psychology belonged to the 'pull yourself together and snap out of it' school. 'Time is a great healer, you know,' would be about the sum of their wisdom. Her father would have suggested she take up a hobby in order to occupy her mind.

She still felt terrible about David. Hurt had given way to anger and, when that subsided, to a great sense of loss. She couldn't believe he could have been so awful to her. Over and over again she kept playing back the things they'd said and done together, trying to find the cracks in the wall, the little fault lines that might have been a clue to the impending earthquake. She found none.

On the Monday, having confirmed her flight the following day, she drove back to London and packed her things at the flat. There were several brief messages from David on her answerphone asking her to ring him but she didn't feel like talking to him. It was her wounded pride that stopped her – why should she do anything to make him feel better when he was the one who had done all the damage? Deep down, she would have liked to have dipped into that great whirlpool of emotion that had engulfed them both with such suddenness, and to see just what – if anything – could be salvaged from the wreckage. But she knew that the time was not yet ripe. The pain of rejection was still too strong in her.

The only growth came through pain, she had once been told. Nothing is learned passively. Well, she had been through the pain barrier and survived, and was a stronger person for it. She flew out with the dance troupe, as scheduled, on Tuesday morning. It was tough for her at first but, among creative people and in a foreign land of such richness, she found her rough edges slowly began to be smoothed down, like pebbles in the sea. Gradually, the feeling of loss began to subside, and she started to channel her energies into her work.

The photographs she took of the dance were among the most expressive she had ever taken. Strongest of all – because they were the ones with which she identified most closely – were those reflecting sadness, pathos, tragedy. Some were exuberant and joyful, but it was to those encapsulations of the darker reaches of the mind that she felt most drawn. In recognising those feelings in the dancers, and translating it into the language of form and texture and tone, she began to sublimate some of her own most powerful emotions. As a result, she began to sense that the healing process had begun.

One night, near the end of the tour, she was sitting

with members of the troupe in a Kyoto sushi bar. She was feeling more stable now, and had regained much of her old composure and sense of self-control. She was talking to the assistant choreographer, a wry but charming northerner called Paul. He was slightly older than her, a brilliant dancer in his youth but his career had been impaired by a serious ankle injury incurred, of all things, while playing an impromptu game of football on the rehearsal stage at Sadler's Wells. Though he still performed occasionally, he was devoting much of his creative energy to encouraging others to make the movements he could no longer achieve.

'How do you feel about it?' she asked him.

He shrugged, and smiled a smile that had no malice in it.

'I'm not bitter, you know,' he said. His Yorkshire vowels were flat and very working-class still and he made no attempt to hide them. She found this lack of artifice very attractive. 'I'm just as happy doing what I do now.'

'And what do you think you've learned from it?'

He thought for a while. That was another thing she liked about Paul – he didn't just say the first thing that came into his head. When he said something, you knew he'd given it due consideration. David was like that. The troupe respected him for the way he said what he meant, rather than trying to be amenable, even if he did ruffle feathers.

'I think – I know this sounds daft – I think I've learned not to be afraid. We're always afraid that terrible things are going to happen to us, aren't we? Usually, at the end of the day, they're not that bad, really. We just imagine they're going to be worse than they really are. My dad was regular army and he said there's no such thing as bravery, just that some people have got a more realistic appreciation of danger than others. Everyone else is taking cover or running around flapping like headless chickens, and your so-called hero is just an ordinary chap who happens to have grasped that things aren't quite as bad as everyone else seems to think. So he just acts normally and all of a sudden everyone's slapping him on the back and pinning medals on his chest.'

'So where does that leave you? I mean, you're not in the army.'

'Not, but I got wounded in a different way. It seemed pretty bad at the time, you know, but I survived. When I damaged my ankle it seemed like the end of the world for me and in a way it was. But look at me now – I've come through it, I'm alive, I'm out here in Japan and all the blokes I went to school with are on the dole or filling shelves in supermarkets. I'm not fool enough not to know there'll be other things that will go wrong, but I'll be able to cope right enough. I know I can get through it.'

She slept with Paul a couple of times, before they flew back to England. Making love wasn't out of this world but she liked him and – not least because of what he had said to her that evening in the bar – she could relate to him, as she could to David. He had a hard, muscular body which he knew how to use but most of all she liked the feeling that she was back in control again. She was doing things that she wanted to do rather than those that were expected of her. Paul made few demands on her, didn't expect her to be his property. When they got back to Heathrow, both knew it would be unlikely they would ever see each other again. It was like a holiday romance for adults, and she wished she'd had that kind of strength to enjoy it for what it was when she was a teenager – she'd have avoided those dreadful nights in a beach hut at Frinton-on-Sea, for a start. The recollection made her laugh – something she couldn't have done three weeks ago. She had wondered why that boy had never replied to her letters, and why her parents were reluctant to let her go away the following year with the same girls. Now she knew.

Scarcely a moment still went by, though, when she didn't think of David, but she knew now that she could survive without him, that the damage would not scar her for life. When she returned to her studio she found no more messages from him. Sooner or later, their affair would have to be resolved one way or the other, but the moment was not yet ripe. She knew she couldn't go on ignoring him for the rest of her life, that one way or another they would have to wind things up properly. There were too many loose ends lying around – there was a whole pile of her stuff at his cottage, for instance, and she had some of his things in London. She worked late, several nights in a row, to get Philip de la Salle's photographs into shape. It was strange, looking at them now. How different her expectations had been, and yet it was not much more than a month ago. She was pleased with the photographs and it showed in the care with which she printed them, but she felt a complete detachment from them. It was their life, but it wasn't hers. No way.

She rang Liam Forbes-Chalmers, as was the arrangement, to tell him they were ready. He sent his driver round for them. Emma wrapped up the package of prints and negatives with so much tape that it could easily have withstood an earthquake.

Later on, he rang with his customary charm to thank her. He is a grade-A shit, she thought to herself, but she could understand why she had been attracted to him. She felt she could cope with people like him now. When he asked her out, she was not reluctant to accept. She knew how to handle snakes.

They ate at a little place, not long opened, in Covent Garden. This time, there was no fancy footwork under the table, and they were hemmed in by other diners. She knew, as he knew, that it was over between them, almost before it had started. There was no need to say anything – the understanding was implicit. They could relate in other ways, as friends – he wasn't totally awful. She didn't want another relationship, not yet at any rate. Using all the courage that Paul had helped her find in herself, she was still assessing the damage David had caused her. It was like the aftermath of the minor collision she and Liam witnessed between a taxi and a Mini as they waited to cross the road outside the Royal Opera House. The cars were soon on their separate ways, dents and all, but the bits of broken tail-lights were still lying in the road, and needed sweeping up.

Bow Street was busy now, with the crowds that were streaming out of the Opera House. It took Liam some while to hail a cab. In the end, he took out his mobile phone – he probably took it to bed with him, she reckoned – and stood in a doorway, phoning a private company. She looked at his face in profile, the way his hair fell about his temples just as David's did. Suddenly she felt sad and empty. She glanced down, not wanting the passers-by to see the tears that she could feel welling up in her eyes. When she looked up, there was Liam standing holding the door of a cab on the other side of the road.

She dodged quickly between the passing cars.

But it wasn't Liam. It was David. They looked at each other in absolute amazement. All traces of hostility vanished from her heart.

'What are you—?'

'I kept trying to ring you. You didn't reply.'

'I've been in Japan for most of this month.'

'Yes, I know. I had tickets for the opera. I went with friends. I wasn't expecting—'

'Neither was I.'

Even in the streetlights, she could read so much from his eyes. They stood there looking at each other, their private language saying things that words could never convey. She didn't have to say anything. She understood. Before she even knew she wanted to be there, she found herself in his arms.

'Come back with me,' she said. She could feel his tears mingling with hers as they ran down her cheek. 'Tonight. Come with me.'

'Of course I will,' he said.

They got into the cab together. She squeezed his hand. It felt soft and warm. She kissed him, and held on to him tighter than she had ever held anyone in her life.

In the cab he told her about the episode with Gabrielle, how it had happened, how he had reacted, the anger and despair that he had subsequently felt. She didn't tell him her side of things until later – perhaps when she was sure of him, at last. He, in the meantime, didn't tell her how Lisa Doulton had tried, unsuccessfully, to entice him round for an evening of decadence – he felt he'd punished himself sufficiently well not to need her whips and leather gear – nor of how, when he finally felt like coming out of his shell, Kirsty Fenwick had phoned him out of the blue. He'd gone down to Wales and spent a revitalising couple of nights with her only the previous weekend. That he could handle – there were absolutely no strings, it was a simple physical relationship and he knew it would never turn into anything like the business with Gabrielle. The weekend had done him good – in the first, traumatic aftermath of the bust-up with Emma, the last thing he had felt like was sleeping with anyone. Free of sexual frustration and with something of his old self-confidence beginning to emerge, he felt more like himself again.

As they were driven through London's late-night traffic, his mood veered wildly between elation and a curious exhaustion – elation, because he had regained that which he had felt was lost to him forever, and exhaustion, because he had expended so much mental and emotional energy in trying to resolve his own feelings at their deepest level. The elation, inevitably, triumphed. They went to Emma's flat in St John's Wood – 'I don't do this with every man I pick up off the street,' she had told him, and he believed her. She could hardly unlock the door fast enough.

Never having been there, he had no idea what to expect but in her living room the soft, natural colours were instantly soothing. There was much emphasis on texture – again, natural materials like hessian and plain wood and thick woollen rugs – and the lighting was carefully arranged to bring this out. There were some photographs on the walls – he quickly recognised, long before he studied the signatures, work by Ansel Adams and Angus McBean – but what really caught his attention were the stone carvings. There must have been a dozen or more of them, on tables and mounted on the walls, ranging from heavy medieval gargoyles to primitive tribal art. Lying on the floor by the empty hearth, looking for all the world like a slumbering pet, was a two-feet long fossilised lizard.

When he turned round Emma was standing in the doorway, wearing the black silk cami-knickers he'd bought her in Whitby. Sheer black stockings set off her long and elegant legs to perfection.

'I think we've got something to celebrate, don't you?' she said, looking him knowingly in the eye.

Holding her gaze, David reached out and traced a line of white-hot fire from her throat down between her breasts, across the shimmering silk that enfolded her rib-cage and down between her parted thighs. Her pussy felt hot and slightly damp to the touch. Words were superfluous.

Taking his hand in hers, Emma continued to look intently at him, at his eyes, his face, his body. Then she pressed herself against him, warm and trembling slightly. Above her perfume he could trace the unmistakable aroma of her arousal. He wrapped his arms around her, crushing her to him, running his fingers through the blonde hair that seemed to have grown, even in the month since he had last seen her.

Moving together like dancers in a slow, sinuous mambo of desire, their tongues probing the inner recesses of each other's mouths, David felt himself melting and becoming as one with her – physically, mentally, emotionally. He became aware of the urgency implicit in his penis, rubbing hard and ready against her silky pubic mound.

They broke apart for a second. He felt Emma pulling

on his arm and then he was in the bedroom with her, tearing at his clothes as she shed hers, desperate to be naked as she now was. As he moved to cover her trembling body, she spread her legs to accommodate him. She raised her knees, and he caught a glimpse of the dusky cleft between her thighs – even in that split second, the lips were plainly visible, swollen and puffy with desire.

For once there was no subtlety between them, no sophisticated lovemaking strategy designed to enhance the sensations of the moment. For had he not, in his imagination, played through this scene again and again, the longed-for reunion, the final affirmation of all that he had believed in? He had imagined over and over the feel of her tender skin against his own, the sensation of hands and lips as they explored each others' most intimate places. All that was known to him, understood, taken as read. All that was needed now was the consummation.

She took hold of his penis in her hand and, tensing the muscles of her backside and raising her hips from the bed to meet him, she guided him home into the warm, pouting folds of her vagina. Lifting his head, awash in a welter of emotions, he had little consciousness of his actual physical movements as he thrust forward into her.

They lay as they were, poised above the abyss, barely moving at first. Conqueror and conquered, hunter and hunted, lover and beloved – each was both at once, each knew to the depth of their being the very last atom of the other. They gazed into each other's eyes, unveiling their souls to one another, ablaze with a passion of an intensity that neither had ever known before.

Softly moaning, Emma began to twist her hips in a snake-like, undulating movement. He could feel her tensing the inner muscles of her vagina as she gripped his penis in her sheath. He moved in and out of her, filling her completely before withdrawing a little. Everything was happening automatically now, and everything was the way he had always hoped it would be. He floated away, aware of nothing beyond the experience of having sex with the woman he loved. Nothing else existed for David at that moment. Nothing else mattered.

Her vagina was already contracting in short, pulsing spasms even as he reached his own nirvana. His seed flowed deep into her welcoming body and then he was still.

# A selection of Erotica
## from Headline

| | | |
|---|---|---|
| SCANDAL IN PARADISE | Anonymous | £4.99 ☐ |
| UNDER ORDERS | Nick Aymes | £4.99 ☐ |
| RECKLESS LIAISONS | Anonymous | £4.99 ☐ |
| GROUPIES II | Johnny Angelo | £4.99 ☐ |
| TOTAL ABANDON | Anonymous | £4.99 ☐ |
| AMOUR ENCORE | Marie-Claire Villefranche | £4.99 ☐ |
| COMPULSION | Maria Caprio | £4.99 ☐ |
| INDECENT | Felice Ash | £4.99 ☐ |
| AMATEUR DAYS | Becky Bell | £4.99 ☐ |
| EROS IN SPRINGTIME | Anonymous | £4.99 ☐ |
| GOOD VIBRATIONS | Jeff Charles | £4.99 ☐ |
| CITIZEN JULIETTE | Louise Aragon | £4.99 ☐ |

*All Headline books are available at your local bookshop or newsagent, or can be ordered direct from the publisher. Just tick the titles you want and fill in the form below. Prices and availability subject to change without notice.*

Headline Book Publishing, Cash Sales Department, Bookpoint, 39 Milton Park, Abingdon, OXON, OX14 4TD, UK. If you have a credit card you may order by telephone – 0235 400400.

Please enclose a cheque or postal order made payable to Bookpoint Ltd to the value of the cover price and allow the following for postage and packing:
UK & BFPO: £1.00 for the first book, 50p for the second book and 30p for each additional book ordered up to a maximum charge of £3.00.
OVERSEAS & EIRE: £2.00 for the first book, £1.00 for the second book and 50p for each additional book.

Name ............................................................................................................

Address ........................................................................................................

......................................................................................................................

......................................................................................................................

If you would prefer to pay by credit card, please complete:
Please debit my Visa/Access/Diner's Card/American Express (delete as applicable) card no:

| | | | | | | | | | | | | | | | | | |
|---|---|---|---|---|---|---|---|---|---|---|---|---|---|---|---|---|---|
| | | | | | | | | | | | | | | | | | |

Signature ................................................... Expiry Date .........